The Book of Souls

Justice
1

Jaycee Moule

The Book of Souls

Justice
1

ISBN number 978-1-84914-486-5

First published in Great Britain in 2015 by
CompletelyNovel.com
Copyright © J Moule 2015
Front, spine and back cover designed
by copyright © Ana Grigoriu 2015
The two scriptures that were used are from The NIV
Bible.

Acknowledgements

I'd like to thank my husband, daughter and son for putting up with the countless missed meals and endless hours with my head buried in my laptop as I've been writing this book. Without your support and understanding, I wouldn't have been able to do this. I love you all to the moon and back.

To my mum and dad whose love and encouragement have kept me going through some very tough times, I love you both so much. Also a special hug for my mummy Moule, who helped me discover who the real Jesus is, you will always hold a special place in my heart, and of course the rest of my family for always being there too, love you lots guys x

A big thank you goes to my friends: Jo H, Helen & John W, Sally and John WJ, I don't know what I'd do without your wise words and help, you guys are so special. And a big thank you to all the church people who have been praying for this to happen.

I mustn't forget about those special few teenagers who became my readers and critics over the couple of years it's taken to write this adventure: Emily Ore (We will never forget the laughs we've had with these few words, 'I'm dying, I'm dying!!') Hannah & Lizzie Norton, Lizzie Barraclough and Anna Hayward. Thanks for your time and I hope you all enjoy the finished book.

PROLOGUE

And I saw the dead, small and great, stand before God; and the books were opened - Rev 20:12

Resting his hand on the carved edge of the cavernous mouth, the angel hesitated as he peered into the pit which existed in the depths of the earth, below the heavens, yet above the abyss of perdition. He'd never experienced fear before, but with each step he took, it brought him closer to his destination and the unknown emotion wavered on the edge of his mind. The stagnant, damp smell of age filled his nostrils and within a heartbeat, he had strolled into an imposing cavern. Over the centuries the zigzag of stalactites and stalagmites had formed pillars reaching from the vast ceiling to the uneven ground. He circled, sword raised high, its light reflecting off the stone columns and curtains. It was then, in the distance, that he spotted the four tunnels, each the same width and height, and each giving off a sense of trepidation. Closing his eyes, the young angel folded his wings against his back and emptied his mind, drawing on His grace.

Within the silence, he sensed a faint residue of God's Power lingering in and around the opening furthest to his left. Snapping his eyes open, he smiled, knowing that the one he hunted was close, so very close. The angel sauntered towards the opening, shrugged and entered, his father's command still ringing in his ears, *"Return what is Mine from the one who has betrayed me."*

At the same instant, he felt the tunnel wrap itself around him, sucking energy from his whole being until his strength waned and he fell to his knees. Splaying his fingers across his chest, the angel gasped for air as he watched the light from his sword die. Several times he tried to stand, each attempt sending him sprawling back to the ground. Never in all the countless centuries had he felt such weakness. He was a being consumed with power, a being always in the light of The Creator. Now he understood how his fallen brothers were imprisoned here; without God's light, they were nothing but powerless creatures.

He laid his head back against the wall of the cave and waited. Never before had he experienced darkness like this. He'd no idea in which direction he was gazing but suddenly a glimpse of light seeping out of some of the rocks ahead of him, caught his attention. He watched the spark as it sizzled along a crack in the ceiling, growing in intensity until the angel had to shield his eyes in the cuff of his arm, then within the blink of an eye, a shimmering presence hovered a few inches from his face.

"This isn't a permitted place to be." A voice from within the light boomed.

"I didn't have a choice," the angel replied, while peering over the top of his arm. "I seek The Book of

Souls, which was stolen from the Almighty when its Keeper fell to earth. I know the thief is imprisoned here."

Unseen hands pulled the young angel to his feet. Light tendrils, like long fingers flickered across the angel's breast plate and traced along each arcane letter of his name, before they lingered on his face.

"Thwarter of demons," the voice said, in recognition.

The young angel felt a surge of power enter his body at the instant the Being spoke his true name and nodded

"My orders are to return the book to the throne room of Our Father." The angel's midnight-black hair fell forward onto his brow.

The light shifted position. "You are too late, it was taken by another."

"What do you mean?"

"I was forbidden to stop the boy." The light dulled for a second.

"The boy, a mortal boy?"

"The Enemy, Satan, used a child to steal the book from the fallen Keeper."

"But how?" the angel asked, in a voice faint with disbelief. "No human or fallen angel can enter this place, then leave it whenever he desires. The book should've been safe here."

"One who has the same blood running through his veins as the Son of David ... *can*."

The angel knew the Celestial Being spoke the truth. However, in the hands of The Enemy, 'The Book of Souls,' which was to promise life, would now be turned into a book of death, an abomination.

He had to find the boy, whatever the cost.

CHAPTER ONE

Maya peered up into the shadowed eaves of the Norfolk church lych-gate and cringed. The sight of dusty cobwebs and dead spiders with their spindly legs clustered in the crevasses, made her shiver. She hated spiders. Praying that the wind wouldn't dislodge them, she ruffled her fingers through her mass of red curls before wrapping the collar of her Jacket around her neck.

"Where the hell are they?" She squinted down at the bright numbers on her mobile phone: **19.30.** "Why do I bother?" Maya gave a large sigh. *And why did I agree to this in the first place?*

Just then, the faint crunch of shoes on gravel startled her. She crossed her arms, rubbing them while straining to see through the descending fog, but Maya couldn't make out anything further than an outstretched hand. Twisting her head so she could focus her hearing on the footsteps alone, Maya tried to visualise each of her friends fitting into them. *It isn't Ben, because the gravel isn't being kicked up by his foot dragging along the ground and it isn't Harriet either, she's always in too much of a hurry, and would never, ever walk that slow. As for Jess, her high heels would be a dead giveaway.* She brought her fingers to her mouth and chewed a nail. Maya never chewed her nails, for she didn't see herself as that type of person, the kind jumped at their own reflection, at least not until now.

1

She chuckled to herself. *Maybe it's Sam then. He's the only one with the inclination to turn this into a joke.* Her gaze drifted towards the path and as she stared, Maya noticed four florescent stripes rise and fall in a ghost-like fashion low to the ground. With a gulp, she bit into her bottom lip and waited. *I don't like this! I don't like it at all!!*

Without warning, a figure tore through the fog. Maya took a step back, not realising she'd been holding her breath until a sigh gushed from her. With abrupt clarity, Sam stepped under the cover of the lych-gate and stopped in front of her.

"Dammit, Sam!" She struck his arm with the flat of her palm.

He flinched back, faking a wounded look. "Hi, to you too."

"It's not funny, you scared the life out of me." Maya pushed her hair from her face. "Anyway, where are the others? I thought everyone was supposed to be here at seven?"

"Yeah, sorry about that." He pushed the sleeve of his jacket up and glanced at his watch. "I kinda got held up."

"Well, you're always late, so that's nothing new, but you still haven't answered my question."

He lifted his gaze to meet Maya's. "Okay! Give me a chance to finish. Just as I was leaving, Jess sent me a text saying she wouldn't make it."

"I didn't think she would, not with that cough she's had all day. And by the expression on your face, you're going to say that Ben and Harriet have changed their minds too, right?"

"You're good." He nodded, causing a strand of brown hair to fall in front of his right eye. "Ben messaged me an

2

hour ago. Apparently, Harriet told him that it was, 'too cold and foggy.' Can you believe that?"

"Yeah, actually I can, coming from her."

"He also asked me around his instead, mentioning that Harriet would be there, but he didn't say you were coming which I thought was strange. I'm assuming they forgot to invite you?"

"Really? Well that's noth ..." Maya stopped short before she said something she would've regretted like, *'well that's nothing new ... that's Harriet all over, particularly when it involves me.' Sam didn't need to know about her latest outburst. However, as this was her idea, then she's got one hell of a problem.*

Sam's cheek muscles stood out when he clenched his jaw momentarily in deep thought. Maya watched as his eyes narrowed and his lips pursed. *He's even cute when he's angry!*

"Bloody hell!" He said, as if a great discovery had flashed across his mind. "You know, she's a vindictive cow sometimes. Do you think she planned all this at lunchtime knowing that Jess wouldn't make it because of her cold?"

Maya shrugged.

Raising his arms to grab tufts of his hair, he walked a few steps out from the covering of the lych-gate. "Knowing her, she probably checked the weather forecast for tonight, then told Ben to text me in the hope I'd take him up on the offer, leaving you out here on your own." He dropped his arms and turned to look at Maya. "I can't believe she'd go this far, Maya. I know she's been on your case lately, but this is unforgivable."

"It's okay. Just forget it. She isn't worth the hassle." *If it wasn't for Jess, I wouldn't have to put up with her in the first place.*

Maya lifted her head to look over Sam's shoulder and at the fog beyond. Straightening, she wiped the back of her hand across her brow. *But why does she dislike me so much?* And then she remembered spending the odd hour mulling over the same old question, and only coming up with the same old answer ... jealousy, it had to boil down to jealousy, because Maya never confided in her, never let her get close; Harriet didn't like that. *Yet I don't tell Jess or Sam everything either. It's best that way, trust in no one and you won't lose friends or family that way.* The truth hurts. The truth of what she'd witnessed nine years ago, hurt then and it still hurt now.

"Maya?" Sam bent forward, a confused expression covering his face.

Turning away, Maya blinked and pushed those memories of the past back into the depths of her mind and glanced at Sam. *At least he's still the same old Sam I've known since primary school.* Except now that they were both sixteen and in their first year of sixth-form, her feelings for him had changed. No longer was she irritated by his constant teasing and infuriating jokes. Instead, Maya found herself drawing images of his delicious caramel eyes, perfect tanned body and gorgeous scruffy hair on an imaginary canvas in her mind. Even now, her gaze followed a tiny bead of moisture rolling down a strand of his hair, onto his left cheek and along the line of his jaw before it came to rest on the tip of his chin. If only she could be that tiny drop caressing his face, unfortunately, her wish was shattered by the annoying swipe of the back of his hand. Their eyes met. Maya turned her head away, the picture destroyed, but not forgotten.

Sam levelled his head with Maya's. "Hey, you're right you know. I shouldn't let her bug me and neither should you. I'm here, aren't I?"

"Yeah, you are, and thanks." She brought her hands up to her lips and puffed her cheeks out to blow warm air on the tips of her fingers. "But they're right about one thing. It sure is cold out here."

Sam grinned. "Yeah, you wouldn't think we'd get crazy weather like this at the end of March."

Maya chuckled for the first time that evening. "What's the plan then?"

"Oh ... right ... yeah. Well, we could go to the social."

"No, we can't." She shook her head and huffed on her fingers again before continuing, "It's closed for the weekend, some sort of electrical fault, that's what my mum told me anyway."

"Great!" He tightened his arms around his body and leant back against the flint wall.

"So, how about a walk?" Maya suggested. "I could do with warming up."

"Really!" There was a humorous glint in his eyes and his mouth twitched with amusement. "I know a really good way to warm you up, Maya, much better than any boring old walk." The words floated from between his lips as his grin turned to a smile.

Maya's breath froze and her body tensed. Did he really just say that!? He's obviously joking! Right?

He clapped his hands, making her jump. "You see, I can still shock you." He laughed and with a springy

5

bounce, headed off with long, purposeful strides down the path.

Maya shook her head and called out to him, "I'll get you back, Sam Brown. Just you wait."

"Sure," he replied with a chuckle.

Crossing Church Road and stumbling over a patch of uneven grass, Maya eventually reached the track that led down to the embankment. She stopped for a moment to wrap her quilted jacket around her body and cursed as the cold air still managed to penetrate the thin fabric. However, her mind still happened to be on his last innuendo. *Damn! What if he meant it? He's like the fittest guy in school. No ... no!* She tossed her hair across her shoulders. *I'm just being stupid, he wouldn't think of me like that, like his girl.* Staring ahead, Sam's silhouette disappeared through a thick patch of fog ahead.

"Sam, wait," Maya yelled.

"Scared of the dark?" his voice came as a bodiless whisper, until he broke through the fog.

"No." She paused for a moment's reflection. *Now what do I say?* And a few seconds later an idea came to her. "No, I'm not, I ... I was just wondering why you were heading towards the river, that's all?"

"Why not?" He shrugged.

"Well, this fog's getting thicker and ...." A sudden wave of apprehension swept over Maya.

"And what's the problem with that?" he interrupted.

"Because ...." She eyed him in startled interest. *Is he smirking? Oh my goodness, he is!*

Maya shut her mouth, she wasn't prepared to give him the satisfaction of seeing her afraid again, even though in daylight the embankment was a dangerous place to be.

Bending forward, his face almost touching hers, he said with an impish grin, "I'll look after you."

Maya placed her hands over her cheeks to hide her embarrassment, her eyes narrowed. *I bet you will!*

Trailing several steps behind him, she twisted her head searching for the unseen eyes she'd felt haunting her for the past five minutes and hoped with every second that her emotionally stretched imagination was just playing tricks on her.

"Sam ...." she called out in as quiet a voice as possible.

However, it hadn't been quiet enough. The trees to her left shook violently and a growl that sounded like no other creature she had ever heard before, pierced the air. An unseen wall of force enough to drive breath from her body in a gasping grunt, brought Maya to an abrupt halt. She screamed and slapped her hand over her mouth. Sam appeared in front of her, his chest heaving as he stood staring blankly at her for a moment, then he placed his hands on Maya's shoulders and drew her toward him. They huddled together, hardly daring to breathe, every single sound now emphasised by their silence. High-pitched squeals of laughter circled them, twigs fell by their feet. Maya glanced up at Sam, his tanned face now a deathly-white.

This can't be happening ... not here, not now.

A jolt of unease stabbed Maya's stomach as she watched lumps of mud being ripped from the ground by invisible hands. They molded the earth into what looked like legs and then a torso. The breeze kicked up leaves and twigs to shape a face that held no resemblance to a human at all with its thick and furrowed skin, and its eyes were sunken, almost lost under the rise of its bony brow. Yet, Maya couldn't drag her gaze away from them. *It ... it can't be! It can't be the same one as before, but those eyes, they are ... the ... the ... same!*

Sam grabbed her arm, his fingers digging through the thin fabric of her jacket, however, when the monster snarled, any pain he caused disappeared within an instant, and at that precise moment, a memory flashed before Maya's eyes; she'd seen it before, when she was seven, when all this had started. She had been in the living room with her little brother as her mummy was in the kitchen, and her daddy was in his study. The goose bumps on her arms, the chill in the room and her breath freezing in the air were all the same now as they were then. *Why is it here? Why has it returned? Is it after me now?*

The monster bared its teeth in what could only be described as a smile. The skin on the back of her neck prickled as the beast raised its arm and pointed a clawed finger at her. Without warning, a bolt of lightning struck the ground behind Maya and Sam, the shock paralysing them both for a few seconds. A pillar of light appeared and intensified, forcing Maya to shield her eyes in the cuff of her arm. She knew that she should be consumed with terror, but somehow her fear ebbed away as the light sizzled by. Taking a peek over her arm, she saw the beast's wings uncoil, but she still didn't feel the panic she had felt earlier. *Is that light doing this to me because right now, I should be screaming ... or running ... or doing something to get far away from here? Except, that light is so ... so ....*

"RUN - *NOW!*" A powerful voice cracked the air.

But I don't want too! She stood rigid, completely transfixed by the alluring light.

"RUN. Run to the church." The voice demanded again and as the words sank in, Maya felt a familiar shiver of awareness.

A whoosh of fear rushed through her as she pushed away from Sam's embrace and stood there trembling.

"RUN TO THE CHURCH."

Swallowing, she took a deep breath and grabbed Sam's arm, giving it a sharp tug, but he didn't budge, he simply stood there resembling a zombie with one arm limply pointing in the direction of the monster. When Maya took a second to glance into his eyes it only solidified the Zombie look with his once brown eyes now made completely white, from the reflection of the iridescent beam.

"Sam, what do I do? SAM, PLEASE!" Maya shouted. She glanced across at the light and then back at Sam's expressionless face. Taking a step closer, she slapped her hands on his broad shoulders. "Sam, come on. Snap out of it," she yelled above the racket and when he finally blinked, a sigh escaped her. "We need to get to the church!"

Sam shook his head and rubbed the back of his neck. His gaze flitting from Maya, then to what had held him captive and back to her. He grabbed Maya's wrist and seconds later, they were running away from the ear-splitting roars that snapped at their heels.

The church was three hundred yards away, yet it felt more like miles with her cold, achy legs struggling to carry her. *We won't make it!* She wanted to cry out, *'It's too dark! Too foggy! We'll never find it!'* But it was eventually the sickening anguish and not her aching muscles which made her stumble, pulling Sam down with her. Straight away Sam dragged her back to her feet and they were running again.

He reached the medieval oak door first and grabbed the iron handle with both hands. Breathing heavily, Sam twisted, then pulled and finally smashed his shoulder up against the wood. After his third attempt the door flung wide. He hit the floor hard, the air punched from his lungs in an explosive grunt. Maya tumbled forward, landing in a tangled mass of arms and legs on the cold flagstones beside him. For a moment neither of them moved; Sam was still gasping to catch his breath and Maya could only hear her own pulse thrumming through her eardrums as she tried to deal with her own pain. Eventually, Sam raised his right leg and kicked the door shut with a resounding thud, leaving them both surrounded by eerie shadows.

Wrinkling her nose from the stink of mouse pee which lined her nostrils, Maya tried her best to ignore it as she sat there blankly staring straight ahead. She twisted around when her thoughts were interrupted by a small arc of light to her left and saw Sam with his mobile phone stretched out in front of him.

"Who're you calling?" she asked.

He ignored her, his fingers tapping away with increased annoyance. "Bloody thing," he grumbled. "I can't get a *flippin'* signal in here." He turned to face her, his brow lined with a frown and then he made a gesture with his chin towards the door. "What the *hell* was that thing out there?"

Maya shook her head. She didn't know how to answer. Instead she sat upright, stretching to relieve the ache in her back and in a weak voice asked, "What if that thing comes after us in here?"

CHAPTER TWO

Before Sam could reply, they were both scrambling towards the entrance. The bolt shot home and Maya sighed as she slumped back down, landing on her backside. A red-lock of hair fell in front of her eyes, but she left it dangling like a ripped veil and peered at the pews beyond. *I've had enough of this.* Climbing numbly to her feet, she limped over to the nearest row of wooden seats and sat down. Sam stood, stretched and joined her.

In the darkness her thoughts drifted back to the evil creature; how it had felt the same as before, how her body had reacted in the same way ... horrific, frozen panic ... and it looked like the same *thing* she'd seen nine years ago when her brother had been snatched. She closed her eyes. *But it can't be ... It just can't.*

Sam nudged her painfully in the ribs and said in a nervous whisper, "Is it me, or is it getting lighter in here?"

Raising her head, Maya followed his widened stare. He was right! At the opposite end of the church the stained window above the altar, had lit up. She watched as a patch of light swelled across its surface, forcing shards of rainbow colours to reflect across the walls. Without warning, the pews rattled beneath them and the pulpit lifted off its base. Wrapping her arms around the carved lion at the end of her pew, Maya clung on tight while the whole bench wrenched itself free from the bolts securing it to the floor.

"Not again!" she cried out.

Sam pried her fingers apart and pulled her to her feet. "There," he shouted and pointed towards a gap in a pair of ceiling to floor curtains before putting his arms around her waist and pushing her in their direction.

A cold draft lifted Maya's hair as she stood waiting for her eyes to adjust to the gloom of the bell tower.

"Sam, where are you?"

"Down here, near the curtains."

Maya turned to see Sam's dark form kneeling down and peering through a sizable tear in the fabric. Stepping forward, she soon found her own moth-eaten hole to spy through. Putting her face to the cloth, Maya stared out into the church. Her breath caught in her throat. *No way, it can't be! What's it doing here?* The same light which had aided their escape earlier, floated through the window and hovered in front of the altar. Sam jumped to his feet and took a step back, a shadow of alarm touching his face. Maya forced herself to remain still and not flinch backwards, she needed to figure this out.

"What's it doing?" he asked, with a distinct note of distress.

"It isn't doing anything ... Oh no ... wait!" Maya backed up.

"What is it? What's happening?"

She turned to face him. "It's gone! It just vanished!"

"Are you sure?"

"Of course I'm sure."

The tread of approaching footsteps made Maya fix her eyes on Sam's, and when they came to an abrupt halt, they both kept quiet, neither wanting to make the first move or say the first word. Holding her breath, silence followed: no strained breathing, no scurrying of mice, nothing, until the trapped air in her lungs escaped with a hiss as her body unwillingly relaxed.

"Hello." The voice was melodic, strangely soothing. "I know someone's in here."

Sam swore beneath his breath. Maya glared back at him, shaking her head in confusion.

"Do you reckon it's the vicar?" she whispered.

Sam shrugged, pulling out his mobile phone, his fingers tapping nervously at the buttons.

"I won't bite you know. You can come out."

However, as if hypnotised, Maya parted the curtains and stepped forward without a backward glance. *Why am I doing this? Why does it feel right, feel safe?* Guided by the glow from Sam's phone, Maya's breath sort of ... stalled when she saw the person standing before her. *Wow, he's gorgeous, no ... that's the wrong word for him. He's perfect, it's like he's just come from a modelling shoot in his Burberry-style coat and jeans.* An arched eyebrow indicated his humorous surprise, except Maya ignored it and continued her appraisal under lowered lashes, unaware that she was still staring. *How his midnight-black hair complements his face perfectly ... and those eyes of his ... a turquoise-blue, the kind of blue you just want to jump into and lose yourself.* She swallowed.

The guy's exquisite, there's no other word for it. The stranger tilted his head to catch Maya's gaze and smiled. She stroked her arm and felt her skin flush.

His eyes narrowed as he looked down at her and said, "Are you alright?"

That voice, those eyes, sent a rush of adrenalin through her body which was unbelievable, exhilarating, exciting and dangerous all at the same time; a mixture of sensations she hadn't experienced before.

"Yeah, thanks. Er, who, are, you?" Maya asked between stutters.

Sam strolled over and stood beside her, folding his arms across his chest.

"Oh sorry, I'm Leo and you are?"

"Oh ... Um ... hi, I'm Maya." She blushed again. "And this is," she began to say when Sam rudely cut her off.

"How'd you get in?" Sam inquired. Yet Maya noticed an edge to the tone in his voice.

Leo turned and pointed toward an arched door on the side of the building. "Through there," he replied. "I heard the thunder or whatever that noise was, and this was the closest place to head for."

"You knew it was unlocked then?"

Maya snapped her head around to face her friend, her gaze alarmingly direct.

"No, but then I'm assuming you both are here for the same reason." The corner of Leo's mouth lifted into a lopsided grin and his eyes expressed more challenge than curiosity.

However, Sam ignored him and continued with another question, "I haven't seen you around here before?"

"No, I doubt you have."

Oh my goodness! I don't believe this! What is Sam's problem? Maya glanced from Sam to Leo and noticed that against this fit stranger, Sam's good looks bordered on ordinary. Her expression dropped. *Is he jealous? Is that what it is?* She raised her head, peering out towards the back of the church and on to the arched window behind the altar.

"Do you reckon the ..." she stopped mid-sentence. *Oh crappit-crap, if I mention the word monster, Leo's going to think I'm a complete nutter.* She glanced at Sam before continuing, "Do you reckon the storm's over yet?"

Sam shrugged, yet his arms remained folded across his chest and his gaze stayed focused on Leo.

"I'll go and have a look," Leo offered.

"Only if you're sure?" Maya squeaked unintentionally and she waited until he'd left before glaring back at Sam. "What's the matter with you? I can't believe how rude you're being."

"Just leave it." He snapped.

"No, Sam, I won't just leave it, because you're acting like a spo ..."

The door closed with a thud making Maya jump and cutting her attack off short.

"It looks okay out there," Leo called as he approached. "The fog's still thick though."

"Great, let's get out of here," Sam replied and by the

16

time he had finished his sentence, he had already marched past Leo and left Maya in the company of the good looking stranger.

Maya gaped at Leo in astonishment as he moved towards her with extraordinary and silent speed. *Oh no, please don't blush* ... but that's exactly what her body did, being a red-head with porcelain skin, it always betrayed her. There was something so delicious about him, and she couldn't say what it was, but it frightened her.

"Do you want to get out of here or are you planning on staying?" He chuckled.

Maya gave a brief nod before briskly heading for the door. She stepped outside without looking over her shoulder to see if Leo was following behind.

Although there were no signs left of the so called storm, the fog hung between them like blown flour. Maya closed her eyes, trying to steady the sudden and irrational feeling of fear that plagued her. *What if the monster's hiding out there somewhere, waiting for me to be on my own? No way am I walking home by myself.* Suppressing a sigh, she re-opened her eyes and was greeted by Sam standing a few inches from her.

"Come on, I'll walk you home," he offered, as if sensing her anxiety.

"That won't be necessary." Leo stepped between them, his voice strangely neutral. "I'll make sure Maya returns home safely."

Sam balled his hands into fists, a suggestion of annoyance hovering in his eyes. "Are you kidding?"

Oh for crying-out-loud! Not again. Yet when Maya

took a moment to think about it, it did seem a strange remark from someone she'd just met, then that thought faded away as if it had never been there in the first place and at that same instant and as if by magic, Maya knew she would be safe with Leo. She reached out to place her hand on Sam's arm, but he flinched it back and shook his head.

"I'm sorry, Sam. But I know I'll be okay with, Leo, and I can't explain why I know this right now," she said, feeling slightly apprehensive to what she was about to do. She glanced back at Leo for a small sign of assurance. *Am I crazy! I hardly know this guy and I'm choosing him over Sam, yet it feels right and I ... I really don't know why, or why I should let him walk me home.*

Leo nodded, but said nothing.

"But, Maya, you've only just met the guy."

"I promise I'll look after her," Leo spoke with blatant honesty, making sure Sam understood his intentions towards Maya.

"Yeah 'course you will ..." Sam pointed at Leo, giving him a steely stare before turning back to her. "Are you sure you'll be okay?"

"Yeah, 'course," she replied, with a slight nod, yet Sam's reaction bothered her. *This isn't like him, then again ... it isn't like me either.*

Sam leaned into Maya, his face close to hers and whispered, "Know that I think you've made the wrong decision." He bowed his head, his face carefully neutral and without further comment, withdrew into the fog.

"Sam, wait." But he didn't stop or reply, leaving Maya

alone again with Leo.

Ten minutes later, Maya stood in front of the gate to her garden with Leo standing behind her. She pushed her thumb down on the latch and shoved the gate wide enough for them both to step through. Before placing her hand on the door the same thought that had bugged her during her walk home resurfaced, *what if Sam's concerns were right and Leo is a weirdo or ... worse ... he had something to do with that monster?* Turning, she peered up into those blue eyes of his and noticed that they were full of an unquenchable warmth, a warmth that she would never know, but could only dream of. Leo smiled and Maya quickly diverted her gaze, suddenly feeling embarrassed for thinking such thoughts. *It was a stupid idea. There's no way he would've been involved with such a horrible monster ... what was I thinking.*

"Thanks for seeing me home," she said, lowering her head.

"No problem."

"I guess this is goodbye then." Heat rushed to her cheeks. "Will I see you again?"

Leo reached for the handle, his arm brushing against hers as he pushed the door wide. "Good night, Maya."

The sweet intoxicating musk of his body drifted up to her nose, catching her breath. *Oh cripes! Everything about him is so perfect. Which is all so wrong. No-one is perfect.*

"You haven't answered my question," she told him and tossed her hair over her shoulder. She wasn't prepared to let him leave until she got some kind of an answer.

"Probably." His fingers tightened their grip on the handle and he gestured with his other hand for her to enter the room. "I'll see you soon."

"You promise?" She wiped her sweaty palms down her coat. *Why am I behaving like this? I sound like some love sick kid who's been hit by a love potion.*

"I promise we'll see each other again, Maya. Good night."

Keeping her eyes fixed on Leo's tall frame through the glass-panelled door, Maya steadied herself on the welsh-dresser to loosen the laces on her boots and within the split second it took for her to bend down and pick them up, he had gone. *How the hell did he do that? No-one moves that quick.* Maya peered out into the fog, hoping to catch one last glimpse of him and after a few seconds, she sighed and held onto his promise, that she would see him again.

With an expression of confusion still on her face, Maya took slow deliberate steps back towards the kitchen even though she continually stared at the spot where Leo had just been. Now that he had gone, the horrific realisation of what had happened returned in a rush. Swaying sideways, she reached out for the doorpost to steady herself. Her stomach tightened and the blood drained from her head with every memory of the evening lying jumbled in her mind. Maya tilted her head back, resting it on the wall behind her and closed her eyes in the hope of chasing those thoughts away. *Stay calm! At least Sam saw it to, and although he isn't about this weekend, I think I can cope until Monday.* She placed her hands on top of her head and took in several slow measured breaths sniffing in the comforting scent of coffee and roses before opening her eyes again. Lifting her foot over the threshold to the kitchen, she stubbed her toe on the bottom of a steel bucket containing flowers and alerted her mother of her arrival.

Ouch!

"Mind the bucket, dear," her mum called from the lounge.

'It's a bit late to warn me now,' Maya silently cursed and hopped on the spot before replying, "Yeah, thanks mum, I think I found it."

Breathe, Maya, just breathe and count to ten. She forced a smile on her face and limped through to the lounge. Her mother sat in her usual comfy chair, her feet resting on a footstool and a Portmeirion mug of coffee warmed her hands. Maya sat back in the striped armchair opposite and settled her shoulders against the cushions.

"Did you have a nice time?" her mother asked.

Maya nodded, it was easier to lie. *No way is she going to believe me anyway ... she wouldn't understand ... I hardly understand it myself, because this shouldn't be happening again.* And as Maya sat there, images of the monster kept intruding her thoughts, clouding her mood, making her feel angry.

"Are you okay, love?"

Snatching her gaze away from the fire, Maya glanced across at her mum. "Yeah sure, it's just been a weird night. Is Dad home yet?"

"No, he had an emergency meeting at work, won't be home until late." Her mother placed her mug on the bookcase beside her.

"Yeah, that's what he always says," Maya mumbled, not intending her mother to have heard even though it was the truth.

Since her father's new position as managing director of Lotus, he made every excuse possible to keep away from Maya. But it hadn't all started with the new promotion or since their move to Wicklesham, it was way before both of those events and Maya didn't feel she could go there just yet.

Her mother interrupted her thoughts with, "Now, you know that isn't true."

"Oh, but it is, and the fact is, he still blames me and you won't even admit it."

The guilt and hurt that ate away at her every day was building up inside her now, and the more she sat there thinking about it, the more annoyed she got. Maya shifted in her chair to look at the row of photos lining the mantel piece, her gaze pausing on the small gold-framed picture of her brother Jack, which had been taken on his fifth birthday, two hours before he was grabbed. The guilt she had felt that day, washed over her now. *Could I have stopped it?* Her dad believed she could, if she had only shouted or screamed to warn him, he reckoned he would've been able to run from the study in time to save her brother. Except, he had no idea the fear that had crippled her ... that had controlled her ... that had prevented her from uttering a single sound, and ever since then, he could barely look at her.

Maya's mother sat forward, her brown wavy bob curtaining her round cheeks. "Now you know that isn't the reason he's hardly here. He's working every hour he can, so that we have a nice home. You've got to stop thinking he blames you, because he doesn't." She tucked her hair behind her ears, her gold-rimmed glasses slipped to the tip of her nose. "He thinks the world of you, Maya, and loves you to bits. You do know that, don't you?"

Maya wanted to say, *'No, Mum, I don't really,'* but it wouldn't help. She snapped her head around. "Well, he's hardly around to show it." She dropped her gaze and wiped the tears from her eyes. *Damn it, why am I having this argument now?* Taking in a deep breath, Maya took control of her emotions before pushing herself to her feet. "I'm sorry."

She stepped over to her mother and gave her a kiss on her forehead. Standing slightly slumped over, Maya told her mum, "I'm sorry. I don't know what's come over me. I didn't mean what I said, about Dad."

Her mum's hands caught Maya's shoulders and she lovingly pulled her into an embrace. "We both love you very much, don't you ever forget that, because you mean the world to us."

"I won't."

A moment later, when she was released, Maya straightened and strolled towards the stairs. "I'll see you in the morning." She said, giving a little wave and climbed the stairs.

Maya left her room in darkness and picked her way

23

across the carpet toward her bed to perch on its edge. She wished she could tell her mother that the monster tonight resembled the one which took Jack, but Maya knew she couldn't, like she couldn't tell her that she was still haunted by that day, knowing that it would break her heart. Maya took in a deep breath and exhaled slowly. *Anyway, my parents didn't believe me then, so why would they now.*

While she sat there, images of her brother's disappearance began to re-emerge. For years Maya had buried the memories deep in the back of her mind, except now they were unbound and free to torment her once again. She sat rigid and observed the whole devastating event playing in her mind, like a movie on a big screen. Maya could see Jack, then five, sitting with his legs crossed on the carpet, giggling, his little body bouncing with excitement as he watched his favourite cartoon on the television. A smile extended across Maya's tear-streaked face, he looked so real, so alive. Then she caught sight of her seven year old self sitting in the armchair opposite him. She was busy playing with the doll in her lap. Maya remembered that doll, she'd loved that doll. A chill entered her body, she knew what was about to happen. She opened her mouth to shout a warning, except nothing came out. Her heart stopped just as it had on that day, the fear that had crippled her then, crippled her now. Her skin broke into a cold sweat as a gassy mass emerged behind Jack and increased in size, solidifying into a grotesque monster. The same monster. It gawked at her younger self through ugly, orange eyes and then its Master

24

appeared. Maya's body trembled as once again the skinny man stood with her brother's limp body hooked over one arm. She remembered the man's face as clearly as if he stood in her room right now. His chiselled chin, high cheekbones and straight black-hair were unforgettable. The man's dark eyes stared into hers and an evil grin pulled at the corners of his thin lips. He placed a bony finger in front of them, 'Shh' the sound gushed from his mouth before he vanished, taking her brother with him.

Maya closed her eyes as the flood of emotions filled them. No one had believed her when she'd explained what had happened. A doctor had nodded, saying, 'There, there everything will be alright,' but it wasn't; some evil individual and his ugly pet monster had taken her brother and it would never be alright. Five years later, her dad insisted that they move in the hope that a change of scene would stop her nightmares, and they had, except tonight, they'd returned. However, this time it was different, this time she wasn't alone, Sam had seen the creature too. Maya wiped the cuff of her sleeve over her eyes and sniffed. *I don't understand it all.* She wrapped her duvet around her, brought her knees up to her chest and began to rock back and forth until sleep enfolded her.

The sweat that trickled down her back was immediately cooled by the wind's pummelling hands as Maya ran along the moonlit path. She allowed herself a quick glance back to find that the obscure form pursuing her, had managed to gain ground.

"Stop," a young voice shouted, a boy's voice.

25

She glanced back again and her heart missed several beats. A boy of about thirteen maybe fourteen, no younger, no older, could just about touch her if he wanted to. *I've seen him somewhere before, but where?* Her foot caught on a twisted root and for a few seconds she felt weightless until she landed belly down on the ground. Rotting vegetation pushed up against her as she skidded to a halt. Spitting out the dirt, her hair fell forward revealing a vile worm dangling from a few coiled strands. She screamed and flapped her hands through her hair, dislodging the soggy thing.

Lowering her arms, Maya had expected to touch damp soil however, to her surprise they had landed on cushioned fabric. *What the hell's going on? What's happening to me?* Brushing her hair from her face, she found herself back in her room lying across her bed with her duvet heaped under her arms and there was no sign of the worm.

"It was a dream ... a flippin' dream!" She gasped.

Except, this time the dream had been different from the ones she'd had in the past, those were nightmarish and about her brother. This dream had been so real that even now she could still smell the lingering odour of rotting vegetation in the air. Maya wiped the moisture from her forehead with the edge of her duvet. *It's happening again, the monster, the nightmares. It's all starting again.*

CHAPTER THREE

The tumbled down village consisting of eight small cottages and a derelict church, had a deserted air in the late afternoon. A boy crept around the corner of a stone cottage and peered across at its rusting gate with the name 'Thistle Cottage' written in grey letters. His gaze followed the cottage's brown withered hedge until he stopped and noticed that every piece of vegetation belonging to the place, had had the life sucked right from it. But it didn't just stop there; the rest of the nearby homes had that same death by suction appearance to them as well. *Go figure that out,* he thought.

Staring up into the murky sky, the boy saw a small figure skim across the cottage's roof before landing clumsily on top of its dilapidated chimney pot. The creature tucked its wings close to its back, coiled its tail around its legs and stared ahead. All of a sudden, it froze and with its saucer-shaped eyes, glared down at the boy.

It screeched out in its high-pitched voice and twitched nervously about. "Masters ... theys coming. Yah must goes." It insisted as it stretched its wings wide to take to the air, but instead toppled from its perch to land at the boy's side.

The scrawny looking creature grasped the bottom of

the youngster's woollen jacket and started to tug him towards the woods and away from the drive opposite which would lead them back home.

"Pleassse...."

"Okay, Skip." The youngster snapped, brushing the creature away like an annoying fly.

Skip jumped back, his pointy ears drooping in a dejected fashion before twitching his nose to sniff the air.

"Hide, theys are so very close."

The boy wheeled round, searching for a place to hide. Powering forward into a sprint, he headed towards a hedge several metres to his left and flung himself head first through a gap at its base. Flesh peeled off his palms as the full force of his body pushed him along the stony undergrowth; debris stung his face and flew up into his mouth until he eventually came to a halt in the churchyard beyond. *Note to self; shut your mouth next time.* When he slid to a clumsy halt, he pushed himself to his knees.

"Crap!" He swore, spitting in all directions before he blew on his palms in short blasts to ease their sting.

He peered through the hawthorn hedge and spotted six burly figures emerging from behind Thistle Cottage. The youngster drew in a deep breath when they came to a halt on the opposite side of the hedge to him. He froze, listening to their deep guttural groans. *Great! Fantastic! Why the hell has Fallan sent this lot out for me? Surely one's enough?* He puffed the stale air out of his mouth and took another gulp. *I'm so screwed.*

One of the guards turned towards the woodland, staring high-up into the trees and after a snapped order, they all marched off in that direction. As the boy took a few uneven gasps of air, he caught a glimpse of Skip flitting amongst the tree-line and grinned.

"Thanks, mate, I owe you one."

Peeking quickly over the hedge to make sure there were no other guards hanging around, the boy chuckled at his small victory while watching the last guard disappear. He tucked back down and winced as he got on his hands and knees to crawl through the gap again, and once on the other side, he rose stiffly to his feet and he set off at a sprint, running along the dirt track leading to the manor house and the place he called home.

The first thing that caught his attention as he approached the grey-brick manor, were the lights that glistened throughout the lower level. Yet, it was the single light on the second floor, shining like a beacon that brought him to a skidding halt. *I don't remember leaving that on this morning.* He scratched the top of his head. *So, I wonder how long it took Fallan to finally discover that I'd disobeyed him again.* Scuttling behind a large stack of firewood, he looked across at the front door and spied two guards standing in his way. They were everywhere, even by the doors leading to the cellar. *What's going on around here, what's with all the guards all of a sudden?*

With a long groan, he sat on the damp ground, pulled his knees up to his chest and wrapped his arms around his legs. This morning Fallan had threatened to lock him up in his room *forever* if he left it for any reason today, so what better excuse did he need than to do just that.

But forever is one hell of an exaggeration, thought the

boy and he gave a little chuckle to himself.

Yet his smile quickly turned into a frown when he peered around the woodpile and took another look toward the main door. He exhaled with agitation at the sight of the guards milling around. *Surely they're not all out just for my benefit.* Leaning back against the logs, the youngster tightened his arms around his chest. The thought of running away seemed his only option now, but he couldn't do that to Skip again. He squeezed his eyes shut, the mere thought bringing back that cruel moment in time; he could see himself now, chained to a wall with that rusted collar clamped around his neck so he couldn't turn his head away from the horrific torture his friend was receiving. Fallan stopped only at the point when he could hardly recognise the small creature. *Why would anyone do that to a defenceless being, and why hadn't they punish me when it was my idea in the first place?* He wiped a tear away with his sleeve and opened his eyes.

Without warning, a hand grabbed his arm making him smash his elbow on the edge of a log as he wrenched it away.

"Ouch!" the boy cried out, but quickly clamped his mouth shut.

"Sorry, masters." Skip flinched back.

"Shh." The boy glared at him, and listened for approaching footsteps, but he could only hear the faint muttering of voices travelling from across the yard. He sighed and gave a slow lopsided grin at his friend.

"I'm sorry, Skip," he told his friend as he scratched between the creature's ears. "Don't worry, it's going to be okay." Tilting his head back, the boy peered into the pink-hued sky just as a flurry of sleet began to fall. "What is it with this weather lately?"

"You can't hide behind there forever, boy." A deep guttural voice growled.

Skip leapt onto his young master's lap, wrapping his arms around the boy's neck and clung on tightly.

"*Crap,* it's Fallan." The boy spluttered and stared into his friend's wide eyes.

"Show yourself ... NOW." Fallan bellowed.

Peeling Skip from around his neck, he then went to shove him off his lap, except Skip wouldn't let go. His friend thrashed out, pulling at the boy's hair and clothes until the youngster fought back. He had never seen Skip this terrified and in the end had to settle with leaving him wrapped around his left leg. Dragging himself around the woodpile with Skip digging his heels into the ground, made him regret getting his friend involved in his antics again. *I've got to change my ways, for Skip's sake if nothing else.* He stopped in front of the man who was his keeper.

Snowflakes covered Fallan's black hair, turning it white for the few seconds they lasted. His lank body towered above them both, a lethal calmness was in his eyes as he glared down at the boy and then at Skip, who in turn peeked out from between the youth's legs.

Fallan pointed at the whimpering creature. "You," he said, with unconcealed contempt. "You, I will deal with later. Get out of my sight, pest."

There was a moment's hesitation before the boy felt his friend release the hold on his leg. He watched as Skip

31

folded his wings against his back and padded on all fours, like a chastised dog, towards the house.

Fallan started to circle the youth, the man's expression darkened with an unreadable emotion. Determined not to show his fear even though he hadn't seen Fallan this angry before, the youth straightened and held his head high in defiance.

"If it was up to me, you would be crushed beneath my feet right now, like the squirming maggot you are." Snarled Fallan, a vein popping visibly in his forehead. He stopped abruptly in front of the youth, throwing his hands above his head. "Why ... why do you disobey me and insist on leaving the safety of the house. At fourteen, you should know better. It's beyond my comprehension."

"I ..."

Fallan gave the boy a stinging slap across his face, stopping him mid-sentence. "I am the *one* talking and you *will* listen."

Reaching forward, Fallan grabbed the back of the boy's jacket giving the youth no time to react. Dangling from the thin yet powerful man's arm, the boy wondered how someone so scrawny-looking could lift him off his feet with such ease. *What the hell does this guy eat for breakfast?* His attempts at freedom were completely ignored, even though he kicked and hit his target several times much to Fallan's growing annoyance, but it did nothing at all, except make the man tighten his grip, which in turn, forced the zip on the boy's jacket to bite into his throat. Each breath came in short gulps while he was hoisted up the main staircase, down a corridor and eventually thrown into his room. Fallan glared at him, mumbled a few strange words and when he'd finished, he turned and slammed the door shut. With a clunk, the key turned in the lock and the room became his prison.

For several minutes he sat on the floorboards where he'd landed, wondering what would happen next and what reprimand Skip would receive. *I hope they don't beat him up like they did the last time we got caught mucking around.* He grimaced from the knot in his stomach knowing that Skip would suffer for his foolishness. *If only they'd take it out on me instead, I'm the one that decided to do it, not Skip. I hate them all, every stinking one of them and especially Fallan.*

"I'll get my own back on you Fallan. You just wait." He spat, as he rubbed the burning sensation from his grazed knees.

He eventually got to his feet, let his jacket fall to the floor and peeled off his wet trainers. Throwing himself onto his four poster bed, he pushed his head deeper into the feather pillow as he peered up through the torn canopy and on toward the vaulted ceiling. The usual rank smell of the moth-eaten drapes surrounding his bed wafted down and he found it impossible to focus on anything other than the stench. With a sigh, he rubbed his nose and sat up before grabbing the faded counterpane. He hauled it over to the gargantuan fireplace, slumped dejectedly into the nearest chair and tucked the orange cover around his chilled body. With a blank expression, he stared at the blackened wall of the hearth. He didn't feel right. An unusual heaviness pulled at his eyelids and a peculiar sensation coursed through every muscle, making it increasingly difficult to move. Yet it didn't scare him, although it felt like his body was shutting down bit by bit. Squeezing his eyes shut, the boy searched for the image of the horse in his dreams, the horse that carried him far away from the house and beyond, to freedom. He seized that memory as his body succumbed to the strange exhaustion.

Jolts of electricity shot throughout his muscles, forcing his sleep-encrusted eyes to snap open to see broad, hairy hands wrapped around his arms. Tilting his head back, two men in dark-blue mantles were dragging him along a corridor. *These guys are huge. Where the hell are they taking me?* The boy decided to keep his body limp, his eyes closed and tried to shut out the pain from his bare heals scraping along the stone floor. After a while they came to a halt in front of a plain oak door. He heard the sound of muffled voices coming from within the room and listened.

"You're losing control of the boy, Fallan," a male voice rattled. "And you want me to leave him here with you."

"He's bored, Bazriel, not out of control," Fallan answered, in a lowered voice.

"Bored!" Bazriel roared. "You expect me to accept that as your explanation of his behaviour?"

"The boy needs playmates, General."

"Playmates," Bazriel boomed again. "Huh, don't make me laugh. He's a human, a pet to toy with." There was a pause and then the boy could hear feet shuffling toward the door and him.

The boy swallowed a lump down his throat. *I'm no one's pet to toy with,'* he cursed in silence.

"His mind is getting stronger however," Bazriel said, with satisfaction. "It's time we awaken his gift now, so he can persuade humans to sign their names in 'The Book of Souls.'"

"Yes, My Lord," Fallan replied, in a subdued voice.

What's the Book of Souls? A creak startled the boy and a waft of air brushed his hair as the door swung inward.

"Bring him in," Fallan snapped the order.

The guards dragged him into the room and dumped his seemingly unconscious form onto a wooden chair. A thick hand slapped against his chest and forced his spine up against its spindled back. Another hand, thinner and more refined, gripped his chin and raised his head. All the while the boy kept his body as relaxed as he could, and when the cold hand left his face, he allowed his head to drop back to his chest.

"He's still asleep. The spell must've worked better than I'd thought," said Fallan. "I haven't used the incantation on a human youth before."

"You fool." Bazriel spat.

A shadow darkened the light in front of the youngster's eyes and he could tell that someone had crouched down in front of him by the hot, stinking breath warming his face.

"Don't toy with me, boy." The man's voice was hushed, but demanding and had the same rattle on its

35

edge as earlier, it was the person that Fallan had addressed as Bazriel. "Your games won't work with me. Open your eyes."

Instantly the boy's eyeballs felt as if they were on fire. He snapped them open. Yellow irises with black pupils stared back at him, mesmerising him into a hypnotic state. His soul laid bare in the grip of Bazriel's power. Pictures and memories jumped uncontrollably in front of his eyes. This bald, fat, horrid guy was searching for something, and he could do nothing to stop him.

"Hmm." The older man, Bazriel, leaned in closer. "Ah ... there we are. It's time for your gift to awaken and be used."

Crap, what can he see, what the hell's he on about? My gift? He felt his heart jump, smacking against his ribs as currents of electricity surged through his head. He wanted to run, to get away, except he couldn't move. Sharp, burning bolts shot through his mind. Bazriel grinned.

"Stop it. Please." The boy screamed.

Bazriel's smile widened. Fallan stood watching, his tongue wiping across his cracked lips with delight.

"Your suffering will cease when you decide to stop fighting me." Hummed Bazriel.

But I'm not fighting you! Then he remembered the games he played with Skip, where he would imagine an object, picture every detail perfectly in his mind, then look into Skip's eyes, placing the image in his friend's thoughts and *will* him to go and fetch that item. No words were ever spoken, but Skip would always retrieve what he had asked for. What if he could do the same thing to Bazriel and stop the pain?

"You have no idea what you're capable of, do you?" Bazriel placed a swollen, aged hand on his young captive's shoulder and watched as the youngster's body began to shake.

Glaring into Bazriel's eyes, the boy began to form images of every nasty thing he could do to the old man; like stabbing him in the heart, or shoving him in a fire, or blowing him up into a thousand tiny, microscopic pieces. He bundled each picture together and threw them into his captor's mind. Bazriel's eyes enlarged, his face paled.

I did it ... It worked! The boy continued to stare into those evil eyes, which were now rimmed with bulging blue veins and he waited for his own agony to stop.

However, Bazriel shook his head and wiped his hand over his brow. "Oh ... nice one, boy, except your little mind games won't work with me." He purred and dug his ringed fingers into the youngster's arm.

A burning sensation tore through the teenager's chest and escaped out through his skin. He couldn't bear it anymore and his weakened body slumped in the chair, tears streamed down his cheeks, his mind void of all thoughts, while he was held under the old man's will. Finally, he could take no more and collapsed, giving up any fight he had left in him, but he wasn't unconscious yet.

"Good." Bazriel's features twisted into a maddening leer. "Now that I've woken his mind to his power, we can get on with our plan."

The boy's body shuddered from the sudden release of

Bazriel's control, both physically and mentally.

Through a half closed eye, he watched the blurred figure of Bazriel turn to face Fallan. "One of our former brothers has made contact with the girl."

"So why don't we just get rid of her?"

"Don't you think that hasn't crossed my mind, that I haven't already tried to do that," he told Fallan in a full throated voice bursting with outrage. "My last attempt to destroy her while she was taking a walk with her little friend, got thwarted by this former brother of ours, and now his vigilance has increased. Though I do have another plan in progress." He turned back to gaze at the boy. "I think the girl would be of greater use to us alive." He smiled, but it soon dropped into a frown. "However, if this angel uses the girl to find this boy, then our problems will truly begin."

The boy raised his hands and rested them on either side of his face, pressing his palms against his temples to try and relieve the pressure, but it ended up making it feel worse. Electricity sparkled inside his skull and an excess of power pushed against the back of his eyes. He felt poised between life and death, and was unaware that his movements had alerted Bazriel, who swirled around, approached and rested his hands on the youth's shoulders. Flinty eyes cut into the boy's soul, tearing down any barrier he had managed to form as if it was an annoying spider's web to be swept away. Bazriel dropped to one knee in front of him, his chubby, shovel-like hands moving to either-side of the boy's head.

"Grab him. Hold him still," Bazriel barked.

The guard by the door approached. The youngster growled, yet it came out like a weak whine. His arms were wrenched behind his back causing the muscles in his already tender shoulders to rip. He kicked out with both feet, missing Bazriel by a few inches and his grazed heels smacked down on the concrete floor, sending a sharp jolt through his legs.

Bazriel chortled. "It's nice to see you have spirit, boy, because you're going to need it."

The spit from Bazriel's mouth splashed in stinging beads across the teenager's face and again the old man's touch scalded the boy's flesh before entering his mind. With no barrier or strength left to fight, words the boy couldn't comprehend were spoken in a language he didn't recognise or understand. He cried out, yelling for the old man to stop. Every part of the boy's physical form felt on the verge of exploding and then without warning, it all ended, just stopped dead, and Bazriel struggled to his feet with a malicious grin pulling on his face.

"Now, he can be used, but first he must rest before he is introduced to The Book." Bazriel took several protesting steps to stand beside Fallan. "Nazual," he called out softly, wiping sweat from his brow with the back of his hand.

A breeze lifted the stale air, making Fallan's hair fan out from his face. The boy watched as a form materialised by the door. A sallow, scarred-faced man with the haunted look of someone who had seen many battles, now stood before them.

"General Bazriel," Nazual greeted him.

The old general shuffled towards him and halted. "A former brother of ours is getting in the way of Our Lord's plans."

"Which brother is that?" enquired Nazual, with a hint of excitement in his deep voice.

"The one they call The Thwarter of Demons."

Thwarter of Demons, who the heck has a name like that? The boy raised his eyes to find the stranger staring straight at him.

Nazual tilted his head and gave an exaggerated wink his way and a smile formed on his thin lips. "The one Our Lord still desires to turn?"

"Yes." Bazriel rubbed his bald head before placing his hand on the other man's shoulder. "I need you to keep an eye on him for me."

"It will be my pleasure, General."

"You will watch him, nothing else, is that understood?"

"Yes."

"The right time will come when you can face him again, my old friend."

Nazual bowed his head and gave a wicked smile.

"There's one other thing you can help me with though, before you go." Bazriel's plump lips curled into a perfect curve.

Nazual raised his eyebrows with interest.

"Fetch the hounds. They're going hunting." He laughed a humourless vicious sound before turning and pointing at the limp figure of the boy. "And you." He gestured to a guard with his chin. "Return the boy to his room and let me know when he recovers."

CHAPTER FOUR

The following Monday morning, Maya stood at the entrance of the six-form building, searching for Sam amongst the bustling crowds of pupils. Hoisting the strap of her tote bag further up her shoulder and cradling her books in the cuff of her right arm, she craned her neck to peer above the heads and spotted Harriet by the main office scouring the notice board. *Okay, I'll talk to Sam first, then Harriet. Keep it simple, Maya, you know you can do this.* Her brow narrowed as she continued to stare at Harriet's back, her gut tightening with every second that went by due to the pent up anger she'd held on to over the weekend. *No ... I can't. Just look at her, she probably doesn't regret a single thing she did on Friday night.* Maya took a deep breath and straightened her shoulders. *Well, after today, bitch, you're going to wish you never knew me at all.* Maya took a step forward, then stopped as if she'd been slapped across her face. Harriet had spun round and now stared straight back at her, and all Maya could see was amusement flickering in the eyes that met hers. Before Maya could react, Harriet stiffened, haughtily tossed her head, and walked off in the opposite direction without even having the common courtesy to offer an apology.

"What the ...." Maya snorted as she watched Harriet

disappear around a corner.

Taking a deep breath, trying to steady her anger, Maya glanced across the foyer and saw Sam standing with one hand in his pocket, chatting to a new guy, who for some reason regarded her with the strangest unreadable expression before tilting his head slightly and winking at her. Maya frowned in return and when Sam glanced up, catching her gaze, he said a quick farewell to the new arrival and strode towards her.

"Need a hand?" He asked, raising his arms to relieve Maya of her books, whether she wanted his help or not.

She saw a slight glimmer of uncertainty behind his eyes, then it had gone and before she could utter a single word, he turned and strolled off towards the room they'd commandeered last year and named the Snug. *Surely he can't still be in a mood with me over Leo?* Maya had waited all weekend to discuss the events of last Friday evening with him, but seeing Sam now, she wondered whether she should mention anything about it at all. *What if he's like everyone else and thinks I'm crazy?* She swallowed and shrugged. *Whatever, I've got to know what he saw.* Trailing after him, she threaded her way across the corridor and on towards their room.

Stopping in the threshold, Maya noticed Ben shifting uneasily on the sofa along the far wall. Not ready to forgive him for his part either, she gave him one of her disapproving stares. *That's right, you better squirm.* But her attack was diverted by Sam throwing her books down on the top of the coffee table with a thud. Turning, she rested her hip against the doorpost and waited for Sam to crash land in the worn-out armchair, before glaring back at Ben. *I wonder why Harriet isn't with him like her usual parasitic self. And what the hell was with that new guy and his weird wink.* She glanced back at Ben, who immediately lowered his head.

"Sam, who were you talking to just then?" Maya asked.

"What?" he barked.

"The new guy, who was he?"

"No-one."

"Sam, he's got to be someone."

Ben stood, briefly interrupting them. "You guys look like you need to be alone," he said, his movements stiff and awkward as he approached Maya. "I'm sorry about Friday night, Maya." He took a deep breath trying to steady the shakiness in his voice. "Harriet planned it all, getting us all to meet at the church and then not turning up it was all her idea and I don't know why she did it. Anyway, I'm sorry." He looked at her with his soft, puppy dog eyes. "You know what she's like." He tried to relax his face into a smile but it wasn't quite working and it appeared more like a grimace.

"It's a real shame that Harriet isn't adult enough to come forward and apologise for her own actions, but thanks Ben, I knew it wasn't your fault anyway. Don't worry about it anymore."

"Thanks, she told me not to say anything, but I'm not like her." He glanced back at Sam. "I've got to meet up with Harriet now in the language block before the bell goes, so I'll catch you guys later, okay?" He finished and turned whilst hoisting his trousers over his belly.

So that's where she's hiding, and poor old Ben does what he's told as usual. I don't understand what he gets out of their relationship, if you can call it that. Sam had a puzzled look on his face as he flicked his hand in a quick wave. Maya stepped aside so Ben could pass and waited until he was lost amongst the crowd before returning her attention back on Sam whose shoulders slumped when their gaze met.

"Look, I'm sorry if I sounded a bit off with you, it's just when that new guy saw you ... he started asking a lot of questions." Leaning back, he crossed one leg over the other. "Anyway, what was Ben going on about?"

"Don't try changing the subject."

"I wasn't."

"Focus on the new guy and tell me what his questions were about?"

"You."

"Me? He was asking questions about me? Whatever for?"

Sam shook his head. "All I know is that his name's John Latruce, he moved here from Suffolk a week ago and when he spotted you standing in the main entrance ..." He shifted uncomfortably in his chair and repositioned his legs.

Maya walked to the table, pushed her books to one side and sat down on its edge. "What sort of questions did he ask?"

Sam sat up straight. "Whoa, just hold on a minute. Are you interrogating me?" He smiled suggestively.

"Oh, for goodness sake, Sam! Be serious for once in your life."

He groaned, tilted his head back and answered, "Okay, um ... he wanted to know your name, then where you live and did you have a boyfriend." He pointed at her. "And no, before you ask, I didn't answer them."

"But why? Why does he want to know that kind of stuff about me?"

"How am I supposed to know?" His eyebrows raised and he chuckled, "Perhaps he fancies you."

"No way!" She gave him a slap across his arm. *That's a really sick thought.* "This really isn't the time to be joking, Sam."

He rubbed his arm, his smile fading a fraction as he looked at her.

Clearing her throat, Maya glanced back at the door, making sure there was no one about before continuing her next onslaught of questions. "Anyway, I've got something important to discuss with you, concerning Friday night."

"What about it?" Sam straightened and regarded her with sombre curiosity.

"You know ... the creature down by the river, the thing that scared the hell out of us."

"What creature?" Sam raised an eyebrow. "What are you on about?"

A cold knot formed in her stomach. "You're kidding right? Please don't tell me you can't remember."

"Can't remember what?"

"The winged monster and the pillar of light."

Sam gave her a sidelong glance of utter disbelief.

46

"Okay, if you don't remember them, do you remember meeting Leo in the church?"

He shook his head.

"Do you remember any of it?"

Sitting forward with his arms resting on his thighs, he began rubbing his hands together. "You must've had one hell of a crazy dream that night."

Maya sat quite still, staring at him, tongue-tied. *But it happened, you were there, Sam. Why can't you remember?* Her eyes widened. *Is Leo a figment of my imagination as well? NO ... no, I don't want to believe that.* The mere thought of it was like a stab in her heart. *But if Sam can't recall any of it, then who am I going to talk too? I'm not crazy, I'm not.*

The school bell shrilled through the classroom speaker, startling Maya, and for the first time since talking to Sam that morning, she became aware of her surroundings. Sitting back in her chair with her palms flat on the table, she glanced down at the open pages to her exercise book and sighed loudly. *Great! It's taken me an hour to write the date. Pinton's is not going to be impressed with that.* She raised her gaze, peering at the empty chair opposite, and it was as if someone had smacked her in the face with a table-tennis paddle, switching on all the mechanics in her brain. *Jess! Dammit ... I can't believe I haven't even notice she's not been here all day.* Delving to the bottom of her bag, Maya pulled out her mobile phone and tapped out a quick message.

Jess r u ok?

Shifting in her seat, she waited for Jess' reply, but the

47

sound of someone drumming their fingers on a table behind her became too annoying to ignore. Twisting, she jerked upright when she spotted John Latruce in the far corner amongst the shadows and he stared back at her with his obsidian black eyes, then he smiled, except there was nothing good intended in that smile, it wasn't warm or friendly, but cold and dangerous. Maya returned to face the front of the classroom and shivered when John started up the drumming again. *What's his problem?* Her mobile phone vibrated, giving a welcome distraction just as the final bell rang. Gazing down at the screen, she read:

I'm ok, still getting over the cold, c u 2 moz x J.

Dropping the phone back in her bag, Maya grabbed her belongings and headed towards the school car park, and her mum's waiting Volkswagen Polo.

Tuesday morning, Maya entered the snug and saw Sam, Ben and John standing in the centre of the room discussing football. She looked at Sam. *Typical guys, the mere mention of football and they'll forgive just about anyone of anything.* Maya peered towards the back of the room and spotted Jess sitting on the sofa, her legs crossed and her face buried in an anthology book. Jess always presented herself immaculately and today was no exception; she wore a smart pastel skirt, matching jacket, and a pair of heels that were to-die-for. She looked great with her shiny-blonde hair, not a strand out of place. Maya dumped her bag on the table as she approached and Jess peered over the top of the hardback to greet her with a smile.

"Hi, it's good to see you back. How're you feeling?"

enquired Maya.

"I'm good thanks. Who's the new guy?" Jess gestured with her chin towards the weasel-faced John who now blocked the doorway.

"That's John, why?" Maya proceeded to sit down beside her.

"Do you know him?" Jess asked, with a twinkle in her eyes.

"Not yet, but they all seem to be getting on," answered Maya, while continuing to look directly at him.

His shoulder-length hair clung to his face like a hood, one side hiding his left eye and a look of veiled amusement crossed his face for a split second when their gaze met. He winked and Maya hoped that that was for Jess' benefit and not hers.

Closing her book, Jess gazed longingly up at John. "He's cute, don't you think?" she stated, but didn't wait for a reply before continuing, "I saw him in the village shop on Sunday. He kept eyeing me up and even bought me a box of chocolates. How sweet is that?"

"Really?" Maya replied. *Is she serious! There's no way I'd describe him as being ... cute!*

"Don't sound that surprised." Jess chuckled, as she shoved her book in her bag and stood. "Look, I've got to go. I'll see you later."

Maya gave her a forced smile and a tense nod while she watched Jess sashay towards the door and stop in front of John. She shifted her bag to sit protectively halfway across her chest. *That seems a weird move if you fancy someone. Why is she afraid of him, yet propelled towards*

49

him at the same time? Was there something in that chocolate he gave her? Cripes, what am I thinking? Love potion in the chocolate, how crazy does that sound?

"Hi, um, have you got English next?" Jess asked him.

He nodded, superficially.

"I'll walk you there then, if you'd like?" she suggested.

"Yeah sure," he answered with an impersonal nod.

What's he playing at?

Before they left the room, John twisted his head to look directly at Maya. *Oh my goodness! There's that wink again. What a creep. Yet, he's the least of my problems because I really don't know what's come over Jess. She's never had that kind of reaction towards a boy before, not since she started her A-levels and vowed not to chase the opposite sex until she'd finished them at least, and I've always admired her commitment for making that decision. Except now, out of all the fit guys she could have, she thought John was cute. Seriously!*

"Strange, very strange," Maya mumbled to herself.

Maya struggled to ignore Jess' continued flirting throughout the following two hours of double art, it was sickening to watch. Every time she took a peek at them, John would smile and wink back at her in a creepy, perverted kind of way. She shivered. *Something's not right with John Latruce, but I can't quite work it out, not yet anyway, and why can't Jess see it? It's as if she's been blinded by some sort of powerful spell.* Maya shook her head and glanced down at the still-life drawing of a vase of flowers she hadn't quite finished. *Maybe it's just me being bitchy and John happens to wink at everyone.* She

50

shrugged and added pencil to paper, following the curves of the vase and while gazing at the reflections thrown across its surface she saw a face with sky-blue eyes appear, a face she could recognise anywhere, staring straight at her.

"Leo," she said in a startled whisper just as the bell rang, making her flinch.

Maya continued to look at the glass vase as the last person left the room, but the image of Leo only lasted a matter of seconds. Stretching across the table to shove everything in her bag, Maya stood, scraping the chair across the floor as she pushed it back. Hoisting the strap of her bag over her shoulder, she grabbed her art folder and spun round towards the door. Her heart leapt with surprise. Pressed back against the doorframe with his thin arm stretched across the opening, was John. Maya took a deep breath and approached.

"Excuse me," she asked politely.

John didn't budge. His head hung low, a thick strand of hair had fallen in front of his right eye and a smile pulled on his lips. When she stepped closer, he didn't look up or move, however, the menacing smile stayed.

"Hope you're okay?" His lip curled.

"What are you on about?" She placed her art folder across her chest.

"We haven't had a chance to talk, have we?" He purred, while leaning forward.

Unable to hold back her frustration, Maya glared at him. "Move..." She snapped.

John's head shot back, smacking against the wooden frame, yet instead of a grimace of pain, he burst out

51

laughing. Shivering at the notion of any part of her body touching his, she pushed her folder up against his arm, except he still didn't move. Maya skipped back, a flicker of apprehension coursing through her. His high-pitched laughter pierced the air, then he fell silent and sniffed before lowering his arm to wave her through.

"There you go, pretty." His voice purred again.

Stepping in to the hallway, Maya held herself steady until she got around the first corner where she broke into a sprint, the echo of his laughter fading into the distance. Skidding to a halt, she peeked over her shoulder and sighed with relief that he wasn't following. Maya bent forward, clutching her stomach with one hand, she caught her breath. *That guy is seriously screwed up. I've got to warn Jess somehow, tell her what a psychopath he is.*

When Maya arrived home that afternoon, she headed straight to her room in silence, flung herself on her bed and stared up at the ceiling. She had to work this out; what with John's odd behaviour towards her, Jess' strange infatuation with him and Sam's loss of memory which had all started after being attacked by that monster. She had to do something to find out what it all meant. Perching her laptop on her stomach, Maya searched the internet for anything that might resemble what she had seen down by the river. She typed in *winged beasts,* then *demonic creatures* - of which there were fantasy art drawings on there - but nothing that resembled the beast she'd now seen twice. Frustratingly, images of historical mansions kept appearing on the screen and the only reason for that, Maya thought, was due to the gargoyles and grotesques figures that were dotted around the buildings. The image of a substantial gothic building called Cripply Gorge Manor caught her attention and she stared at it for several seconds, feeling oddly drawn toward the place. When Maya finally turned the computer off and sat up, those few seconds staring at that house had somehow turned into thirty minutes. *That's weird! Why was I so hooked on that place?* She laid the laptop beside her and stared vacantly at a patch of uncluttered carpet, struggling to clear her thoughts.

A whisper of cold air fluttered across Maya's skin, forcing a shiver under its touch. Her vision blurred and it had nothing to do with her weariness. Rubbing her eyes, she blinked and the scene seemed to steady, then once again it blurred, everything in her room lost its definition, appearing distorted and vague. Shutting her eyes, she counted to ten, snapped them open again to find herself in darkness. When her vision had adapted sufficiently to the gloom, she stood in a tiny clearing, crammed in by four walls made from trees. Maya glanced up into a ceiling of branches, her breath quickened. *What happened? How'd I get here, wherever here is?* Lowering her gaze, she spotted a narrow animal track to her left, which disappeared through the thick undergrowth. *What do I do now?* She turned a full circle, her heels digging into the grass. *Maybe if I close my eyes again, I'll be back in my room.* Screwing her eyes shut, she began counting to ten, but before she even got to the number four something rustled in the thicket to her right and then behind her. Her eyes shot open. *Wh... what was that?* She bit into the corner of her bottom lip and felt something tighten in her chest, but this time she knew it was fear.

In a nervous panic, Maya whispered, "The track it is then." And marched toward it.

"Wait ... please." A boy's voice echoed from behind her.

Maya didn't stop, ferns brushed against her legs as she continued along the track, her pace quickening. *That's the same voice from that dream the other night. But this isn't a dream ... no way, because I didn't fall asleep this time and I know I'm still awake now.*

The trail led to an opening. Sparse trees stood to her left and on her right was a thick clump of bracken, ivy and nettles which blocked any route of escape. Halting at the edge of the trail, Maya felt a shiver of unease stir deep down inside her. She wiped the sweat from her brow and straightened to look around, checking whether the boy had followed. Just then, a head peeked from behind a tree trunk in front of her before darting back out of sight. She stared at that spot for a while, praying that it had been a figment of her imagination. However, when her gaze returned to the clearing again, the boy now stood in front of the coppice opposite her. *He isn't real, he's just in my imagination.* Unable to move, Maya stared at him for those few seconds, then somehow he mysteriously appeared a couple of metres from her. Her gaze roamed along his disarrayed, tangled hair which complemented his handsome square face, a face that looked oddly familiar.

"Hi," Maya said, in a whisper.

His hand rose to her face, but before he could touch her, the vision faded and the familiar aroma of her perfume masked the rank odour of decomposing leaves with each intake of air. Maya blinked several times, her vision clearing and she realised that she now stood in front of her bedroom window with her feet buried beneath a pile of her clothes on the floor.

Her pulse still racing along with her muscles aching. "The boy was real. No way was that just a dream!"

CHAPTER FIVE

A week later during third period, Maya sat by herself on the opposite side of the classroom to Jess and John. If John hadn't made that hit on her after art last week, she wouldn't be in this situation right now. It was his fault that she had to spend her whole time evading him as well as lying to the others. *Life is so complicated these days, it sucks.* Her mind was firmly set in deep reflection as she glanced across at Jess, remembering that only a few weeks ago, things were so different between them. At that very moment, John reached out to push a silky strand of Jess' hair behind her ear, *that's okay,* Maya thought, except, he then looked up to fix his eyes on Maya, who stiffened under his withering glare. She swallowed, lowering her head to read the messages carved into the surface of the table. *How the hell can I get her alone when he's always there? I need to tell her what his creepiness did to me last week?* The bell for lunch echoed throughout the room startling Maya. As she gathered her belongings, the crescendo of conversations and chairs scraping along the floor made it harder to concentrate on a plan.

"Hey, Maya, are you coming to lunch?" Jess called to her from the doorway.

Maya scratched her head, brushing her hair out of her face and turned to look up. "You guys go ahead. I'll catch up."

She gathered her things and stood, wishing she had an excuse to get out of lunchtimes altogether. Maya felt physically sick knowing that creepy John would be watching her every move while she ate again. *Why don't my friends including Sam, see how he is around me?*

When Maya arrived at the refectory ten minutes later, she saw Jess and Harriet sitting at their usual table alone. Picking up her tray, Maya weaved her way towards them and slid the tray onto the table, pulled out a chair, sat down and positioned her food in front of her. Stabbing at a piece of pasta with her fork, Maya chewed a mouthful of the cheese bake and wished she hadn't bothered, because the aftertaste of disinfectant from that one mouthful still lingered in her mouth. Pushing the tray to one side, she sat back in her chair and watched Jess nibble at the corner of her sandwich. Turning to look towards the canteen, Maya wondered if the guys were waiting in the queue, but she couldn't see them anywhere in the refectory.

"Where's the guys?" she enquired, shifting around in her seat.

Jess swallowed before answering, "They went to the gym to that new club they're running."

Harriet sat back in her chair, her fingers twirling around her pony-tail. She tightened her hair-band and raised her eyebrows into a cocky expression.

"So, Maya, please do tell us why you've been ignoring us lately?" There was that edge to Harriet's voice again, that certain bitterness that hung on the end of all her sentences these days toward Maya.

Maya choked on her drink, then coughed to clear her throat. "I'm not."

"Yes you are, because you haven't joined us in the snug lately, so what's going on?"

"What the hell's this all about? There isn't anything going on, I swear."

Jess placed her arms on either side of her tray, a clouded, puzzled look appeared on her face.

There was a moment of astonished silence. Maya needed to think of an answer and needed it now. "I've just got a lot on my mind. Most of it's down to my course work, that's all, pretty boring really. Anyway, Harriet, what's it to you? I mean, you're hardly seen round the snug these days either," she replied, biting down her rising anger by taking several large gulps of her juice.

Harriet raised her chin with a cool stare in Maya's direction. "Yeah, right."

"Leave it you two." Jess snapped and gave Maya a forced smile. "If she doesn't want to tell us the real reason, Harriet, it's up to her."

Choking again on the juice, Maya lowered the bottle, banging it down on the table. *What does she mean? Has John said something to her about me?*

"Anyway, while I've got you both here," Jess continued, "I've got something to tell you."

Maya straightened and saw a flicker of mocking amusement showing in Harriet's expression, Jess' pretty face on the other hand, was shadowed by her sullen

58

mood.

"John's asked me out," Jess casually told them.

"Okay." Maya nodded, trying not to show her distaste. "And what did you say?"

"I said yes ... of course." Jess glanced across the room, a smile suddenly warming her face.

Refusing to be distracted, Maya asked, "Are you sure about this? It seems pretty quick."

Harriet's eyes narrowed, her jaw tightened and she glared back at Maya, who in return gave Harriet a look with an equally challenging expression of her own.

"I don't believe you, Maya!" Harriet said in a hushed growl.

"What?" Maya snapped back. "I'm just saying what you're probably thinking."

Harriet sat straight, her face turning red.

Maya continued. "He isn't right for you, Jess. He's trouble."

"To be honest, I don't care what you think. We're going out with each other whether you like it or not."

And at that exact moment, Maya knew she was losing her friend, she could feel it, because it felt like another fragment of her was being ripped from her heart as several other friends had in her past.

Harriet flung her chair across the floor as she stood. She jutted her lower jaw forward and leaned halfway across the table to slam her hands down directly in front of Maya.

"Why don't you think before you open your mouth next time?" she shouted. "You're unbelievable. It's none

59

of your business who Jess goes out with." Harriet looked at Jess, her expression changing instantly to one of serene sincerity. "You go for it, Jess. Take no notice of her. She's just a jealous bitch and a complete loner." She stood straight, ignored Maya and stomped off.

What's the matter with everyone? Am I the only one who can see what's going on here? Even Sam's not been himself lately as he follows John around like a lost puppy.

Maya glanced back at Jess. "Okay, I'm sorry, but this isn't like you or Harriet, and what's with her anyway?"

"What do you mean, not like me? And what's the matter with me going out with John anyway?"

"You said, that you'd wait until after your exams before considering having a boyfriend. Has John forced you into this decision?"

"Of course not, what have you got against John anyway? He said you were difficult to talk to, that you kept avoiding him."

"That isn't true. He threatened me after art last week. He wouldn't let me out of the classroom." *There I've told her now. Surely she'll believe me.*

"I told him to wait for you and have a chat, but you can't let anyone get close to you." Jess leaned across the table, her knuckles turning white as her grip tightened on either side of her tray. "You're always in your own little world."

For the first time Maya could remember, she was at a loss for words. Jess was right, she didn't let people get close, but there was a reason for that and that reason had something to do with that monster and her brother's disappearance.

Suddenly, Maya thought she caught a glimpse of Leo and twisted her head to get a better look. However, her gaze fell on John instead who was in the process of paying for his lunch. Diverting her gaze, she searched the refectory and disappointment added to her already darkened mood when Leo was nowhere to be seen. *Why am I kidding myself? Maybe every one's right and I am crazy. What with conjuring up Leo's reflection in art the other day and now here, maybe I do need help.*

John's lean body snaked between the queuing year eights as he sauntered towards their table. Stooping forward, he dropped his tray next to Jess', wrapped his bony arms around her shoulders before his pale lips attached to her neck like a blood-sucking leech. Lengthening her neck, Jess parted her lips for a kiss. Maya cringed. *She's besotted with the creep and there's nothing I can do about it.*

John pulled his mouth away from her delicate flesh. "So how's the most gorgeous girl in this dump?" His voice created that strange throaty purr sound again, and when his gaze caught Maya's, he winked.

Shuddering, Maya stood and grabbed her bag. "I've ... I've got to go to the library and get a book before lessons start." She gave a false smile. "I'll catch you guys later." Then swivelled round on her heals and with a brisk walk, threaded her way purposely towards the main door.

Entering the library, Maya hesitated by the front door, the unnatural silence bringing a chill to her body. *Where is everybody? This place is usually heaving.* Brushing her hair back from her face, Maya strolled over to the reception desk and spotted a hand written note lying on top of the register;

No study time today. However, you may return or collect books, but make sure you leave its title and number below.

Back at 2pm.

Mrs W.

Well, that explains why no one's around, but it's still pretty odd because why isn't Miss Shear-Butter here instead. Maya shrugged, turned and dumped her bag on one of the ten tables neatly positioned in a semi-circle around the main desk. She glanced out across the vast room and saw row upon row of tall wooden shelves stacked high with thousands of books. Peering up between the aisles, Maya's gaze flashed across the white signs hanging by chains from the ceiling.

"Fiction, nonfiction, biology, art and ah, there it is - history."

Her fingers glided across the books standing on the middle shelf, until the spine of one book caught her interest. Pulling the rather battered hardback out, Maya wiped her hand across the embossed cover.

"Maya ...." her name was called in a lingering whisper.

Her head shot up, her eyes wide.

"Maya ..." the voice whispered again, mockingly.

She looked left and then right. "Hello ..." she called softly, but heard no reply. "Hello ... is anyone there?" she repeated, her last words barely audible.

"Maya ...." The voice was hushed, yet deep and menacing this time.

Hearing nothing but the wild thrumming of her pulse, she crept in the direction of the door, but all of a sudden, she came to an abrupt halt. A figure stood at the end of the aisle blocking her path, it was John Latruce.

"We meet again." A strange smile touched his lips. "Little Maya, all on her own-some." He swaggered towards her, his boots thudding across the wooden floor - surprisingly bearing down heavily compared to their skinny wearer - his eyes abnormally dark.

Maya backed away, unable to peel her eyes from his.

"What have you got there?" He stared down at the book in her hands.

"Oh this ... it's nothing," replied Maya, turning the book casually over.

Just then, John seized the book, ripping it from her grasp and peered down at the cover. "History of the occult," he said, with a grin as he opened it, rifling through the pages. "What're you doing with this?"

Snatching the book from his sweaty grip, Maya retorted, "Just doing some research and it happens to be none of your business." She slammed the book shut and cradled it close to her chest, turned and retraced her steps.

"You and I have got a lot in common." He gave a little giggle of evil satisfaction. "I like all that occult stuff."

Maya quickened her pace, turned the corner and gasped, John once again stood blocking her way.

"We could be friends, Maya, very good friends."

Spinning round, Maya sprinted down another aisle, the main desk fifteen metres from her now, and she knew her escape was just beyond that. Tightening her hold on the book, she returned to a quick walk, but suddenly, John came at her in a blur, pushing her back up against the shelves. The book slipped from Maya's grip as pain erupted in her spine. John caught both her wrists in his grasp, forcing them behind her and clasped them in one of his hands, while his free hand reached up to brush her hair from her neck. Maya desperately tried to turn her face away from his, but he caught her chin, forcing her to look at him.

"Get off me," she demanded, trying to keep her voice level, but she could already feel her body betraying her by trembling, half with fear, half with anger.

His nose touched hers and his putrid breath hit her nostrils, leaving a metallic tang in her mouth while his hand brushed across her cheek, then down to her throat.

"Now that we're close." He smirked and leaned forward, his lips brushing the surface of hers.

"Get off me, you *creep*." She spat in his face.

"Oh, feisty little thing aren't you." He made a strange gurgling sound half way between a cough and a laugh, then the cords in his neck stood out violently. "So tell me, Maya, why are you avoiding me? Is it because you fancy me?"

64

"Get lost." She felt the pressure on her windpipe slowly increase, silencing her.

"You're jealous that Jess and I are going out, aren't you?"

His grip caused any reply to wedge in her throat. However, she could hear his heavy breathing as his mouth caressed her neck.

Lifting his head, he glared straight into her eyes. "You won't come between us you know. Jess is mine, and you won't be able to change her mind. Is that understood?" A swift shadow of anger swept across his face. "And if you think your life is lonely now, wait and see what I can do if you say anything to make Jess doubt me."

Maya shut her eyes, she had to think of a way out of this situation and think of it quickly. Her knee struck his groin with amazing speed and accuracy, forcing John to release his grip. She glanced down at his bent over form, then the book laying on the floor by her feet. Picking it up, she gripped the hardback in both hands and lifted it above his head. With a mighty swing of her arms and a thwack, the book connected with its target and Maya watched as John's limp form crumpled to the floor. She didn't wait to see if he was okay, why should she, after what he'd just put her through. Instead she turned and bolted towards the front desk, grabbing her bag on the way out. Fleeing through the door, she took a quick glance back to see if John had recovered and when Maya turned her head to look forward again, she came to a sudden and abrupt halt. The book flew into the air, her bag skidded across the grass, and she fell backwards landing on the concrete path on her backside.

A deep and furious blush whooshed through her when she peered up to see Leo standing over her with a look of concern written on his face.

"Are you okay?" he asked, as he held out his hand.

"Yeah."

Maya gasped as an indescribable sensation sparkled up her arm the instant her hand touched his. Once she was back on her feet, she released her hold and felt heat radiating off her face. *Oh for crying-out-loud! This is so embarrassing.*

"What are you doing here?" she asked as she bent down to retrieve her belongings.

"Oh." He looked momentarily down at the path, then back at Maya. "I was having a guided tour, but the guy who was showing me around, pointed out the library and told me to wait here. And that's what I was doing until you ran out and ...."

"You're coming here ... to this school!" Maya interrupted in breathless amazement.

A smile pulled at one corner of Leo's lips. "Yes, I start after the Easter break. My dad and I moved into Wicklesham last Wednesday."

"Really?"

"Really," mimicked Leo.

Oh cripes, this is too good to be true, but I'm staring at him again. She fiddled with the clasp on her bag, then glanced back towards the library. "Can we get away from here?"

66

"Sure, where have you got in mind?"

"Anywhere that's not near this building."

Five minutes later they ducked under the bus shelter and Maya waited for Leo to sit on the bench beside her. He sat sideways, his midnight-black hair falling forward, slightly obscuring his eyes but it didn't take away how they brightened a couple of shades of blue, and for a few seconds her attention was completely absorbed by his gaze.

"I'm a good listener." The warmth of his smile echoed in his voice.

"What?"

"I'm a good listener," he repeated with infinite serenity. "Why were you running from the library?"

"It was nothing, really." Maya lowered her head as John's attack resurfaced. *Why did he have to bring that up? He wouldn't understand even if I told him.*

"Didn't seem like nothing to me." He placed his hand on her arm. "What's troubling you?"

Maya swallowed and gazed down at his hand. After a moment's reflection, she had planned to tell him, 'I'm fine, there's nothing troubling me,' although when she opened her mouth, the wrong words blurted out. "I think I'm going mad, I really don't know what's going on with me?" She slapped her hand over her mouth. *I can't believe I just said that!*

Leo shuffled closer, his hand still resting on her arm, while Maya stared straight ahead. "Maya, don't be afraid. You can trust me."

Can I though? Can I trust someone I hardly know?

"Tell me what happened?" Leo asked, in a hauntingly tranquil whisper.

Biting into her bottom lip, Maya turned to face him. Their eyes met, and she saw something flicker deep within them, things she couldn't imagine anyone ever living through: pain, suffering, war, famine and death, and then it had gone, leaving tenderness gazing back at her. She wasn't alone in her suffering, he had experienced it to, and one day she hoped he would tell her about it.

"It ... it's to do with John Latruce."

Shaking his head, he replied, "I don't know the guy."

"Right, sure. Well ... he attacked me a few minutes ago in the library, that's why I ran out." Maya looked away. *Why am I telling him all this?* Heat from his hand sizzled pleasantly up her arm forcing her to peer into those blue eyes again and then the details she would've kept hidden, gushed out. "He pushed me up against one of the bookshelves, grabbed me by the throat and tried to kiss me."

Leo's eyes darkened. "What!?" His voice deepened a few tones. "How did you get away?"

"I brought my knee up and smashed him in the groin." Maya noticed Leo cringe. "Then I smacked him over the head with that book." She gestured with her head to the book sitting under her bag, "And ran."

Leo arched an eyebrow. "Remind me not to get in a fight with you."

Maya managed a weak smile.

He leaned closer. "You sound as if you're having a rough time."

With every word spoken or movement that Leo made, Maya couldn't stop staring at him and strangely, she began telling him about the night they'd first met in the church.

"I saw a monster or something evil down by the river, and Sam saw it too. It was huge and it had bat-like wings and massive fangs ... and." She stopped, surprised by his calmness. *He isn't laughing!*

"Go on."

"I've seen it before. When I was seven ..." she trailed off.

"And?" There was a questioning look in his eyes.

"No one believed me then, but it's starting all over again. The dreams."

"Dreams?" interrupted Leo.

"Yeah." She fell silent, she'd said too much already. "You must think I'm crazy, nuts, whatever."

His eyes searched hers. "No, you aren't crazy. I believe you."

Maya pushed a stray strand of hair from her cheek, a surge of hope lifting her spirit, because at last, someone believed her.

"Really?" she asked, not quiet believing it herself.

Leo grinned and nodded encouragingly for her to continue. "You said you saw the creature when you were seven, what happened?"

"That's when my brother was snatched," she replied, while looking blankly down at her shoes.

"I'm sorry to hear that. Are they still looking for him?"

Her eyes narrowed and she raised her head again. "They?"

"The police."

"Oh, they stopped searching for him four years ago, or that's what my parents reckon."

"That's pretty rubbish. I'm really sorry."

They fell silent for a few seconds. *Why am I telling him everything, I've only known him for a couple of hours at the most, yet it feels so right. At last I'm not alone.*

"I wish I could help in some way." He lifted his hand of her arm and combed it through his hair.

"You have. You're the first person I've spoken to in a long time about any of this, thanks." Maya placed her hands on the wooden slats of the bench and pulled herself to its edge. The warmth of his touch lingered, but she missed the actual contact of his hand and the comfort it brought. She turned to face him. "I'd better get going."

Leo smiled and inclined his head. "Yeah, me too, I'll probably see you around the village. If not, I'll see you here after Easter."

"Yeah, I'd like that. Oh, were you in the refectory earlier?"

Leo shook his head and stood. "No, I haven't been in there yet. Why, is it any good?"

Well that answers that question. I'm conjuring him up in my imagination now.

"It's okay if you don't need to eat, I suppose," she answered, with a chuckle before turning and strolling off towards the Arts Building, taking the odd glance back to see if Leo was still standing under the shelter, disappointingly he wasn't. *Only another two lessons to survive and then it's the start of the Easter break and project Leo.*

Maya buried her head in her books through the next couple of hours avoiding John's glances. Yet annoyingly, throughout the last thirty minutes, he threw tiny pieces of rolled up paper directly at her whenever the teacher's back was turned. Lifting her gaze to glare back at him, Maya was caught unawares to see a flicker of amusement showing on his face as their eyes met. Sitting forward again, she rested her chin in the cup of her hand wondering how she could wipe that smirk off his face when John went marching by to leave his work on the teacher's desk. On his return, he slowed to an amble and as he reached her his face turned grim, and his hand clasped around his throat, mockingly strangling himself. Alarm and anger rippled along her spine as every cell in her body wanted to rearrange that smug smile of his, yet, she knew he was warning her off, threatening her again. Maya composed herself, smiled instead and then lowered her head to continue her dissertation on street art, while wishing for the final bell to hurry up and ring.

John's threat stuck in Maya's thoughts the whole journey home and even now as she stood in front of the back door to her home, she still couldn't get rid of it. *Would he really carry it out, whatever the threat is?* Keeping a firm hold of the book, Maya flung open the door, dodged the flower-laden buckets and stomped into the kitchen. She dumped everything except the book on the table and paused to take in a deep, shaky breath. At last, two weeks without John tormenting her had finally arrived and the greatest part of it all, was the fact that Leo now lived in the same village and just around the corner from her, well nearly.

Her mother clattered her way into the garden-room, laden with a bucket full of flowers. "I'm on the rota for the flowers again this weekend," she called in a muffled tone, whilst dumping her load on the tiles and pulling out two large mixed bunches. She stood straight and sniffed in the fragrance of the cream coloured roses. "Maya dear, will you be okay for a couple of hours while I'm at the church?"

"Yeah sure," Maya replied, her hand already withdrawing from the biscuit barrel with a handful of chocolate digestives. She turned and headed into the lounge, hurling herself onto the sofa and opened the book.

An hour had past and Maya hadn't found a single picture of the creature that resembled what she had seen. Witches were mentioned, along with a page on how to invoke spirits and a small paragraph or two about demons, but nothing describing a monster that grew out of the earth. Maya groaned and tossed the book to the floor. Nothing gave her the answers she wanted. She closed her eyes, her thoughts drifting back to Leo and how she had told him things she hadn't told anyone. Surprisingly, he'd listened and with genuine concern, not questioning or dismissing a single word she'd said, unlike her father. And then there were the visions of him: the first one being in the vase during art, just before John stopped her from leaving the classroom, and the second, when she caught a glimpse of him in the refectory, again happening just before John's latest attack. Yet, Leo had told her that he hadn't seen the refectory, unless he was lying. *But why would he lie about that? And why do I want to see him so much? It's just how Jess is with John, she can't keep away from him.* Maya wiped her hands over her face.

Leo had been there every time: At the church that night, then his image in the vase and outside the library. They've got to be working together. A sickening feeling entered Maya's stomach. *But they're completely different, Leo is kind and understanding, and John is ... well ... a lunatic who ought to be locked up. Leo couldn't, wouldn't be involved with him.*

Gazing out through the lounge window, Maya caught a glimpse of an image dashing across the glass, she gasped and straightened. Just then, the dark shadow shot past again, except this time it made the latches rattle. Jumping, she tucked her feet under her and huddled into the cushions. The black mass splattered across the window panes, blocking any light for a few seconds before it lifted off, chased away by a blaze of light. Maya's fingers dug into the armrests as she tried to stop her body shaking. *What the hell was that?* She sat there, not daring to move, a minute past and then five, but whatever it was, it didn't return.

CHAPTER SIX

Bang ... bang ... bang ....

"Maya," her mum shouted up the stairs. "Sam's here, luv."

"What?"

"Sam's here."

"No way!"

Maya rolled over and glanced at her clock. *Eleven-thirty-five?! Oh for crying out loud! That can't be the right time. And what's Sam doing here anyway? Unless he's here to have a go at me as well.* She kicked her duvet to the bottom of her bed.

"I'll be down in ten," she called, as she rammed her legs into a pair of jeans and pushed her arms through a burnt-orange, t-shirt.

Maya sat in front of the mirror, brush in hand and anti-frizz spray in the other. She shook her head, knowing that the next few minutes would be taken up in outright war with her mass of curls. *I really don't need this this morning.* Placing the brush back down on the dresser, she sprayed her hair, combed her fingers through it and then stomped over to the mirror to study her reflection.

"That'll have to do," she muttered and flicked her hair over her shoulders. Turning, she left her room and headed downstairs.

When Maya entered the kitchen, Sam straightened and smiled. However, her mother continued chatting, her hands buried beneath a mountain of foam in the washing-up bowl. Sam on the other hand had stopped listening, his gaze fixed on Maya as she leant against the doorframe.

"Hi," she mouthed a silent greeting to him.

"Hi," he replied, in the same fashion with a nod and a mischievous look on his face.

"What're your plans for the Easter break, Sam?" Maya's mother asked, twisting her head to face him. "Oh, Maya, I didn't hear you come down." She pushed her hair back from her brow with the back of her hand, leaving a wet splodge of bubbles behind.

Maya smiled, trying to hold back the laughter inside her.

"Not much," Sam replied, looking from Maya to Mrs Stewart. "My parents are working, which leaves me pretty much up to my own devices during the day."

"Oh right," her mum replied, whilst wiping her hands on a polka-dot tea towel. She glanced at Maya. "I can see you two want to be getting on, so I'll just leave you both alone." Her eyebrows raised in amusement as she strolled out of the kitchen and into the garden.

Walking to the sink, Maya poured herself a glass of water.

"What's so funny? You looked like you were about to explode."

Bringing the glass to her lips, she gulped the liquid down in a thirsty rush. "Oh it's just how she was still talking to you when I came down, she was totally oblivious, that's all. Anyway, why are you here?" Maya asked, placing the glass in the washing-up bowl and spinning around to face Sam.

A large beaming grin warmed his face. "Come with me. I've got something to show you, but it's out the front."

Parked on the road outside her front door with two helmets perched on its seat was a sixties style retro-scooter.

"What do you reckon? It's a pressie from my parents." He buzzed with excitement. "Do you like it?"

"It's great. I love it." Maya said, with a grin. She hadn't imagined Sam owning a scooter before, but in a weird way, it suited him.

"Come on, let's get out of here." He handed her a helmet and put his own on as he straddled the seat. With a push of a button the scooter spluttered into life.

"It won't be against the law then, if I get on the back?" Maya yelled over the rattle of the engine.

"Don't panic, I passed my test on Tuesday."

The new-found freedom was exhilarating. Maya's clung to Sam's waist as they travelled through the village and out along the country lanes. After a mile, they headed down a track that led to a popular picnic area appropriately named, Sandy Gap, consisting mainly of sand, loads of grooves and a multitude of potholes. After negotiating way too many of those potholes, Sam pulled up in a small indent near a crop of trees and turned the engine off.

Twisting round to face her, he asked, "Do you fancy a walk?"

"I don't think I want to," she replied, while staring ahead at the vast expanse of trees. *This isn't a good idea, Sam. If only you could remember what happened the last time we went for a walk, then you wouldn't be suggest this at all.*

Sam removed his helmet and ruffled his hand through his hair. "Come on, I'll keep you safe. I promise. Please …."

Yeah, right … as if you'll be able to do that. Dismounting the bike, she removed her helmet and stood back while Sam pushed the scooter in a gap between two trees.

"So why have you been avoiding everyone these past couple of weeks?" he asked, without any warning as he turned round to face her.

Maya's jaw dropped. "I haven't!" *I knew it. I wonder if Jess or John put him up to this. Except Sam's not the kind of guy to be told what to do.*

"Come on, we haven't seen you hanging around the snug for a while. Is it because of me?" He marched through a stack of nettles, knocking them to one side with his foot.

"No, it's not because of you. It's nothing … it's just me."

Twisting to look at her, he continued, "Don't shut me out. I'm here for you."

"I know." Maya stepped forward, her head hung low as she ambled along the track.

She knew Sam was there for her, but he wouldn't believe what was going on, none of her friends would; she could hardly believe it herself. They ambled deeper, heading in no particular direction, the minutes whooshing by.

Sam's voice became a quiet mumble until he shouted, "Maya, have you been listening to me?"

"Yeah," she replied, without thinking.

"No you haven't, you've been day-dreaming."

Maya forced a smile. "I'm sorry, Sam. I'm just worrying about how long we've been out here. Do you think we should head back soon, before it gets dark?"

"Maybe," he replied, staring down at his watch. "I can't believe we've been out her for four and a half hours. I mean, how does that work?" He lifted his head and looked at her.

She shrugged. *It does seem odd, because it only feels like an hour and a half at the most.*

"I suppose you're right. Let's get out of here, if we can find our way out?"

"Yeah, I was thinking the same thing."

Sam spun around slowly, searching every possible track for the way they had just come.

Scanning the surrounding trees, she began to panic, everything looked the same, it was impossible to keep your bearings in here. Sam came to stand beside her, his arm accidentally brushing hers and for a few seconds all concerns vanished as she gazed into his caramel eyes. He raised his hand to stroke her cheek with his thumb. Her blood rushed to colour her face and she took a step back, but Sam's arm scooped around her waist, drawing her close to him. Maya's breath caught in anticipation as his lips brushed hers, teasing her. His mouth claimed hers and when he pulled her flat against his body, she let out a gasp. But there wasn't that spark, that electricity, like whenever she was close to Leo, her body felt flat, lifeless in Sam's embrace even though she'd fancied him for ages. *What does all this mean ... am I meant to be with Leo? I know one thing; this isn't right, Sam isn't what I want anymore.* She wriggled her way free and stood staring at him. *Maybe if he had made his move a few months ago, things would've been different.*

Sam dropped his arms to his side. "I'm sorry. I shouldn't have done that." He reached out and hesitated when Maya took another step back. "But I'm glad I did." He tilted his head forward and flashed a cheeky grin.

"What do you mean?"

His smile vanished. "I've been wanting to tell you that I ...."

"No ... I don't want to hear it." Maya raised her hand to stop him. What she wanted to say was, 'Not now, not while all this crazy stuff is happening to me,' but how could she when he had forgotten everything that happened.

Sam rushed on, "I can't help the way I feel about you. I've felt this way for ages, except I've never had the guts to say anything." His eyes locked on hers. "I'd hoped that maybe ... you felt the same."

She lowered her gaze. *How do I do this without hurting him?* "I ... I'm sorry." Her tone softened.

She had felt the same, but not now, there were too many peculiar things happening in her life and one of those things was the unexplained feelings she had for Leo. Maya continued to stare down at the ground, drawing a pattern in the rotting leaves with her foot. *Going out with him would complicate matters further. But how do I tell him that?*

Lifting her head, Maya swallowed, trying to dislodge the hard lump stuck in her throat. "I just don't want to spoil our friendship at the moment." She threw up her arms. "I can't do this right now, Sam. We'll talk about it later. Please ... let's just get out of here first." Turning, she strode off, knowing it wasn't the greatest of explanations, yet right now, it was the best she had.

Despite his efforts to conceal his disappointment, Maya could hear that Sam's voice was strained and husky with emotion. "You can't do this right now. What about how I feel?" He called out. "Please, Maya, don't leave me hanging on like this. It'll do my head in."

Maya glanced back. "Sam, don't do this ... not now ... please."

Not wanting him to see the indignant tears that threatened to come to her eyes, she turned away and marched off through the forest, trying her hardest to ignore his continued questioning. Wiping her eyes with her sleeve, Maya pushed through a group of ferns and was brought to an abrupt halt by someone grabbing the back of her coat. Instinctively, her hands clenched into fists and she spun around.

Sam's appearance had softened. He held his hands up defensively. "Whoa, Maya, I just need to say that I like you ... I really, really, like you."

Don't do this to me. The anger she felt waned as his words sunk in. He placed his fingers on her chin, lifting her head and leaned forward for another kiss.

"No, Sam. I mean it. I can't." Maya pushed him away. "I need to get out of here."

He drew in a deep breath and after a few seconds of silence he replied, "Okay ... but I'll keep trying."

Maya watched as he strolled away from her. *This is so hard. I hate it. I hate my life.*

It became virtually impossible to move with any speed through the tangle of scrub. Sam had plucked a thin whip-like branch from a sapling and thrashed anything that got in his path. A nauseating sensation had pushed its way from the pit of Maya's stomach, and travelled up into her throat as the fear of being lost, became a reality.

"Stop for a minute, I need a break," she demanded.

Crouching forward, she removed her black pump and rubbed her little toe. There wasn't a single sound, nothing but complete and utter silence: no birds chirping, no woodpecker hammering, no buzz from insects, nothing except an eerie suffocating silence.

"I don't like this. Why can't I hear anything?" She hobbled closer to Sam.

He didn't move and replied, "I don't know."

All of a sudden, her head snapped up and she spun in one fluid movement to face him, her pump slipped from her hand and dropped to the ground. "We're going around in circles."

"What makes you think that?"

"That." She pointed at a withered tree. "We've passed it three times."

"No way?" He took a closer look at it. "Maybe you're right."

"I know I'm right." She shoved her foot back into her pump with a cringe and a silent yelp.

Sam tugged at the top of his hair until it stood up in wild tufts. He threw his head back in frustration and exhaled before approaching the twisted tree.

"What're we going to do? It's getting dark and there's no way I want to be out here when it does."

Sam approached her. "It's going to be okay. We'll get out of here, I promise."

Crack!

"Did you hear that?" Maya's voice dropped into an urgent whisper.

"Hear what?"

They stood still, listening, but the silence came surging back.

"I must've imagined it." A prickle of unease stirred the small hairs at the nape of her neck. "I thought I heard a branch snap, that's all."

Lowering his arms, Sam stepped away. "That's it. We're getting out of here, right now," he shouted and strode off.

Maya trailed after him, but the stench of rot hitting her nostrils made her come to a halt. Her lips curled as she sucked in the strong reek. The pungent odour of decay was like nothing she had ever smelt before and she'd no words to describe it. Sam approached, his hand covering his nose and stopped to point towards a gap between a mass of brambles on the opposite side of a clearing just ahead of them. A faint rustling sound came from the brambles, and Maya's eyes opened wide when she saw the top of the bushes shake.

Looking around wildly at her, Sam whispered in a broken voice, "I heard that. Did you hear that?"

Maya nodded and froze until something brushed the back of her arm, unnerving her even more. She jumped forward, bumping against Sam, her hand reaching out for his and once found, she held on tightly. Twisting her head to peer over her shoulder, her heart missed several beats as her gaze fell on a black man with startlingly white hair standing behind her.

"What the hell!" Sam snapped, turning to follow her gaze.

"Shh ...." The broad-shouldered stranger held a finger to his plump lips. "Be quiet and don't move," he commanded whilst continuing to stare across the clearing. *Why should I do what he wants, when my body is crying out for me to scream and get the hell out of here?* A gentle breeze brushed Maya's hair from her face. The silence was interrupted by the breaking of twigs and the soft padding of feet. *What the hell's that?* Maya shifted her weight, her legs trembling beneath her. The man placed himself to her right.

83

"Whatever you're about to see, you mustn't scream," he urged in an authoritative, guttural tone.

CHAPTER SEVEN

The hairs prickled on the back of Maya's neck. Sam squeezed her trembling hand tighter in his grip and pulled her to his side. There was still a bit of daylight and she could see enough to spot a dark shape pushing its way through the brambles, completely ignoring the clawing thorns. The man stooped forward, hands outstretched, ready as if to fend off an attack.

"When I tell you, I want you to run." He raised his arm and pointed to her left before continuing, "In that direction."

As she gaped at the creature that punched through the bushes ahead, every nerve in Maya's body screamed out for her to run now and not when the man would order them to. Never before had she seen a beast like it; it resembled a wolf, but much bigger, its coat was jet-black and shaggy, its eyes were a fierce red, yet its snout lacked any fur at all. The creature pulled its muzzle back to reveal razor-like teeth and a low growl emanated from deep within its chest. It stopped, swinging its head from side to side in a similar fashion to a caged animal, except its gaze never left Maya. She slapped her hand over her mouth and tried not to scream, the distance between them and the brambles seemed that much shorter now. *Why is it staring at me?* She bit her lip, piercing the flesh. A tiny trickle of blood rolled down her chin, but her hand remained clasped over her mouth.

Maya and Sam didn't move.

They didn't dare.

The beast's head lowered and drool dripped from between its discoloured fangs as it waited to pounce. *I can't bear this. Why doesn't it just get on with it? Is it afraid of the man?* The last rays of light faded as the animal crouched down on its haunches, howled and sprang forward. It came at them in a blur, covering the ground effortlessly with its long gait.

"Now," the man shouted, before the beast smashed into his chest, the force of its attack carrying them both into the trees behind them.

Sam pulled Maya in the direction the man had pointed. "Keep running," he shouted, dragging her behind him.

Something dark appeared to Maya's right, running parallel to her. She flashed a quick glance and saw another hound. It didn't close in, but it kept pace, smoothly covering the ground as she struggled to keep her footing. Another one arrived to her left and for a split second, Maya's focus on the ground drifted, giving the hounds an opportunity to rush at her legs and knock her down. Air exploded from her as she landed on her front, each breath a strangled gasp. One of the dogs leapt towards her, this time its jaw clamped around her right ankle and the beast hauled her along with ease.

Maya couldn't hear her screams anymore; no sound

seemed to escape from her mouth at all. Using her free foot, she kicked the dog's broad head several times, and dug her fingers into the dirt, trying to slow its progress down, but in the end, the pain in her ankle was too much to ignore, and it took everything she had to stay conscious. Glancing up, Maya could see two hounds circling Sam. He managed to hit one across its muzzle with a fallen branch, making the animal yelp as its jaw broke. The other dog lowered its shoulders, ready to pounce and she could see that with each beat of her heart, Sam was weakening. He thrashed the branch about feebly, each strike missing its mark as the muscles in his arms gave way.

Terrified, desperate and exhausted, Sam looked up and yelled, "Maya," before the final attack.

The animals' howls of excitement pierced Maya's ears.

"SAM ..." she screamed, her eyes filling with tears. "Please God, not Sam." And then she could see him no more as the dog pulled her around a bend. There was no fight left in her ... the hounds could have her, at least then she would be with Sam.

Squeezing her eyes shut, images of every person Maya loved flashed before her eyes and paralysed her whole being with misery and hopelessness. She said a silent goodbye to each one of them as the dog continued to haul her along until it unexpectedly released its hold, its whines suddenly slicing through the air. With the little strength Maya had left, she lifted her head and looked behind her. A dark-haired man with his back to her stood over the beast, his right foot pressed down on its chest and the tip of his flaming sword aimed at the creature's heart. The animal snapped its jaws, but the man was stronger. He peered down at the hound and spoke in a strange language that Maya didn't recognise. The dog's howls echoed through the trees as the sword struck. The sound of flesh and sinews ripping tightened her throat as she tried to stop herself from vomiting. Then the man turned.

Maya gasped and swallowed. *No, it can't be .... It can't be!*

Leo left his kill, walked over to her and knelt down. His sword fell to the ground and disappeared. Reaching forward, he wrapped his arms around her, lifting her close to his chest. Maya's salt soaked eyes peered into his as he stroked her hair.

"Sam. Is he ... dead?" She croaked weakly with fresh tears rolling down her cheeks.

"Shh ... everything is going to be alright."

He stood with Maya cradled in his muscular arms. She caught a glimpse of movement in the nearby thicket and watched blurry eyed as two figures pushed their way through. The white-haired man from earlier appeared first, his coat splattered with a black blood-like substance, the other person was a very handsome blonde guy, so handsome he was beautiful.

"Go and get the boy," Leo ordered. "I'll take Maya back to the house and I'll meet you there."

The men vanished right before her eyes and a white mist was left hanging in the air. Maya stared blankly at where they had been standing, she could've sworn she'd heard the faint sound of fluttering wings, but as she tightened her arms around Leo's neck and rested her head on his shoulder, she succumbed to the heaviness her body felt.

When Maya opened her eyes again, she was lying across a sofa in a high ceiled room with white cornices, picture rails and curtains patterned with gold and white swirls. Looking around, her gaze stopped on a gold framed painting that hung above the fireplace. The scene depicted a battle; not a battle of human warfare, but that of a heavenly battle, angels in the sky, swords ablaze, were fighting against demonic creatures. The sound of ripping fabric startled Maya, making her peer down towards her legs and she saw Leo kneeling on the carpet inspecting her ankle. Her face twisted with disgust at the sight of the swollen bite marks, until Leo covered them with his hand.

He raised his head. "What were you doing out there so late?" His tone was unsympathetic. "Don't you understand the danger you put yourself and Sam in."

Tears formed in Maya's already bloodshot eyes as she relived her last vision of Sam being mauled.

"Sam?" She whispered his name, hoping he might hear, but her thoughts were redirected to the increasing heat in her wound. She yelped and pulled her leg away.

"I don't understand your stupidity, and of all the places to take a stroll, you choose somewhere that hardly anyone goes." Leo sighed and looked up at her. "People are dying and that could've been you tonight."

"It wasn't my fault. We ...." Maya began to explain, but was cut short by Leo's raised hand.

He shuffled closer and took her left hand in his, she went to pull it back, but hesitated when their eyes met. *If it wasn't for him, I'd be dog food by now. There's no way he's just an ordinary guy.*

There was a short pause before Maya asked, "Who are you? What are you?"

"You know who I am, and you now know *what* I am."

Maya shook her head, her hair fell in front of her eyes and she glanced through it, from him, to the painting, then back to meet his gaze. Her imagination raced, all manner of questions rushed through her mind; *he'd killed the hound, yet, how could he over-power an animal that strong? How'd he know I was there in the first place?* Her memories of when they'd first met now made sense; he had said the light in the church the very first time they met was lightning, however it had arrived just before he did. *Could he also be the pillar of light down by the river? And what about the images of him before John's attacks, had that been his way of warning me when something bad was about to happen? I'm so confused.* She glanced back at the painting. The flaming sword of an angel flashing through the clouded sky. *The flaming sword! He'd killed the hound with a sword just like that one and then it had disappeared when he placed it on the ground!* Her eyes widened. *He can't be!*

"Go on, say it," he encouraged her.

What if I'm wrong?

"Go on," repeated Leo, his blue eyes sparkling. "Say it."

Maya opened her mouth and then snapped it shut.

90

She swallowed and coughed before stuttering her answer, "You're a ... a ... an angel." She lowered her head. *This is so crazy!*

Leo bent low to catch her gaze and squeezed her hand in a gesture of support. "That wasn't that painful, was it?"

"I don't believe it!"

Tilting his head, he flashed a comforting smile. "It's true. I am an angel."

"Why didn't you tell me sooner? I've told you things I haven't told anyone else and you couldn't tell me who you are."

"Would you've believed me?"

Maya laid her head back on the arm of the sofa, unsure of how to answer. Truthfully, he was right, she wouldn't have believed him. Her eyes searched his. "Why were we attacked? Why is all this happening to me?"

"I don't know why the hounds tried to drag you off, lucky for us they did. Hell hounds usually kill their prey." He lifted his gaze. "All I can assume is that they've changed their plans."

"Hell hounds?" Maya gasped. "And who's changed their plans?" *None of this makes sense.*

"The fallen ones and their demons."

"Demons!" Maya's face was expressionless and ashen. "Seriously?"

Leo raised his eyebrows. "Yes."

"Why me?"

"I can't answer that at the moment."

"What kind of an answer is that?"

"It's the only one I have."

And before she could continue, a white mist began to form in the corner of the room. Maya glanced back at Leo, but he paid no attention to it. The guy in the Burberry trench-coat and with the white-hair materialised first.

"The boy?" Leo asked, without turning his attention away from Maya.

"Afriel will be here with him shortly." The broad-shouldered angel approached and peered down at her. "Is she alright?"

"Yes, Zach, we arrived just in time. You did the right thing in calling me." Leo stood and placed a hand on Zach's shoulder. "How're you?"

"I've been in worse situations," replied Zach, with a self-satisfied grin plastered across his face.

And as the two angels discussed the events of the fight, the sound of beating wings alerted them to another arrival. Embraced in the slender, yet powerful arms of the blonde-haired angel was a limp, bloodied body.

"Who is it?" Maya went to push herself up.

"Leo!" Zach said, indicating her with arched eyebrows.

Leo stepped forward, grabbed the top of Maya's arms and gently forced her back in the chair.

"I'm sorry about this," he said, holding her down.

"Sorry! Just let go of me." Her body shook, half with fear, half with anger.

"No can't do, sorry."

"Leo, you're frightening me."

"That wasn't my intention." Lines of concentration

deepened along his brow and under his eyes. "But you don't need to see this, Maya." He let go of her right arm and tapped her forehead with his finger.

In an instant, Maya's body relaxed into the cushions, her focus no longer on Leo or the others but on the stars or the galaxy which consumed her vision of the phenomenon that veiled her eyes before her lashes sealed her in that wondrous scene.

CHAPTER EIGHT

The boy opened his eyes and although his vision was blurred, he recognised his room and the saucer-shaped eyes that stared down at him. He turned his head a tiny bit, which forced a surge of pain to shoot through his entire body. Grimacing, he wormed his arms from under the cover and watched them flop weakly by his side.

"Is master's okay?" Skip asked, and prodded the boy's arm for about the ninth time with a bony finger.

"Please, stop that."

With protest from his aching limbs, he pulled himself into a sitting position and pushed his back against the cold headboard.

"Did something happen to me, since the last thing I remember was Fallan finding us outside and then locking me in here."

Skip jumped off the bed and with his head hung low, he strolled over to the fireplace, his tail dragging on the floor. He picked up a metal rod and began stabbing at the burning logs.

"So something did happen then?" The boy stated.

Skip spun on one foot in the process of denying everything when the bedroom door flung wide and Fallan marched in.

"Good, you're up," the man said flatly. "Get dressed, we have visitors. You ..." He pointed at Skip who had ducked behind a chair and was growling back at Fallan. "You stay here and don't you dare leave this room." The man glanced back at the dark-haired boy. "Madame Pillsbury-Gaunt has prepared something for you in the kitchen. Once you've eaten, come to my office. Bazriel wants to see you." With a sweep of his long coat, he turned and left the room.

"Nice to see you too," mumbled the boy.

As he swung his legs over the edge of the bed, the boy's stomach churned with an unfamiliar burning and he winced as foul-tasting liquid scorched the lining of his throat. He hadn't felt these sensations before; come to think of it, he'd never been ill. Gritting his teeth he placed his feet on the floorboards and stood. Every step was as though a knife stabbed into his heels. However, after half an hour, he had managed to wash, dress and leave his room.

The boy crept down the worn staircase and along a vast corridor towards the kitchen. Two men were arguing in a doorway as he approached. They fell silent, casting him nervous sidelong glances and waited until he had walked past them before they continued their dispute. A servant scurried by, sweat beaded across his brow from the heavy load of logs piled high in his arms. The gaunt man looked at the boy, fear stark and vivid, glittered in his eyes. *But why? Why's he so afraid? Is it because of the visitors?* For as long as the boy remembered and in all the years he'd lived in the house, they never had visitors. New guards and workers would come and go, but never visitors. *Is this the reason why everyone seemed agitated and even afraid?*

He hesitated in front of the kitchen door before pushing it wide, regretting the fact that he had to enter at all, let alone eat something in the filthy pigsty. His gaze travelled across the stacks of old papers, bags, pots and pans, to vegetable peelings and scraps of uneaten food, until they landed on Madam Pillsbury-Gaunt the head housekeeper who had already placed a plate of food on the table. Pulling up a chair, he sat down and began chewing on a mouthful of sausage and mash, only to be watched impatiently by the Old Hag. *Maybe calling her an 'old hag' is a bit harsh,* he thought for a split second. *Nah,* he smirked and let it go with a shrug. Madam Pillsbury-Gaunt came up behind him with her hands folded across the top of her huge bosoms. She observed every mouthful he took with increased annoyance, her impatience growing with every minute.

With only the last few bites of his meal left, she finally snapped. "That's it. You've had your fill," she bellowed, in a low man-like voice.

The youngster flashed a glance at her and held back his laughter as her round face flushed and her top lip rolled up to reveal stained and broken teeth. Snatching his plate from the table, she threw it forcefully and accurately into the fly-covered sink.

"Get out of my kitchen you impertinent human," she yelled, her grubby hands shoving him off the chair.

He dodged the swipe from her pudgy hand and sped

from the kitchen, his laughter easing his pain.

A few minutes later, the boy stood at the closed door of Fallan's office. Something wasn't right. He didn't know what, only that it felt anxious.

Before he got a chance to raise his hand to knock, a voice boomed from within the room. "Come in."

It didn't sound like Fallan, although for some reason he did recognise it. He pushed the door open and the first person he saw was Fallan standing bolt upright beside a grey-haired, older man who sat comfortably in Fallan's leather chair that was situated behind his desk. *I wonder if this is that Bazriel guy Fallan mentioned earlier.*

"Come here," demanded the elderly man.

The boy approached, but his gaze was drawn to a large book sitting open on the desk. The older man raised a hand, grabbed one side of the book and slammed it shut, except the youngster couldn't snatch his gaze away. Every inch of the worn cover was adorned with strange symbols that were intertwined with each other. His eyes widened in recognition. He remembered that book, it was the book he'd taken from the caves a few years ago, except the picture on the cover was different now; before, it had been a large tree in full blossom and now, half of it looked bare, gnarled and dying. As he watched, a leaf fell from a branch and drifted gently down to the pile that lay at the tree's base. He knew something important had just happened, yet he didn't know what or the significance of it, only that he felt a deep sadness within his very core.

The boy stared at the swirling patterns across the bark of the tree and began to hear voices, faint to start with and then becoming louder as his mind adjusted. He gasped. Horror struck him in the stomach, it wasn't voices he heard but the undeniable sound of people screaming in anguish and misery. His hands shot up to cover his ears, except the agonising noise persisted.

"Good. I see the book interests you," the older man purred.

"I'll cover it, Bazriel," Fallan said. He stepped forward and placed a dirty piece of cloth over it.

Bazriel stood, grabbed the book in both hands and concealed it with the linen before tucking it under his arm and hobbled with his left leg dragging behind him, toward the door. Fallan grasped the teenager's arm and pulled him out of the room.

"We've got a visitor for you, boy, and a little job," Bazriel told him, while he was dragged down loads of steps and in to a labyrinth of tunnels.

The youth winced as Fallan's fingers dug further into his flesh with each jerk on his arm, making his eyes swim from the tears that filled them. Bazriel halted in front of a plain wooden door.

"Stand here and don't move," he ordered, pointing a chubby finger towards his feet.

The youngster watched as Bazriel turned and entered the room, followed obediently by Fallan who slammed the door shut behind him.

What the hell's going on? They can get stuffed if they think I'm going to do anything with that book. He hissed a silent curse when he pushed his sleeve up his arm and saw five swollen marks that had formed on his skin. Scowling, he rubbed at the bruises and when his gaze dropped to the floor, he spotted rust-coloured blotches trailing from under the door and along the corridor. The boy crouched down and traced his finger around the edges of the largest patch. *What is this stuff?* Just then, the door opened and Fallan glared down at him. Willing each muscle to relax, the teenager stood, cleared his throat and without hesitation stepped into the room.

The first thing the boy saw when he entered, was Bazriel with the book still tucked firmly under his armpit standing beside a young woman who sat at a small table placed in the centre of the sparse room. Fallan shoved him towards an empty chair opposite the woman and as he approached, he couldn't take his gaze from the tears which were beading down her soft heart-shaped face. *What have they done to her?* Fallan's hands slapped down on the youngster's shoulders and guided him roughly into the chair's seat. The boy smiled at the woman, but it only seemed to add to her fear. *Why is she afraid of me?* Bazriel paced forward, placed the book tenderly on the table between them both and removed the cloth. He licked the tips of his fat fingers, opened the book and rifled through the stained pages until stopping at a blank page. Sneering, Bazriel bent forward, offering a silver, engraved pen to the woman.

The boy felt a prickle of unease stir the small hairs at the nape of his neck when her body shook, her eyes widened and a shrill scream burst from her full lips. Fallan, as if taking an unheard cue, stepped closer and grabbed her right hand. Taking the pen from Bazriel, he rammed it into the woman's clenched fist, ripping the skin of her palm in the process.

"Sign your name in the book, bitch." Bazriel's spit sprayed across her face making the slap from his hand which followed sound like a wet flannel landing flat on her cheek.

She cried out as Fallan forced her hand closer to the open pages. Tears rolled down the boy's cheeks and acid rose in his throat. He spun round and dashed for the door. Grabbing the handle in both hands, he pushed down, but the door wouldn't budge, so he kicked and punched, but it still refused to move. Laughter from Fallan and Bazriel echoed around the room. With all his strength, the boy continued to pound on the door. He didn't want to be a part of this. *What the hell's wrong with them? Stupid women, why doesn't she just do it and be done with it?*

He hadn't heard Fallan approach until it was too late to react. The lank man grasped the back of his jumper and pulled the youth back. He kicked out at the man's legs, struggling frantically, feeling the pressure on his windpipe increase from the collar of his top when all of a sudden, he was lifted in the air and shoved back on the seat. The teenager grimaced as Fallan pushed down on his shoulders, preventing him from rising again. His gaze met the woman's green eyes, both blood shot and dilated with fear. She stared back at him in horrified silence.

Bazriel drew near, bent forward and whispered into the youth's ear. "You can stop her suffering." Heat from his breath warmed the boy's eardrum as he continued, "look into her mind. Gently though," he warned. "I know you can do it."

"No. I don't want to," cried the youngster. "I can't."

A sharp stabbing sensation shot down the youngster's back as Fallan's nails dug deeper into his flesh. He didn't understand what Bazriel wanted. *Why are they doing this? Why can't you write her name in the book for her?*

Bazriel whispered in an ancient language something the boy didn't understand and immediately at those words he felt the inside of his head burn. It was excruciating. The older man grinned wickedly before leaving his side, stepping over to the woman. Reaching out, he took a handful of her blonde hair in his thick fist and yanked her head back.

"I believe you can see that however much pain I inflict on this pathetic human, she still refuses to sign her miserable name in our visitor's book." He licked his lips. "I think she would rather die." Saliva formed in the corners of his mouth.

Dropping his hands, Bazriel placed them on either side of her face. The woman's eyes widened, her mouth opened in a silent scream. Blood pooled between her lips, staining her teeth.

Shutting his own pain in the depths of his mind, the boy shouted, "Stop it ... please stop it. Leave her alone you sick piece of ...."

Every ounce of Fallan's weight came pressing down on his shoulders, forcing him to be silent and watch Bazriel as he dipped one of his fingers in the woman's mouth, amongst the blood which now pooled behind her bottom teeth. He then trailed it down her chin before bringing the digit back to his plump lips and sucking on it like a lollipop. The boy gagged when he saw the look of pure delight lighten across Bazriel's face until the sting of Fallan's hand struck the back of his head, diverting his thoughts away from what he'd just witnessed.

Screwing his eyes shut. All his life he'd witnessed strange behaviour and happenings; he'd seen guards change into winged creatures from the slightest provocation on his part, and when he'd first witnessed it, at the grand age of six, it had terrified him so-much-so that he peed himself. Now though, it was a normal occurrence, everyone he knew, except himself and Fallan, had changed their form into some kind of freakish beast at some point in his life. Yet, what was happening in this room was wrong and he needed to do something about it.

Without warning, the shooting pain returned, making his eyes snap open. He glanced at the woman and knew they weren't getting out of this situation alive unless he did what Bazriel wanted.

Fallan stepped aside as Bazriel took his place behind the youngster. Chunky hands grasped the boy's head and tilted it back to face him.

"You will obey me, or we'll kill her. Do you want us to do that knowing that you could've saved her?" Bazriel fell silent, his eyes searching his. He wet his cracked lips again before continuing, "Once she's signed her name in the book, she can go home and enjoy the rest of her sorry, pitiful, little, life. It's all down to you."

Staring across at the woman, her pretty face marred by

her own sweat and blood, the boy knew he had to be the one to save her, he had to obey Bazriel as fighting him was pointless.

"I'll do it," the boy said, in a whisper.

Removing his hands, Bazriel leaned closer to the youngster's ear. "You're doing the right thing," he said in a hushed tone. "Now focus on her eyes, the colour and the shape, then beyond the eyes and into her mind. Remove her fear and encourage her to write her name in the book." He shifted to the youth's side, raised a hand and tapped the open pages of the manuscript with his fingers.

"Why don't you do it?" The boy hissed.

Bazriel punched the table in anger.

"Because I can't ... God gave you putrid human's a free will, and whether I'm charming or not, it makes no difference to this one. My torturer's skills work for most and sometimes my words of persuasion, but this pathetic human is choosing to stand against me." His anger disappeared and a soft smile pushed the corners of his lips up into a synthetic grin. "So, I thought she might respond to a kinder, gentler touch."

Bazriel sauntered over to the woman and squatted down in front of her. He moistened his lips and with a venomous grin licked the blood from her chin, dragging his tongue along the side of her face. She drew back in horror and watched wide-eyed as he smacked his lips together in satisfaction.

"You see, boy, whatever we do to her, she still refuses to sign in the book. We need her scribble in there, as the only good thing about her is the value of her soul." Bazriel reached down and lifted her arm. "If you change her mind before her life-giving blood drains, then we'll let her go."

Fallan sidled to Bazriel's side and pulled a small, gold handled dagger from his coat pocket. Clasping the woman's arm in his hand, he placed its sharp edge on her wrist and sliced it across her flesh. Blood flowed with ease, dripping onto her lap, her mouth remained open, although no sound escaped. Seconds later, she realised what had happened, and looked desperately across at the boy.

"Please. Please ... help me!" Her voice rose to a cry of anguish and then Bazriel slapped her across the face to silence her again.

"Her name's Julia by the way. You'd better get on with it. You wouldn't want her to go and die on you now, would you?"

The boy couldn't peel his gaze away from Julia's blood as it trickled onto the concrete floor, producing a similar pattern to the marks he'd traced his fingers along in the corridor. *Oh crap, someone else has gone through this, had their wrist cut or worse and bleed out onto the floor!* The thought tore at his insides. Looking up, he peered into her eyes, remembering how the sick, old man had said 'that it was up to him, that he was the only one who could save her.' *I've got to do it.*

There were too many shades of green in her eyes to concentrate on one particular colour, so he gazed at her pupils which dilated and contracted as she tried to focus on him through her tears. Then words ... no, thoughts, entered his mind; they were jumbled, scattered by terror, rolling over and over with options on how she would die, how she wouldn't get to say goodbye to her parents and especially ... her son.

Her son. She had a son. A four-year-old son.

Seeing Julia with her arms wrapped around her child in a loving embrace was weird. The boy had never been held like that, had never felt what it would be like to be protected by someone. He had no choice, but to persuade her to write her name in the book, she had to return to her little boy.

Entering her mind wasn't that dissimilar to entering Skip's, he just had to concentrate harder because she had a lot more memories.

I wonder if I can get her to see me as her son, then I'll be able to persuade her to see the book as a colouring book or something like that.

Using the information he'd gleaned about Julia's little boy from her thoughts, he brought her son's image into her terrified mind.

I can do this ... just concentrate dame it.

Her son's curly, blonde hair surrounding his peach-coloured face, his emerald eyes beaming with innocence, now replaced the teenager's own features in Julia's eyes. The boy smiled at Julia and he knew it had worked. Her eyes beamed with love as she looked at her son sitting opposite her. He continued to flood her thoughts with pictures: the fun they'd had at the park, the comfort they felt when she read her son a bedtime story. Julia responded, no longer horrified. He placed an impression of a colourful book, a book with messages from friends and family in her mind and pointed at it. She glanced down, and this time, she didn't recoil from the book on the table. With every minute that ticked by, he saw her weaken. Interweaving his thoughts into hers, the teenager implanted a vision of her son signing his name on the blank pages, and then pleading for his mummy to do the same. Her face lit up as the picture became clearer. She grabbed the pen in her bloodied hand and with a little coaxing from her son, she happily signed the ancient parchment.

The deed was done.

Bazriel grabbed Julia's hand and wrapped his fingers around the seeping wound on her wrist. He muttered a few inaudible words and showed the boy that he'd kept his side of the bargain, the cut had been sealed, leaving a small rosy line. The teenager left her mind carefully, soothingly, leaving images of her little boy, in the hope that she wouldn't again experience the fear she'd suffered this day.

"You know what to do, Fallan. Her soul is Our Lord's now and the sooner he has it, the better it is for us," whispered Bazriel.

Fallan lifted the woman out of the chair and pulled her towards the door.

"When you've finished with her and taken the boy back to his room, I need you to tell Cordal to extend his search for vulnerable people in the cafes and stations around the cities. And then join me in greeting our latest victims ... Oops, visitors. They should be arriving soon," called Bazriel, before looking back at the boy with a smug grin across his bloated, weather-beaten face. "Good work, boy," he said, with a slight tilt of his head. "We will have to do that again, soon, very soon."

Bazriel bent down and locked his gaze with the boy's. No one had the colour of eyes that this old man had. They were as black as coal and not their usual yellow and every few seconds, the youngster saw a vivid red glow sparkle deep within them. It was then that he remembered their first meeting, how those eyes had looked into the very depths of his soul.

"Time for you to rest. You look very tired, very tired indeed," Bazriel's voice hummed hypnotically.

He did feel on the verge of collapsing, yet his mind was alive and uncontrollable. *You can't make me.* Nevertheless, with each word that Bazriel spoke, the boy struggled to move, struggled to keep his eyes open.

"Fallan will be back in a minute to take you to your room." The old man placed his hand on the boy's head to ruffle his hair.

Staring blankly at the distant wall, the boy hadn't notice Bazriel picking the book up and leaving. The single light which hung in the centre of the ceiling dulled before turning off and leaving him alone in complete darkness.

CHAPTER NINE

Maya knew Sam was dead and that it was all her fault. Her eyes opened a fraction, ripping apart dried tears and the first person she saw was Leo.

"Wha, what did you do to me?"

"I did what was best for you." Leo brushed a strand of her hair away from her eyes.

"What was best for me?! You have no right to decide something like that for me."

"I won't apologise for what I did, Maya." He straightened his back and the muscles along his jaw-line twitched. "I was protecting you from a sight I knew would cause you pain."

Pausing for a few seconds, she lowered her eyes and peered at her fingers. Earlier she could have sworn she'd seen one of the other angels carrying someone. *SAM!* Her head shot up again. *Sam, was that someone!*

"Sam, was the person being carried in that angel's arms just before you made me fall asleep, wasn't he?"

Leo nodded.

"Is Sam ... dea ...?" Her throat tightened, she couldn't say it. Now she understood what Leo had spared her from seeing; Sam's mangled and lifeless body, he hadn't done it for any other reason.

Leo shuffled closer.

"Is he ..." She didn't want to believe it. "Dead?"

Leo pushed his fingers through his hair and his lips formed a gentle smile. "No, Maya, he's not, he's going to be okay."

Maya flung her arms around his neck and cried. "Thank you, thank you so much for saving us." She bit into her lip, trying to hold back the tears and as Leo's hand slid down to the small of her back, she yielded to the compulsive sobs that shook her.

Afriel, the beautiful angel that had rescued Sam, stood over them with a confused expression across his face. Maya noticed that his unusual amber eyes, seemed to be searching for an answer.

Leo laughed and gently pushed Maya away from him. "It's okay, Afriel, I just told Maya that Sam's still alive and her hands around my neck were an embrace of joy," he assured him.

The young angel first frowned, then a smile slowly formed on his face as he glanced down at her. Maya sat up straight and wiped her face. *That was weird? Why did Leo have to explain what we were doing? Did Afriel think we were making out?*

"The boy would like to see you." He gestured towards Maya with his chin. "He didn't believe us when we told him that you were safe."

"Where is he?" Maya asked with a sniff.

"He's in the next room," Leo told her, then looked up at the other angel. "You can help Sam into here now, Afriel."

Afriel bowed without further comment, his face

neutral and withdrew. Five minutes later, he led Sam through the doorway, lowered him onto the sofa, and when he seemed satisfied with Sam's comfort, he turned back towards the hallway again.

Dried blood stained her friend's face.

They could've washed that off. At least then there'd be nothing left except his ripped clothes to remind him that he'd just been in a fist fight with a creature from hell.

He gave Maya his usual cheeky grin, a grin that had always made her blush in the past, but not now, because now her heart belonged to another.

"What a date ... huh?" Sam said with a chuckle.

"Yeah, crazy." Maya raised her eyes to Leo. "Is he going to be okay?"

"He'll be fine," Leo replied. "You're both very lucky."

"Yeah, lucky," joked Sam, but when he noticed that Leo wasn't laughing, his smile dropped. "Urgh, thanks for coming to our rescue. I mean, I thought I was a goner when I'd lost sight of Maya until Afriel came out of nowhere and found me."

Leo nodded and shifted deeper into the sofa. Maya watched a frown form on Sam's face when he gazed down at the blood and dirt that covered his hands, then he inspected the rest of his blood stained and torn clothing.

"Great! Look at the state of me." He waggled his finger through a large hole in his jeans and continued, "blood and dirt all over me ... nice."

Why is he making a joke out of it all? Her eyes focused on his face, searching for something. *We've just been attacked by hell hounds, rescued by angels and all he's concerned about is how he looks. Why's he acting as though nothing's happened? What's going on?*

Minutes later, Leo left the room, his excuse being that they both needed to rest, except Maya didn't need to sleep, she wanted answers; answers to why Sam was acting so strange and answers to just how much Leo was involved in this whole situation.

Gazing down at her jeans, she noticed the stains around the tear where the hound had clamped it's jaw onto her ankle and within seconds tears formed as the full horror of the day began to dawn. She rested her head back and closed her eyes. *Sam and I could both be dead right now, our bodies not being found for days. What would that have done to my parents?* Without sensing it, an unusual serenity fell over her, wrapping around her body, warming the chill in her muscles, easing the ache in her heart and silencing her mind.

Maya hadn't realised that she'd drifted to sleep again until she was woken by the soft hum of muffled voices and the shuffling of feet in the neighbouring room. She glanced at the empty sofa opposite and noticed that the indentation of Sam's bum was still in the cushion, so he hadn't been gone long. Just at that moment, the voices grew louder which drew her attention away. *I know it's rude, but hey, how many people get to listen in on a conversation between angels.* Tilting her head slightly to one side, Maya listened in.

"He hasn't sent his hounds out in years, let alone a pack of them." An unfamiliar, deep voice spoke. "If the hell hounds had used the full extent of their powers before we arrived, Leo, the outcome would have been disastrous."

"I know, Gabe, Maya won't be left alone again." She heard Leo reply.

Who's Gabe? But her thoughts were interrupted by the deep monotones of the angel who spoke next, Zach.

"There have been quite a few unusual human deaths lately, which have a certain demonic signature to them," he said. "Um ... do you believe the boy's power is already being used?"

"Yes, I do," answered Leo. "The humans didn't end their own lives, they'd no reason to as their souls were already signed over to The Enemy, and that can only mean the boy's involvement. We need to stop them and soon."

There were loud mutterings of agreement and then Leo spoke again, "We all know that the boy is from the family line of David, and we know what that means."

"I don't," Afriel's musical voice chimed.

"I don't either," muttered Maya quietly to herself.

"No, I don't suppose you do, Afriel, giving that you've just joined this mission. I'll explain," replied Leo. "Certain abilities or gifts were handed down through the generations, to certain individuals of God's chosen family, people from the line of David. The boy is from that blood-line."

"So, The Enemy needed the boy to steal the book?" asked Afriel.

"Yes, he did, as he couldn't enter Tartarus himself."

Who is this boy? Wouldn't it be weird if I knew him?

What if it's Sam? No, Sam wouldn't steal a book, but then he's always around when the attacks happen, and he's here now. Maya cupped her hands on the wall to try to amplify their voices.

"Before I left, Our Father told me that the boy has a gift that needs to be used with care. He has the ability to influence people's thoughts, to make them believe anything he places in their mind. Our traitorous brother, The Enemy, also knew this about him." Maya could hear a hint of anger on the edge of Leo's voice. "He's already using the child to manipulate people. Many have been forced to sign their names in The Book of Souls, and when the deed is done, General Bazriel is killing them or forcing them to commit suicide all because The Enemy can't wait for them to die naturally for fear that they'll find out the truth of eternal life and change their minds which would result in their names vanishing from The Book of Souls, and reappearing in The Book of Life."

"It's a pity Fallan snatched the boy from under our guard at that last battle." The deep voice of Gabe joined in.

"I have been forgiven for leaving my post," Zach interjected.

Leo broke the uncomfortable silence, "I know, Zach, and he wasn't just your responsibility. We were all deceived."

Afriel spoke next. "But what I don't understand is why he's interested in the girl?"

Maya pushed her ear flat against the wall, but just at the most crucial question, the one question she needed to hear the answer to, the room suddenly fell silent. *No, don't do this to me! I need to know why?* She pushed herself up on the sofa, clutching at its back. Except, she heard nothing, not a single murmur or shuffle, it was as though she had imagined the whole conversation to start with.

When Leo entered the lounge a couple of minutes later, Maya sat up straight. She could already feel her pulse quicken and it had nothing to do with Leo's close proximity, but rather down to too many things happening all at once, and all on the same day. She'd discovered that angels really do exist, that they had the power to defeat the hounds and that they were able to snatch Sam back from the brink of death. Taking a couple of deep breaths, Maya nibbled the inside of her cheek and groaned while Leo approached, stopping in front of her. He tilted his head to one side to catch her gaze and without turning away from her, he pointed at the chair in the far corner of the room. She stared in wide-eyed astonishment, mouth gaped open as it hovered towards him in response to his unspoken command to settle behind his legs.

"You look troubled," he asked. "What's caused this?"

Covering her mouth with her hand, she whispered between her fingers, "That ... Chair ... How ... Did ...." And pointed at it as Leo sat down.

"Oh sorry, it's nothing." He waved it off with a flick of his hand. "Forget the chair, Maya, I'm more concerned about you."

There was a long uncharacteristic pause as Maya

114

looked at him warily, and then in a sudden blurt of coherence, she replied, "Apart from being dragged several miles across a forest floor and seeing my friend nearly die ... you mean?" she cut herself off mid-sentence and shifted in her chair. "I ... I think I heard what you guys were saying in the other room." Her hands rested on the top of her head.

Leo raised an eyebrow. "You think?"

"Well!" She swallowed. "Who's this boy you're after? Is it Sam?"

Leo shook his head. "No, it isn't, Sam."

"Well is this boy a demon then?"

"The boy is most definitely not a demon, and I take it you heard the whole conversation?"

Maya blushed.

"Then you would've heard me telling the others that he has certain gifts which run through his family's bloodline, missing out the odd generation."

She nodded.

"Well, we have to prevent those abilities being misused." He moved closer. "Unfortunately, several years ago, our fallen brothers snatched him from under our noses, so to speak."

"Unfortunately?"

His smile disappeared and his eyes narrowed. "They're misusing his power to persuade people to sign their names in a book."

"What's the harm in that?"

"This is no ordinary book, Maya. It was meant for the names of the saved, the same as the other books that are similar to The Book of Life, which is named in the Bible. However, before I could retrieve this particular book from its Keeper and return it to My Father, my fallen brothers got their filthy hands on it, turning 'The Book of Souls' into an abomination." His expression darkened. "Once a person has signed their name on its pages, their soul is condemned to Perdition, unless of course, they become aware of their need to turn back to God." His eyes searched hers. "They need someone to save them before Satan, The Enemy, kills them, Maya."

Maya's blood turned cold, the colour drained from her face, the mere tone of his voice made her shiver. Even though she was talking to an angel right now and had been attacked by hell hounds a few hours ago. Why did she struggle to come to terms with the fact that Satan actually exists?

"What's Perdition?"

"You've probably heard it called by its most common name, Hell."

Maya took in a deep breath. "You've got to stop them, Leo. You've got to get the book and destroy it."

"We can't destroy it, Maya, but we can return it to God. And as for our fallen brothers, we are trying to stop them, that's where your help comes in."

"My help? I'm no good at anything."

"Your dreams are the key to finding the boy, and I know that he's been trying to communicate with you again." He ran his hands through his hair in a detached fashion. "You see, Gabe and I believe that you have an ability to change your dreams, to manipulate them, to

116

make them real."

"Seriously?"

"Yes, I am quite serious, for without you, we can't find the boy who knows where the book is, and we can't stop what's happening. And the stronger his gift becomes the greater number of lives he will affect."

"So they're after me, because I can help you?"

"Yes."

"That's not fair."

"No it isn't."

Maya looked down at the carpet, visualising the deaths of thousands of innocent people, she took in a couple of deep breaths to calm the sudden realisation of the horrific end they would have.

Gathering her thoughts, she asked, "When and if I see the boy in my next dream, should I stop running away from him and try talking to him instead?"

"I'd wait until you've learnt how to safely get back to reality first though." The warmth of his smile echoed in his voice. "I can help you with that."

She picked at the embedded dirt from beneath her nails, trying to take her mind off her turbulent feelings and pulled her legs up to her chest. "How'd you know the boy was even in my dreams anyway?"

"Maya, you forget who I am. We've known about the dreams for as long as they've been happening and you've had one not that long ago, am I right?"

"Wow, you're good. But they're just dreams, aren't they?" She faltered, swallowed and rushed on again, "And anyway, won't the bad guys be able to use this boy in the same way you're asking me to find him, so they can get rid of me."

"No, his abilities are not the same. He is only able to contact you through his dreams and the fallen will see them only as dreams, if at all. It is you that makes them real."

"Why me? Why does he want to contact me?"

"I can't tell you that for your own safety, but we believe he might know what happened to your brother."

"Seriously?" she said, not believing she had heard him correctly.

"Yes." Leo leaned back in his chair.

"But how?" *You better not be lying to me.*

Leo shook his head. "We think he might've befriended your brother at some point and that's how he found out about you."

She looked away and gazed into the fire. *He's hiding something, but what and why?*

She looked back at Leo. "So let me get this right ... that monster and man who snatched my brother were real, they weren't just some figment of my imagination?"

"No."

All the years of keeping everything locked deep inside her, suddenly punched Maya full in the stomach forcing her to gulp for air.

Leo bent forward. "Maya, try and breathe slowly."

It's all true, what'd happened to Jack had been real. I had told my dad the truth. Taking a deep breath, Maya forced herself to laugh as tears formed in her eyes.

"I told my dad the truth all along, Leo, that Jack had

been kidnapped by a scary man and his pet monster. I had told him the truth!"

Leo acknowledged her with a brief nod and handed her a couple of tissues out of a box which sat on top of the coffee table nearby.

Maya wiped her tears away and blew her nose as quietly as possible, straightened and returned to the subject at hand.

"Okay, if I've got it right, you want me to find out where this boy is, so you can get your hands on that book ... and in the process we might be able to find out what happened to Jack?"

"That basically covers everything, yes. The boy and the book are shielded from us by some kind of force-field, but if you can get him to trust you and tell you where he is, then we have a chance to stop what's happening to you, and save many human souls from eternal misery in the process."

Maya shook her head. *But how is Jack involved in all this?*

They didn't speak for a moment as Leo's words gradually sank in. Memories flooded back; she was staring at her seven year old self sitting on the sofa beside her mother moments after the monster and that man had taken Jack. Her dad was kneeling in front of her with his hands resting on her knees.

"Where's Jack, Maya? Where's your brother?" he said in an urgent whisper.

Tears formed in Maya's eyes as she recalled the moment her dad blamed her for her brother's

disappearance. *Why hadn't she screamed to warn them?*
Why hadn't she ran for help?

"Where is your brother?" her dad repeated.

Maya's mouth moved at the same time her seven year old self sobbed, "Mon ... ster took him, Daddy."

Her father shook his head and then he said those words that would keep them apart for nine years. "No, Maya ... there are no such things as monsters."

Maya blinked and the vision cleared. If she could make things right by finding out what happened to Jack, then maybe her dad could forgive her and they could be a family again. Maya sniffed and wiped the edge of the tissue under her eyes. The thought hadn't crossed her mind that the boy in her dreams could be real or alive, yet she would do anything to find out what happened to Jack, and if it meant finding some boy in her dreams to discover if he was, then that's what she would do.

"I'll do it. I'll do whatever it takes." She glanced at Leo and noticed that he wasn't smiling. "When do we start, and how do I help?"

"We'll start in the morning, if that's alright with you. I'll explain then. You've had quite enough to cope with this evening."

She nodded. "Can I ask you something else that's been bugging me?"

Lines formed on his brow, but he still gave Maya a nod.

"What's the matter with Sam? I mean, he's just been attacked, nearly killed, found out that you guys are angels and he's ... well ... acting as though nothing's happened."

Leo's intense turquoise eyes searched hers during the few seconds before he answered, "We couldn't heal him fully, Maya. When the hounds bit him, they injected venom into his bloodstream, we've tried our best to slow it down, but we have no idea what effect it will have on him."

A conflict of emotions followed one another in quick succession across her face. "Are you telling me that he's going to die eventually?"

"No I'm not saying that, and anyway we can stop that from happening, but we have to keep an eye on him. His body will go through some changes, hopefully ones that we can deal with."

"What sort of changes?" she insisted.

Leo shook his head. "Maya, no one has ever survived an attack, so we have no idea what to expect. It could be physical or it could be something that involves his mind."

"When I saw him earlier, he was acting strange, as if he hadn't been attacked at all?"

"That's because he doesn't remember, it's better that way. Afriel made him forget, like when I wiped his memory after the incident down by the river. As far as Sam is concerned, he thinks you both had an accident on the scooter."

"You did that? You made him forget what happened at the river, but why? Why did you do that for him and not me?"

For a shrinking moment, he paused and rubbed his chin. "I'm sorry, it was for his own good, imagine the nightmares he'd have."

"Oh, so it's okay for me to have spent my whole life

121

trying to forget what I've seen. It's alright for me to have spent years getting assessed by some nut doctor." The words tumbled out in a rush and in an instant, a memory sprung into her thoughts: she sat in the doctor's office while he talked to her parents in the corridor. Did they not realise she could hear every word they said.

"It's your daughter's way of coping with the trauma of seeing her brother snatched, Mr Stewart. It will take time, but she will come around eventually," the doctor had said.

"But a monster? Surely this isn't normal?" her father told him. "She keeps insisting that it was a monster with wings and an evil looking man that took Jack. Come on ... that's crazy."

"Has your daughter been reading horror stories or watching them on TV?"

"No, and we've already told you that," her mother replied.

"She's also having nightmares about it, waking up screaming every night," her father's deep voice broke.

"Give her time. That's all we can do," the doctor told them.

Shaking her head, Maya recovered and continued where she left off. "And it's alright that my mum and dad thought I was some sort of mad weirdo." She paused for effect. "Is it?"

"No, it isn't, but we don't understand why these things happen, sometimes. What you are able to see and do are a part of you, and it will be with you until your last breath."

"That's supposed to help me?" She pulled herself to the edge of the chair.

"I can't change what happened to you or your brother." He placed his hand on her arm and gave her a comforting smile. "I'm sorry. However, with your help we might be able to put some of those things right."

Leo's expressive face changed and became almost sombre as Maya tears collected in her eyes.

She sighed before speaking again, "I felt like a right idiot when Sam couldn't remember. He said I'd dreamt it. Thought it was a joke." She blinked and a tear escaped between her lashes, rolling freely down her cheek. "Do you have any idea how hard it is for me to trust anyone and then for them to throw it straight back in my face?"

"I won't let that happen again, but both you and Sam need to keep our true identities hidden."

Her head shot up. "From everyone?"

Leo nodded and lifted his hand off her arm. "Yes, Maya, and especially your parents."

That's not fair, but then I suppose they wouldn't believe me anyway. She peered towards the door leading to the hallway. "Is Sam still here?"

"No, Afriel took him to get his scooter and then followed him home."

He gave her one of his lopsided grins. "Apart from tonight, has everything else been okay? Did you have any further problems with John?"

Maya settled back into the cushions on the sofa. "I've been avoiding him, but Jess worries me. She's been kind of odd lately."

"In what way?"

Digging her right elbow into the armrest, Maya

123

relaxed her head on her fist. "She's changed. She isn't the same. I tried warning her about John and she had a right old go at me, accusing me of making it all up, which is my life's story."

"What do you mean, she isn't the same?"

"She's completely besotted with him, like she's drunk some sort of love potion or something." Maya scratched her head. *Pretty much the same way I am with you.* She started to blush, then promptly continued with, "I sort of wondered if John had something to do with it, because since his arrival, all of this weird stuff started." Maya shifted her legs into a more comfortable position. "I'm really worried about her, Leo."

"Is this the same John who forced himself on you in the library?"

"Yeah."

"Interesting!" His muscle clenched along his jaw-line, yet his expression gave nothing away.

CHAPTER TEN

The next morning, Maya stood on the steps leading up to the porch of the Old Rectory and peered down at her feet. Several terracotta tiles were cracked and rotting autumn leaves were heaped in high piles in the corners. She searched along the wall for a doorbell, her gaze seeing nothing which resembled one except for a long metal rod with an oval shaped handle hanging to her left. Giving a shrug, she took the couple of steps up to the door and the metal rod, and gave it a gentle tug. Nothing happened, so she pulled it again with greater force this time and heard a low clang resounding from within the house. Footsteps from inside drew closer making her heart beat quicken with every step the person or angel took. *Stop being so stupid. You've got what you've wanted all along; a whole day with his gorgeousness.* Maya chewed at her bottom lip as a key rattled in the lock. *So why am I so nervous?* The door swung inwards to reveal Leo standing in front of her, his hand still resting on the door handle.

"Hi, come on in," he said, the glow of his smile warming her.

"Hi," Maya gave a girlish laugh as she stepped onto the colourful tiles and walked into the hallway.

"How did you get on when I left you last night?" he enquired.

"It was okay, my parents were out, so they didn't see me all daubed up, thank goodness."

"That's okay then. Come on through to the study." Leo brushed past her. "I'd like you to meet a friend of mine who'll be standing in as my human father."

She followed Leo into an oak-panelled room with imposing shelves along each wall which were stacked full of antique books. In the corner, two winged-back chairs sat around a circular coffee table with a brass standard lamp behind them. A light that seeped around the door in front of Maya caught her attention, drawing it away from Leo. Her gaze became transfixed as it grew brighter with every second, until it was so intense that she had to close her eyes for a split second, then it died and disappeared. She turned to face Leo who stood with a wide grin on his face.

"He's just arrived," he told her.

The thought of meeting another angelic life form blew Maya's mind. *What's he going to look like, what if he doesn't like me?* She still struggled to form a coherent sentence whenever Afriel or Zach were in the vicinity. *So what effect is this one going to have on me, complete stupidity maybe?* The door opened. Leo stepped closer to Maya and touched her arm reassuringly. Yet, she stood rigid, her heart stopping its usual rhythmic beating as the angel stepped into the study. *He's incredible!* She gazed at the angel who towered over them both. He was handsome, but in a brutish sort of way. His short, perfectly

126

cut, light-brown hair, hugged his broad face and his eyes were as green as spring meadow grass. *Their eyes are so striking, it's like being able to see their whole essence of life, their souls even - if they have one.* Maya's breath gushed out as she remembered to breathe.

"Good morning, Maya." His voice was as big and broad as he was, yet his tone was soft.

"Um, good morning, Mr Err ...."

"White," interjected Leo.

"Mr White," Maya finished saying. *How appropriate, she chuckled to herself.*

"Leo has spoken a lot about you and your adventures," the angel continued.

I like him.

"I've been looking forward to meeting you."

For the first time in a while, Maya found herself at a loss for words. *He's been looking forward to meeting me! Hell no!*

"Leo, would you like me to stick around for a while?" he enquired, politely.

"That would be good, Gabriel, if you can spare the time?"

"Ga ... bri ... el?" Maya gulped, a look of utter shock spreading across her face. "No way, you ... you can't be."

The huge angel smiled and tried to hold back a gurgle of laughter. "No, I'm not that Gabriel, Maya."

Leo on the other hand couldn't contain it and burst out laughing, only to receive a bitter glare from Maya. However, this was the first time she had seen him laugh like this, he looked carefree for once and she liked it. Her anger faded and she threw back her head, and joined in. And for those few minutes, it felt like she was sharing a joke with two ordinary people. How far from the truth that was.

Regaining his composure, Leo rested his right hand on his chest as he began to explain, "The Arch angel Gabriel, who you're thinking of is far more important than my brother here." He pointed at the massive man standing proudly in front of them now. "No offense intended big guy." Leo slapped his hand down on Gabriel's shoulder.

His brother on the other hand cocked an ironic eyebrow back at Leo, but kept silent.

"Gabe is like me, a soldier and protector of humanity."

Maya's cheeks flushed a rosy pink when she recognised that name; Gabe had been one of the angels she had snooped on yesterday and now seeing him, she felt a pang of guilt for her actions.

As the blush continued to deepen and cover the rest of her face, Leo took her hand in his and pulled her towards the door which the huge angel had entered the study by. The touch of his hand in hers had caused a surge of static electricity to shoot up her arm and the sensation didn't fail to make her desire him even more. She didn't want him to let go, but inevitably he would and then she would get that gut-wrenching disappointment, because he was an angel and angels were probably clueless to the needs of those raging hormones that raced through every teenager in the world. Maya turned her head away and took a quick peek back at Gabriel, but she couldn't see him anywhere in the room. He had simply vanished.

Trailing behind Leo, Maya looked around and noticed how the back garden was in complete contrast to the front; here, neatly trimmed topiary bushes lined the gravel path leading down towards the pond and on from that, she could see a well-tended rose garden. Yet, the front entrance with its overgrown trees and unkempt driveway gave an unloved, almost abused feeling. Maya sat down beside Leo on a wrought-iron bench overlooking the pond and watched the insects skittering across its surface.

Her mind for once, fell silent, almost peaceful, then Leo interrupted it with a rather soft tone by asking, "I need to try something with you."

"Try what?" She turned to face him.

"It's a way of getting you to safety in a hurry."

Maya flicked her hair over her shoulder. "Like yesterday, how you got me away from the hell hounds and back here?"

"Yes, but this time you'll be conscious."

"Oh ... right, yeah. Will it hurt?" She took a deep breath and rushed on, "because if it does, I don't know whether I want to try it."

Leo frowned. "I don't think it does. At least nobody's complained about it so far."

"Oh, okay, so what do you need me to do?"

Leo rubbed his hands together, the muscles in his arms flexing and pushing against his all too tight shirt. Maya smiled with contentment, knowing that his attention was all on her and only her right now. It was then that she noticed his dark eyebrows arching inquiringly and knew he hadn't missed her obvious examination and approval of him. Her cheeks coloured under the heat of his gaze.

"I ... I'll transport you ... from one area to another by ...." He shook his head, his black hair falling forward to obscure his eyes and breaking the awkwardness between them. "It's easier to experience than explain. So if you're happy to have a go."

She gave a nervous nod.

"We'll get on with it then."

Maya didn't know what to expect and she had forgotten that her hand was still in his until he gave it a gentle squeeze.

"Don't be afraid," he said, his tone soft and serene.

"Okay, I think!"

"It's better if we stand, then you'll land on your feet." He chuckled.

"Not helping, Leo."

Maya kept her head bowed and her eyes fixed firmly on the ground as she stood.

"I'll start by transporting you into the study and then we'll go somewhere further. Ready?"

"No."

Except, this time, the light she associated with angels didn't happen. Leo began to glow from within. A steady stream of photon particles flowed and arced around them both. He seemed to shimmer, melting into a gleaming phosphorescence. Maya assumed she still had a body, at least she hoped she did, and as she watched, absorbed, he became an amorphous pulsating body of light. She closed her eyes. A warm breeze brushed across her face, lifting her hair, fanning it out behind her. Adrenaline coursed through her body. She felt no pain, only a pleasant sensation, similar to the whoosh you got on the very last dip of a roller-coaster ride.

"Maya, you can open your eyes now, we're here."

She opened one eye at a time, carefully scrutinizing her surroundings, unsure whether they had moved at all. Leo was right, they were back in the study. Gabriel sat in one of the Queen Anne chairs, his face lit by a large grin.

"How do you feel?" Leo's eyes searched hers for a reaction.

"Um ...." Maya patted herself down. "Okay, I think. Oh-my-goodness, that was totally unreal," she squealed in breathless excitement. "Can we go somewhere else, please?"

Leo raised a hand. "Okay, okay, calm yourself. Let's try going to the school library. No one will be there during the holidays."

"Oh come on! Why can't we go somewhere more exciting, like, London or Paris, or what about the Caribbean?"

Maya heard Gabriel whistle, then laugh.

Leo took a step back and raised both his hands this time. "Whoa! Maya, I need to build the distance you travel gradually, so it gives your body a chance to acclimatise or else your insides are going to cause you all sorts of problems."

"Oh," replied Maya, somewhat disappointed, but she snapped her eyes shut again when the light from Leo enclosed around her.

An unexpected darkness smacked into the familiar light. Maya heard a growl and felt Leo's hand release hers. She opened her eyes, but her focus was blurred. A few inches from her left, an ethereal form scurried by, making her jump. Items clattered to the floor, groans could be heard all around her. Then with a thwack, something punched her in the chest, forcing her back against a wall. The air in her lungs discharged in a loud grunt. A distorted shape blocked her vision, she blinked several times, her eyes gradually clearing, yet, she didn't expect the figure she saw to be someone she knew. *What the hell is he doing here!?* John's face was close to hers, except he had changed dramatically; his hair was the same, greasy and black, but his cheek-bones protruded unnaturally, making his eyes smaller, and his eyebrows were raised up his brow an inch higher, giving him a permanent look of surprise. He gripped Maya's throat with one hand, the other pushing against her chest. His breath washed over her face. It was still cold and putrid, the same as she remembered when he last got that close to her.

"Now, you will come with me, human." He purred. "Bazriel's been waiting a long time to have you as his pet."

Maya's throat burnt as his clawed hand tightened. *Leo!?*

Without warning, a figure appeared behind John, causing Maya to jerk back violently. Leo slapped a hand down on John's bony shoulder. The smell of burning

132

fabric and flesh saturated the air. John's claws lengthened, sinking deeper into the tender flesh of Maya's neck. His eyes flashed at her with outrage and in one sudden movement, he retracted his claws, twisted his head and glared down at the red hand print seared into his skin. Maya felt warm liquid trickle down her neck. She brought her hand up to her throat, wiped it and stared blankly down at the blood covering her palm. Within a heartbeat, John had spun round, punched Leo in the chest with such force that it had sent the angel hurtling between two bookshelves and landing with a clatter on top of a desk.

"No!!" Forgetting her own discomfort, she sprang to her feet and leapt onto the demon's back. Maya's fear eclipsed by a wave of scorn and fury.

Wrapping her arms tightly around his tree-trunk of a neck and her legs enfolded partly around his waist. She clung on with all the strength she could muster and what had once been John, loped after Leo completely oblivious to his cursing passenger.

"Leave him alone you ugly demon spawn from hell." Maya screamed.

It was the best she could come up with without embarrassing herself by shouting obscenities in front of Leo. And then she opened her mouth wide and bit down on John's leathery shoulder.

"Maya ... NO." Leo shot her a surprised, angry look and pushed himself to his feet.

John skidded to a halt, gave what sounded like a gurgled laugh, then powered backwards, smashing Maya's back up against the end of a bookshelf. She yelled out, falling to the floor, her hands clutching her stomach. John turned his head and glanced down at her, a sneer forming on his inhuman lips, then he vaulted towards Leo. Maya could only breathe in short gasps and stare blankly ahead. A silent scream escaped her as John flew across the aisle, his huge frame crashing to the floor. The demon laid on his back over a scattering of books, his body twisted and broken. Although he was dazed, it lasted only a matter of seconds. He pushed himself up slowly, snapping and popping bones back into place as he stretched. Light shone all around Leo as he stood in front of John.

"We can continue to destroy this building, but surely you must realise you can't win this fight against me." Leo's voice had a powerful tone rippling through it.

John crouched, screwing his eyes into a squint and flexed his muscles, readying himself to pounce.

"I've warned you once before not to come near my charge. I won't warn you again." Leo glared at the demon. "I don't understand why your Master keeps sending *you* on this insane mission. You don't stand a chance against me. You do realise that, don't you?"

"You don't frighten me, angel," spat John, he placed his right leg in front of him for balance.

"Ha-ha." Chortled Leo, "You're just a small insignificant demon who dreams of grandeur."

With a sudden burst of speed, John uncoiled and pounced at Leo.

"Leo!" Screamed Maya.

However, Leo had been expecting John's reaction and caught him in mid-flight. With a powerful arm, the angel slammed John up against one of the tall shelves. John struggled to break his enemy's hold and after several seconds, he gave up.

"Doesn't feel good, does it, being the victim." Leo snarled.

The demon tried to say something, but his words only came out as grunts.

"Are you trying to speak?" Leo mocked, his grip tightening. "Time you returned to your Master and I somehow don't think he'll be as lenient as I am. Perhaps you've learnt a valuable lesson today," he continued, all the charm leaving his voice, "That it isn't wise to pick a fight with someone stronger than yourself."

Maya looked at Leo in horrified silence for a moment. *Who is the real Leo? I know he's an angel, but all I see is a hot teenage guy, not this powerful being standing in front of me, threatening a demon with such authority.* Leo's body glowed with such intensity that it forced Maya to shield her eyes. Howls of agony spewed from John's mouth, the smell of burning flesh hung in the air again and an almighty bang similar to a thunderclap shook the foundations of the building. The light faded, yet the rancid smell lingered and when she lowered her arm, John had disappeared. Maya covered her mouth, she'd seen a different side to Leo and it frightened her. He wasn't just this loving, caring being that she thought angels were meant to be - he was all-powerful and a killer. She surveyed the damage that they had caused; books trashed, their pages still floating down towards the floor, desks shattered into tiny fragments underneath the shelves which had fallen on them. It was worse than a mess, it was a disaster. She looked at Leo as he approached, he pulled her hands away from her mouth and the light returned to enfold them, along with the familiar weightlessness.

Within a heartbeat, they were back in the familiar setting of the study. Maya whirled round to see Leo standing a few feet from her and noticed red blotches appearing on his shirt. Fresh blood also dripped through his scruffy midnight black hair and ran in beads to freckle his face. She took a couple of steps towards him, reaching out to touch a deep gash below his right eye, but he caught her hand, gently forcing her to lower it.

"You're bleeding," Maya protested.

"I'll heal," he replied in a calm voice. "But I'm more concerned about your wounds, Maya. I'm sorry the demon had a chance to lay his filthy hands on you."

He released her wrist and placed his hands around her neck, his nose almost touching hers, his gaze observing her through lowered lashes. Maya's pulse raced with each warm breath that shimmered over her face, raising the heat she already felt deep within her. She peered down at his lips, which were excruciatingly close to hers, imagining what it would feel like to be kissed by them. However, the increasing heat under his palms distracted her thoughts.

She pulled back. "Ouch ... that hurts!" She accused, and in an instant, any thoughts of a kiss evaporated.

"Stop fidgeting then or the healing won't be complete," he said in irritation as he continued to hold her neck. After a few minutes he removed his hands and touched her chin, tilting her head from side to side. "There, all done. You'll probably want to wash away the dried blood when we get you back home."

"Home, do you think I'll be safe there after what just happened?"

"Don't you trust me?"

"No. I mean ... Yes of course I do."

An arched eyebrow indicated his humorous surprise. "We'll be watching you, Maya, I promise."

Maya opened her mouth to object again when Gabriel strolled by and sat back down in the chair he had rested in earlier.

"I take it things didn't quite go to plan then," he stated.

"No," replied Leo.

"No, is that it, is that all you're going to say?" *I can't believe him. It's like he doesn't care.*

"There was a slight problem while we were travelling, nothing to worry about though."

"We were attacked, to me, that isn't what I would call ... nothing." Maya folded her arms across her chest, her lower jaw jutted forward. "I deserve a better explanation, and what about the library? I can just imagine the kind of trouble we'll be in if they find out it was us."

Leo leant back, eyes wide and held a hand up in a defensive stance. "Okay, Maya, you're quite right, you do deserve an explanation, but you don't need to worry about the library, it will be fine."

"How? It looked like a bomb had landed."

"Let's just say some brothers of mine have probably already cleaned it up."

"You mean ... more angels?"

"Yes, and to answer the first part of your question, so you don't have another go at me." One corner of his mouth pulled into a smile and there was a boyish glint in his eyes. "We were ambushed just as we landed at the school and I sort of had my hands full with three other demons before I could come to your rescue."

Ignoring his attempts to lighten her mood, she replied with a hiss of distaste, "That was John Latruce." Turning, she threw herself down onto the chair beside her.

"That demon ... was John?" Leo questioned, a momentary look of discomfort crossed his face.

"Yes it was, yet how did he know we were going there?"

"I don't know. Except, he might have known you were with me while we were travelling."

Maya frowned, her brow wrinkling with confusion.

Leo quickly tried to explain, "When we transport people, it changes our colour. Each angel's light is different. It's like their own signature, as is the aura around each human. Some of my fallen brothers know my colour and once it's mixed with your aura, I suppose they knew you were with me."

"What do you mean by your fallen brothers?"

"They are our traitorous brothers who fell from grace, with The Enemy."

Gabriel stood and gestured for Leo to take his place.

"You mean another type of angel?"

"Yes and no." Leo came and sat down, bending forward, he rested his arms on his legs. "They were angels before falling to earth, becoming dark and twisted. We call them the fallen ones and you really don't want to meet one of them if you can help it." He tilted his head and gave Maya a superficial smile.

I had no idea things were so complex.

Leo glanced across at Gabriel, a scowl appearing on his face. "Nazual was there, just watching, and when he realised that I had spotted him, he flew off."

Gabriel's eyes narrowed. "I thought you'd destroyed that one when all this started?"

"So did I, but I obviously underestimated him. I should've crushed him when he first fell from grace."

What is it with these two? It's like they're two hormonally charged adolescents that can't wait to get in to a fight.

"You're getting soft in your old age, boy." A large grin stretched across Gabriel's handsomely sculpted features. "There was a time when you'd smite first, then ask the questions."

Leo laughed, sharing an inner joke with Gabriel. He sat straight, ran his hand through his hair, and when he looked back at Maya his expression dulled.

"Who's Nazual?" she asked, as she rubbed at her eyes to clear the blurriness away.

"One of the fallen and someone we thought was still out of action," answered Gabriel.

Out of the blue, Maya went limp, every muscle in her body became unresponsive. Her pulse raced as panic filled her, because right now she couldn't see anything.

"Are you okay?" She heard Leo ask in a panicked tone.

"Help me, Leo ..." her voice came out in a faint, trembling whisper.

She felt Leo wrap his arms around her shoulders and pull her forward, before she fell into a world of emptiness, a place of nothing.

CHAPTER ELEVEN

Since his return to his room, the boy had no recollection of how long he'd been sitting there staring at the flames. He blinked several times to clear the sleep from his eyes and warily pushed himself up but soon wished he hadn't as his vision blurred. Overcome with dizziness, he fell back into the leather seat and wiped the sweat from his brow. *What's wrong with me? I've never felt this crap before.* Gripping a fistful of his shirt at chest level, he tried to empty the haunting images of Julia from his mind except they still continued to claim his thoughts and he hated Bazriel for that.

He pulled at his hair in frustration and peered down at Skip who was lying on the floor in front of the fire. Watching the rise and fall of his blanket-like wings with every breath the creature took. Dropping his gaze, he spotted a dark-purple bruise spreading across the joint to Skip's right wing. The boy shuffled to the edge of his chair to get a better look and noticed that there was also a cut which ran along the full length of his friend's spine, ending at the base of his tail. A sudden surge of guilt and anger rushed through him. Yet again his best friend had suffered the punishment that was meant for him, for his mistakes.

"I'm sorry, Skip," he said softly, so not to wake him.

"I won't let it happen again, I promise."

The boy's gaze lifted to the flames, shapes formed in the rising smoke. His breathing slowed as he sat forward and looked at the ghostly figure of a horse staring back at him. Never before had it appeared like this, in real time, in the here and now. It was a creature of his dreams only and that was where it should stay. So why could he see it amongst the flames? Closing his eyes, he searched through his memories until he found what he was after. Glancing down at his hand, he could feel the animal's muscles twitch beneath it even now; the warmth of its black fur, velvety muzzle and the moist heat of its breath, felt so real. Yet it was all in his mind, like the girl with the red-curly hair who had been a part of his dreams for so many years, they were all a part of his imagination. However, there was something deep inside him, he could sense it even now. He rested his hand on his stomach. The feeling and need to know this girl had eaten away at his thoughts for several days and it had all started with the arrival of Bazriel. Keeping his eyes sealed, he willed himself to the strange world of dreams, to the horse and to the only place he felt free.

It was a quick transition, he was good at it now and within a heartbeat he had arrived at the place that Fallan never knew existed or would ever find. Pine trees lined the four sides of the familiar meadow. He tilted his head back, staring up into the heavens and circled on the spot, his feet digging into the soggy ground. *Wait! This is all wrong. I shouldn't notice whether the ground is soft or that my feet have sunk into it. Not in a dream! What's happening?* He

142

scratched the top of his head for a few seconds before brushing the thought away when he remembered why he was there. He held his breath waiting with excited anticipation for the arrival of the horse. Between the trees to his right, the magnificent beast appeared. A smile creased the boy's face as he watched the horse trot with ease towards him. It stopped in front of him, lowered its head and rested its muzzle against his chest. He placed a hand on the animal's neck, its muscles quivered with delight.

"Hi boy," he whispered, while moving to its side.

Snakes of varying sizes emerged from its mane when he slid his hand along its neck, their tongues flicking to taste the air. It never occurred to the boy that horses didn't have teeth like lions or snakes growing within their manes and tails; after all this was the only horse he'd ever seen and it liked him. The animal turned its head and glanced back at him before snorting and nudging his leg. Stepping back, he watched the horse bow down before he grabbed a fistful of its coarse mane and jumped onto its back. The horse stood and without warning, powered forward into a canter and the exhilaration he felt, blew away any anxiety that had wheedled its way into his mind from earlier.

The horse cantered across land he hadn't seen before. Time didn't matter. There were no boundaries he couldn't cross. No guards chasing him. No Fallan. No Bazriel, just miles and miles of open space. Nobody would ever know that he could travel through the land of dreams, it was his secret and it would stay that way. Yet his thoughts of total freedom kept being interrupted by the image of

143

the girl with the flame-coloured hair, he still wanted ... no needed to share his freedom with her, but why?

All of a sudden, the boy felt pressure gripping tightly around his right arm and when he glanced down a red hand print rose on his flesh. Sensing the boy's fear, the horse plunged it's hooves into the dry dirt and skidded to a halt.

As the youngster sat for a moment in silence, his dream faded and the smell of sweat and cigarette smoke lingered in the air. Closing his eyes for a split second, then re-opening them reluctantly, he spotted Skip hovering in the corner of his room, the creature's mouth drawn back in a snarl, his body bunched up ready to pounce, but at what? *There's only one thing that smells like that*, thought the boy and he quickly raised his hand to warn Skip to settle.

"Get tee-ya' feet, boy. The General wants to see ya'."
A giant of a guard with the blackest of scowls grunted his command and pulled the boy up in a hostile way.

The youngster glared up at the man's dark and aloof eyes and watched as a snarl extended the full length of the man's face. Then the boy returned his gaze back to the guard's eyes and within the first few seconds he had managed to enter the grubby man's mind. The big guy blinked, twitched, sniffed and snorted, trying to resist the intrusion, but he was useless against the boy's growing ability. Seconds later the guard became transfixed, unable to move, unable to think. All of a sudden, the youngster flinched back; it wasn't a man's mind he saw, it was the mind of something horrific, hideous; the mind of an ugly creature wracked with suffering. His stomach churned with the vile images he saw. Bazriel had control of this guard. *What if I can control him like I do with Skip?* He glanced at his winged friend who stared back at him with wide eyes as he peered out from the corner of the hearth, the flames touching, but not burning him. *I reckon I can do it.*

The boy pondered on the idea, then scratched his face, nibbled the inside of his lip and decided to have a go. He couldn't use the guard's past experiences to gain a foothold for there wasn't any, apart from pain. With perspiration beading his forehead, he decided to plant any old thought into its mind; something simple, something to confirm the fact that he had managed to gain a bit of control, at least. The teenager didn't speak, he didn't utter a sound and by thought alone, the guard released his grip on the youngster's arm, turned and left the room.

"Wow!" The boy grabbed at the sides of his head. "No way, it worked. Skip, it really worked!" He erupted with a chuckle and strolled towards the door. He turned, smiling at Skip. "Come on," he called.

Skip stepped out of the flames and trailed after his young master.

Having Skip with him, reminded the boy of their many adventures around the house and he smiled as he strolled down the corridor remembering how Skip was able to get in and out of any locked room, making him a great accomplice in their favourite past-time of a game similar to 'Hide-and-seek.' There was only one rule to it and that was to cause as much chaos as possible. Skip

145

would steal an item from one of the guard's rooms, then hide it in someone else's space. It was as the fights erupted afterwards, when the game truly began. The transformation from man to demon - both grotesque and fascinating at the same time – just helped to take it to a higher level. He glanced back at his friend. They needed to have fun like that again, soon, he owed Skip that much.

The boy stopped outside the closed door to the room where he had helped Julia gain her freedom. Skip dashed down the corridor and around a corner, before peering back at him. He hesitated, hovering his hand over the handle for a few seconds before pushing down and opening the door wide. What he saw as he entered the room, sickened him. There were three people huddled together in the furthest corner: a middle-aged man dressed in filthy, worn out clothing, an older woman slightly smarter in appearance and a scrawny looking teenage lad a few years older than himself. He glanced over towards Fallan who leaned over the table with his left hand placed beside the open Book of Souls. Bazriel pointed the engraved pen at the cowering visitors and indicated with his head towards them. The boy knew what he had to do; he had to persuade each person to sign their name in the book or they would suffer the same torture that Julia had. It was the only way he could save them, but he hated doing it.

Half-an-hour later, as soon as the old lady had signed her name, the two guards' hoisted her out of the chair and were dragging her out of the room in the same fashion as the man who went before her. Fallan was already shoving the terrified lad into the chair opposite the boy. The man and woman had been relatively easy to manipulate, but this lad was roughly his age and he hadn't met someone his age before. The door flung wide, crashing against the wall as the guards' returned and took their place behind the trembling teen.

"What are you waiting for, boy?" Bazriel eyes narrowed as he peered down at his charge. "Would you rather we torture him first, because that would be rather good sport of you."

The lad went to stand, his body shaking. A guard pushed down on his shoulders, forcing the lad's backside to land painfully down on the seat.

Bazriel pulled on the lad's hair, jerking his head back so their eyes met. "What do they call you, human?"

"Michael, sir," the lad whimpered.

"I know a Michael, but he wouldn't be sitting here whimpering at me like a bag of pus, which is a shame really." An expression of regret formed on the old general's face for a second and then it was gone. "Michael wants to play, don't you, Michael." Bazriel turned to look at the boy, then yanked the lad's hair again as he waited for an answer.

"Yes, sir ... yes I do, sir."

Bazriel released Michael's hair leaving it standing in wild tufts. The boy peered into the lad's hazel eyes and watched the pupils dilate as they tried to focus through the tears. Michael was weak as he hadn't eaten much for quite a long time; images of the lad living on the streets under cardboard boxes alone and afraid came forward in his mind. The boy swallowed heavily as he went deeper into Michael's memories. Pain, loneliness and abuse were there in the darkness. *Why would someone who was meant to love you, hurt you in ways that were unimaginable?* He shook his head and blinked several times, trying to get the sickening pictures of abuse out of his head. He felt a hand raise his chin and pull his head sideways. Opening his eyes, he saw Bazriel staring straight at him.

"Don't stop or you'll regret it," he growled beneath his breath and released the boy's chin to take a couple of steps back.

Looking back into Michael's eyes, he entered the lad's mind with ease. *What do I do? I don't know how to do it this time, his whole life he's suffered at the hands of someone who should've loved him.* And then he remembered the love Julia had had for her son. *Would it work? Could such a broken person feel that kind of love again?* The boy started to place images into Michael's mind of the same love Julia had got for her son; of a mother's embrace, of caring, of protection and of her undeniable love. And there it was, the one memory Michael had forgotten because of the pain he'd suffered at his father's hand. It was a letter from his mother that she'd tucked inside the cover of his favourite children's book before her passing. The boy hated this moment, the moment he had to make them sign in the book, the book that contained the screaming voices and then he froze. He couldn't do it. *This isn't right.*

He leapt out of his chair, headed for the door and

yanked down on the handle, budging the door open a fraction before Fallan slapped his hand on it, slamming it shut with a loud thud. The boy turned, ducked under the man's outstretched arm and sprinted for the far corner where he could at least hide in the shadows for a while. *What the hell do I do now?* He hadn't planned to escape and knew that his only chance had gone. He slid to the floor, crouching low, he rested his elbows on his knees and brought his arms up to cover his head.

Footsteps drew closer, then all but one set halted and that one set, belonged to the cruellest being he knew.

"A bit melodramatic don't you think?" Bazriel squatted awkwardly in front of him. "Now, I have two options, boy. The first one involves a lot of pain on your part, yet somehow I think you probably would tolerate it, so let me explain about the second option, and the one I favour the most. I can tell you like our young Michael over there or else you wouldn't be acting this way."

Lifting his head, the boy glared back at Bazriel. *Where are you going with this, old man?*

"Good, I've finally got your attention. Michael means nothing to me though." Bazriel twisted his bulk and waved his hand towards the lad who was now being held down by Fallan. "So, what if we forget about him signing in the book and being freed to return to his life, but instead, we torture him and make you watch." Bazriel traced his fingers along the boy's arm. "We'll start by peeling the skin back along his arms. I think that is one of my favourites."

The expression on Bazriel's face sent a crawling chill

up the boy's back.

The old general continued, "And it always makes them scream without the risk of them passing out." He smiled a self-satisfying smile. "I'll leave you to think about it for a few minutes." He stood with the help of his hands pressing on his thighs. "By the way, the decision is yours, but the time is ticking away, boy," he said with a flick of his hand as he ambled back over to Michael.

The boy put his face in his hands, shaking his head from side to side. *Yet again someone else is going to suffer for my stupid, pathetic actions. Why?*

"Tick-tock." He heard Bazriel's voice mock him from across the room.

Rising to his feet, head bowed, the boy dragged himself over to the chair and sat down. He took in several deep breaths until he was strong enough to raise his head again. With tears stinging his cheeks, he gazed into Michael's eyes and reconnected with his mind in an instant. He made The Book of Souls look like the story book his mother gave him many years ago. Michael watched as the letter was taken out of the cover and opened. He read the message which had been hidden deep in his subconscious and the wariness immediately lifted from his face, leaving a rosy glow on his once pallid features. Fallan placed the pen in the lad's hand and pulled his arm towards the open pages. The boy watched as Michael wrote, I love you mummy, and then he signed his name and another soul was caught amongst those screams.

The boy collapsed in the chair, his body wracked with

exhaustion and his mind saturated with the scars from the thoughts of the three lives he'd briefly delved into. Bazriel crouched down in front of him. His fat fingers lowering to his left eyelid and raising it to peer into the youngster's eye.

Bazriel's face drew closer, his putrid breath scolding the boy's cheek. "Are you still with us in there, boy," he goaded, tapping his finger on the boy's forehead.

The youth couldn't reply, words wouldn't come out of his mouth, just odd groaning sounds. Through his blurred vision, he saw Michael being lifted to his feet and hauled out of the room.

Bazriel chuckled and ruffled the boy's hair. "Take him to his room. My pet needs his rest."

The next thing the boy heard was a door smashing against a wall as the guards dragged him into a room that had a certain familiar musty stench to it. They threw him with ease onto an unmade bed and left him there in this weird semi-conscious state. A few minutes of silence followed until he heard the sound of approaching footsteps thumping on the wooden floorboards. A shadow smothered the little light which shone over his closed eyes and all he could hear was the sound of his own breathing roaring through his head. The faint warmth of someone's breath touching his ear freaked him out; if only he could open his eyes, could move, he could get up and run away. *What's the matter with me? Why can't I do anything?*

"I didn't think you'd be able to pull it off, making three stinking humans sign in the Book of Souls, and now, they all belong to My Lord," the voice whispered. "It makes all this ... worthwhile."

The boy vaguely recognised the man's voice as he patted him on his head. Light returned to his face when the man turned, the swish of his cloak lifting the dust off the floor, that's when the youngster remembered where he'd heard that voice before; it was Fallan. All of a sudden, the sharp point of cold steel prodded him in the side. He tried to cry out but his mouth wouldn't move, not even a twitch, so his yelp stayed silent as the door to his room flung open again and he heard a gasp escape Fallan.

More than one set of footsteps approached this time. Fallan's cloak brushed against the boy's legs as he marched away from his bedside. Someone with laboured breathing approached the youngster and leaned forward. A cool fat hand with metal bands on each finger came to rest on his forehead.

"He's sound," the new man said softly, affectionately.

"Do you want me to wake him, Bazriel?" enquired Fallan.

"No, leave him be. He's worked hard today."

With a thud and a scrape, Bazriel dragged himself away. The loud creaking of leather indicated to the boy that Bazriel had sat in one of the armchairs in front of the fireplace. The rhythmic tapping of metal on wood made him shiver, it seemed to go on for hours, but he knew that it was only a matter of minutes, because Bazriel wouldn't waste his precious time watching over him for any longer. Fallan left his bedside and headed in the same direction. Just then, the smell of rotten eggs wafted by his nostrils causing his throat to tighten and his breathing to come in short gasps. He heard a cough from the other side of the room, which sounded more animal than human, and wondered whether it belonged to the mysterious person who had entered the room along with Bazriel.

Bazriel shuffled in his seat and smacked his lips before speaking. "We need to up the stakes, Fallan."

The boy heard lighter footsteps approach the centre of the room.

"Don't fail me again, underling. After your last defeat, this might be your only chance to regain my favour."

A new person replied, a voice the boy didn't recognise at all, "I won't fail you, General."

The voice had a weird purr hanging on the very edge of each word making a similar sound to the hiss of a snake.

"I've heard that before," Bazriel replied. "Oh, and I suggest you keep your distance from Leo, the Demon Thwarter, this time. I'm sure you remember why."

There was a chuckle from Fallan.

"You are dismissed," Bazriel ordered.

The light footsteps marched out of the room and faded away taking the stench of rotting eggs with them.

"Are you sure Latruce is capable of carrying out your commands, General?" Fallan sucked in a deep breath.

Just then the boy heard a heavy thud as something fell to the floor and listened to what sounded like someone's legs thrashing against the leather fabric of a cloak, and the strangling groans of a man choking. *Bloody hell! He's killing Fallan here in my room.* The boy had to move, had to do something, but still nothing would happen.

"You *dare* question me? You are nothing in this world. I could crush you beneath my feet like a piece of dirt." Bazriel's voice rattled in the back of his throat. "But it isn't my place to destroy you. That is for Our Lord."

Fallan's squirming stilled. "Forgive me." He croaked weakly and stood.

An uncomfortable silence followed.

"You will show me some respect, brother." Purred Bazriel.

Fallan's breath came in short gasps.

"Our Lord made you what you are today, but I can destroy you with the click of my fingers if needed, remember that."

"Yes. Sir."

The chair sighed with relief as Bazriel peeled himself from its frame. Hands grasped the boy's chin, twisting his head slightly to one side. The putrid stench of death wafted over his face, brushing his hair from his brow.

"When the time is right, I want you there to retrieve our trophy."

The boy was patted on head by Bazriel's plump hand before he moved away from the bed.

"Thank you, General. I won't let you down," Fallan replied in a tone that seemed to convey a somewhat false composure.

Trophy? What did he mean, 'retrieve our trophy?'

CHAPTER TWELVE

When Maya came round, she found herself back in her room lying on top of her bed with the sun streaming through her window. She sat up and shuffled to its edge. She leaned over her bedside table and peered at the hands on the clock. Eight-thirty ... she had slept through the night without a single dream which was both great and unusual; she couldn't recall a night without dreaming since Jack was taken. *How long have I been here? I don't even remember Leo bringing me back.* And she sighed as her feeling of disappointment deepened; every part of her ached to be with Leo and she didn't understand why she felt this way, except that she was falling in love with him. *Could that be why I'm so intoxicated by him? Because I'm in love with him? Are angels even capable of loving? And what about Sam, what shall I say to him if he asks me out again?* She shook her head and got dressed before heading downstairs.

Sitting on a cane chair in the garden room, Maya slipped her feet into her Converse pumps and fiddled with the lace. *At least with this search I'll be able to find out what happened to my brother and get the chance to hang out with Leo all day.* Pulling the lace tight, she sat up. *But how am I supposed to do it, to make myself dream during the day? Is that even possible?*

155

Her mother peered from around the kitchen door, her round cheerful face, now solemn, looked oddly, disembodied.

"Can we talk?" she asked.

Maya raised her eyebrows and flicked her long locks to one side. "I'm in kind of a hurry, Mum, can't it wait until later?"

"No, we need to talk now."

"Okay, give me a minute. I'll just finish putting my shoes on."

Her mother's head disappeared back around the door, leaving Maya looking on in a slight state of shock and curiosity. She tucked the end of the laces inside her pumps before standing, adjusting her top, then ambling through to the lounge and sitting on the edge of her dad's chair.

Her mother lifted her head, nudged her glasses up her nose a couple of inches, her mouth opening and shutting again as if she was struggling to find the courage or the right words to say.

"Your father and I, are worried about you." She sucked in a breath. "We've noticed you're having bad dreams again." Pausing for a moment's reflection, she then went on with a heavy sigh, "What I'm trying to say is ... have the dreams returned?"

Maya stared at her in horrified silence. "I ...." she was about to explain when her mother held her hand up, immediately silencing her.

"Please don't think we're angry with you in anyway, just worried." Her mum's hazel eyes narrowed causing her glasses to fall forward.

Maya hated keeping secrets from her parents' in the first place, but it had to be done or they would book her in to see a nut doctor and there was no way she wanted that to happen again. She shivered just thinking about all those endless hours spent nine years ago, talking to a stranger who in the end, hadn't believed a word she'd said in the first place. She knew the truth, and no one could change that fact however hard they tried; demons and fallen angels really do exist.

"Both your father and I have heard you shouting out at night," stated her mother.

How am I going to answer her? I can't have her knowing that that flippin' monster has returned again. She scratched her head. *What am I worrying about? She wouldn't believe me anyway.*

Maya cleared her throat. "It's nothing, Mum. I am having weird dreams again, but ...." She watched as her mother's face dropped.

"We know you still miss your brother, we all do and that will never go away. Every day I hold him in my heart, and I know he's there with me, but it gets harder to remember him, his little giggles and the kisses he used to place on my face every night. I miss him so much and I know you do too." Tears formed in her mum's eyes. "Hold onto those memories and not the scary ones of his abduction. It might just help you get rid of the terrifying dreams you're having, dear."

"I know, but it's not *those* dreams, like when Jack was taken." Yet the dreams were tainted by the past. "It's just stress with some of the course work I've been set. That's all."

"Are you sure?" Her mum wiped a tissue under her nose. "You know you can talk to us about anything, don't you?"

"Yeah sure, and I will if those nightmares return." Maya nodded and gave her a fond smile. "Can I go to Leo's now?"

"Leo's?"

"Yeah." Maya saw her mum's confused look. "I'm sorry, Leo moved into the Old Rectory with his dad last week and he's starting at the college after Easter."

Her mother's brow wrinkled with suspicion.

Don't do this to me, Mum ... don't go all protective on me now. "Sam's going to be there to." Maya threw in, hoping it would sway her mother's decision.

"Does Sam know this Leo then?"

"Yeah, of course he does."

"Okay." She murmured her approval. "But, just remember we're here for you."

"Yeah, I know." *Except, as usual, Dad isn't!*

Maya stood, gave her mum a peck on her forehead and left with a quick farewell.

Maya strolled alongside the privet hedge surrounding the memorial green in the centre of the village. On the far side of the small triangular green, she noticed a huddled figure perched on the edge of a bench. Thinking nothing more of it, Maya continued on her way towards Leo's,

158

until that person's head jerked up to stare straight back at her. Maya sucked in a large gulp of air. It was Jess, and there was something wrong about the way she sat there, hugging herself and rocking back and forth; something that she couldn't walk away from. *I'm sure Leo will understand.*

Squatting down, Maya looked across at her best friend and noticed her set face, clamped mouth and fixed eyes. She couldn't believe what she was seeing; Jess' pale skin looked translucent, her hair hung in greasy, thick strands, shielding her hollow eyes and she wore black trousers with a black polo-top. Jess never wore black and had told everyone she hated the colour due to its link with death and anything associated with it. In the past, Maya had tried to dig a little deeper by asking her if something had happened to make her fear death so much but Jess would just glare back at Maya in return, snort, and storm off without mumbling a single word. *So why is she dressed from head to toe in it now?*

"Jess," she said, feeling slightly uncomfortable. *How did you get like this so quickly? Last week you looked fine, a little pale, but not like this, like your life-force has been sucked from your body.*

"Yeah," replied Jess, in a weedy tone and not her usual confident voice.

"What's happened to you? Did John do this?"

Jess raised her eyes and glowered at Maya. "No." She snapped. "John loves me."

Maya instinctively rested her hand on her throat, she knew exactly what John was capable of.

159

Jess went on with a heavy sigh, "He's gone. I can't find him anywhere. His house is empty and he won't answer his phone. I can't live without him." She lowered her head into her palms and sobbed.

"Sure you can. You don't need someone like him in your life. Look at what's happened to you since you've been with him." Maya stretched her hand to push back Jess' hair. "He isn't worth it."

Raising her head, a look of hatred blazed in her eyes. "You don't know anything about him."

"Oh Jess, if only you knew the truth about him. He's dangerous."

"Get away from me." Jess growled and slapped Maya's hand away.

"What?"

"Go on, leave. You're no friend of mine."

"But ... please, Jess, you can't trust him." Maya sat back on her heals.

"You fancy him, don't you? You're jealous."

"That's so not true." Maya stood. "You've got it all wrong. He's ...."

"Shut up and leave." Jess shouted and lowered her head to gaze at the ground around her feet.

"John's done this to you. He's evil. I know you won't believe a word I'm saying, but you're better off without him."

"Shut up," Jess said with an animal like growl again.

Taking a step forward, Maya placed a hand on her friend's shoulder. Jess shrugged her off.

160

"I'll be here for you, whatever happens. Just call me, please." Maya waited for a reply but didn't receive one and with a pang of regret, she turned and headed back towards the gap in the hedge.

Glancing back one last time, Maya gasped. Jess had gone, the bench sat empty. *What the hell! That's impossible! How'd she move so quickly?*

Standing at the front door of the Old Rectory, Maya's excitement of seeing Leo had been marred by her conversation with Jess. *I should've done more, but how do I help someone who doesn't want it?* She tugged down on the metal bell rod and in an instant the door opened with Gabriel gesturing for her to enter with his usual wide smile.

"Hi, sweetie." He greeted, but his expression soon dropped into a frown. "Is everything okay?"

"I need to talk to Leo," Maya replied.

"Okay." Gabriel shut the door behind her. "However, he's not here at the moment. So if you can wait for him in the study, I'll give him a call." He pointed upwards indicating to Maya that Leo was on heavens business. "Sam will be here soon though."

He led Maya down the hall, through a small sitting room on the left, and opened a door to their right which led into the familiar study.

She sat counting a row of books, trying to forget Jess' predicament for now or at least until Sam's arrival or Leo's return, which ever would arrive first. By the time she'd reached the nineteenth book, muffled voices came from the hallway. Maya sat up straight as the door flung wide and Sam waltzed in.

"How're you doing?" he asked and sat down in the chair beside her.

"Good ... you?"

"Yeah," he replied and relaxed back in the chair. "This is pretty unreal isn't it?"

"What do you mean?"

"All this ... angel stuff."

"Oh, yeah ... I suppose so," Maya answered, glancing down at her nails. "What do you remember about it?"

"What? You mean the accident?"

So you still don't recall being attacked by hell hounds. It was like Leo said, 'he will only remember an accident.'

After a significant pause, Sam turned to look at her, opened his mouth to speak, then froze.

"Is something wrong?" Maya asked. "Or are you trying to impersonate a fish?"

"Funny." He gave a short chuckle and bent forward, rubbing his hands together. "You said before all this happened, that we would talk about the conversation we had the other day ...." He paused again, licked his lips and waited for an answer.

Maya glanced back at him. "What're you on about?"

"I'm on about what I asked you in the forest." Sam sat back again and tugged at the top of his hair.

Oh my goodness! Please don't tell me that you've spent all night thinking about that, surely not? Yet, in the back of her mind she knew this conversation was bound to happen at some point, although she had hoped under the circumstances, and with what he'd been through, that Sam might have forgotten. "You mean about ... you more than liking me?"

Sam nodded, an inexplicable look of withdrawal came over his face.

"I ... I told you then, that I don't want a relationship yet. Not while all this stuff is going on." She looked away. "I'm sorry."

"Is that the real reason?"

"What do you mean?"

Their eyes met again.

Sam took in a deep breath. "I'm not stupid. I can see the way you look at Leo, you can't take your eyes off him."

Maya's mouth opened wide. "I don't believe you just said that! If you think there is anything going on with Leo or that I'm in love with him, you're crazy," she told him, trying resolutely to keep her temper as she stood. *But he's right. I am in love with him. And how the hell did he know?*

Sam held his hands defensively in front of him. "Okay, I got it wrong, sorry."

"I don't want to talk about this anymore. I've got too much on my mind as it is." Maya turned and her gaze fell on Leo who stood in the doorway. *Please tell me he didn't hear all that? Oh how embarrassing!*

To her surprise, Leo showed no reaction even when he asked her, "Gabriel said you wanted to talk to me about something that was pretty urgent. So shall we take this into the lounge?"

"Yeah, that sounds good."

163

"Excuse us, Sam," Leo said.

"No problem, you guys go ahead, I'll be fine here ... on my own." Sam twisted his neck to take a look at the books. "Oh will you look at that, a book on the Architecture of Historical Buildings, just what I've always dreamt of reading. Go on, shoo! Go and do your thing." Sam waved them off with a boyish grin on his face.

Leo sat down in one of the armchairs and she shuffled towards the sofa, slumping into its soft cushions.

"So, how're you?" he spoke in a tone that seemed to convey a somewhat fake composure.

"I'm okay, apart from on the way here, I saw Jess sitting on a bench at the Memorial Green and she looked awful. She's lost lots of weight, her hair is a mess and ...." Maya raised her hands to the side of her face and met Leo's gaze. "And I'm worried about her."

His expression softened and for the first time since she had known him, he looked at her in a new way. His gaze flicked across her stricken face as if he was seeing her for the first time, taking in every detail of her features. His eyes widened and then he blinked, turning his head to one side and coughed.

"What's wrong?" asked Maya.

"Nothing." He shook his head and rushed on, "You were telling me something about Jess."

Like that was nothing. What did he just see? Maya swallowed and recovered herself. "When I tried to warn her off John, she nearly snapped my head off. She ... she even growled at me like some sort of animal."

"I see. Well, you tried. Maybe you could phone her later. Anyway, John won't be around here again for a while, not after our fight in the library."

"But you need to do something about Jess! You're an angel, you can sort it."

"Zach has tried, believe me, she doesn't want to know or doesn't want our help and there isn't much we can do about that."

"What do you mean?"

"That's the way it works. People are free to choose."

"But at least have Zach watch over her."

"Zach has been, since the moment you ran out of the library and bumped into me."

Maya's eyes widened. "So you've known all along about John and you still let him mix with my friends."

"I didn't know about him until that moment at the library when I smelt his demon stench on you, then Zach informed me that his scent was even stronger on Jess. That is when I had him watch her. But Zach's duties have changed now. As I said, she doesn't want to know."

I never thought angels could be so cruel. Aren't they all meant to be about saving lives? Anger rose from deep within her. "I don't agree with that, she's my friend and she needs our help. So, here's the deal. I won't start searching for the boy until you send someone to keep an eye on Jess again."

Leo's eyes narrowed and dulled a few shades. His expression darkened with an unreadable emotion and for the second time, Maya caught a glimpse of the dangerous side to him, and she wasn't sure how she felt about that.

"This isn't a game you can flick in and out of. It's imperative that we get the book as soon as possible, because, while we're playing around here, people are being killed right now, as we speak." He took a deep breath, trying to steady the anger from showing in his voice.

Maya swallowed. *Stay strong ... he needs you.* Folding her arms in front of her chest, she glared back at him for what seemed forever. However, just as she was beginning to hate herself for her outburst, his face softened and his eyes returned to their usual vivid colour that she so loved.

"You're not going to change your mind, are you?" he sighed.

She shook her head.

"Okay, I'll have someone keep an eye on her."

Maya smiled and unfolded her arms. "Thanks."

"Now can we *please* start looking for the boy?"

She nodded and tilted her head back. Through the window, the rays of springtime sun poured down on her olive face. Now feeling satisfied that she had seen to her friend's safety, her thoughts wandered back to the strange moment when Leo didn't seem himself. *That look he gave me was the first human expression I've ever seen from him. He was actually eyeing me up even if he denies it.*

"Are you okay to start?" he asked, moving closer to her.

Maya smiled. "Sure."

She tried to clear her mind, which wasn't easy whenever Leo was close.

"Alright, firstly, I need you to clear all thoughts from your mind and take deep, calming breaths. If you can hear the sparrows chattering in the bush outside the window, then focus on the loudest one and us its song to help guide you to your dream."

She could only hear his sexy voice caressing her eardrums. *This isn't going to work ....*

"Maya, concentrate. Think of the birds."

Even the sound of his voice had a warming effect on her body.

"Maya, please."

Her eyes snapped open. "You can read my mind!"

"Of course not, but if I could, I wouldn't need too. I can tell your mind isn't clear just by the tension in your body, that's all."

"Oh." She grinned and blushed. "I'm sorry. I'll try again."

"Let's try something else," he suggested, and shifted his chair so he sat dead opposite her, his knees almost touching hers.

"You promise I won't see dead people, just this boy, right?"

"I promise." His eyes searched hers, his expression serious again. "You remember when I mentioned how angels each have their own colour, like an aura. Try looking at me and see if you can make out my colour." He tilted his head ever so slightly to one side. "Do you understand?"

"Yep."

This is so embarrassing. I can't just sit here staring at you while you're looking, it's not how it's done, it's weird. And as if on cue with her thoughts, Leo relaxed his shoulders, closed his eyes and sat motionless. Biting into her bottom lip, Maya's gaze caressed along his face, his broad shoulders, then on to his well-fitting T-shirt that stretched in all the right places across his chest, defining almost every muscle and then allowed her eyes to drift lower ....

"Concentrate." He murmured.

"Yeah, I am." Her eyes shot back to his face.

What is an aura meant to look like anyway? Maya mumbled quietly to herself as she tried to conjure a picture of one in her thoughts.

Squeezing her fists into a tight ball, she stared without blinking for several seconds willing something to appear, however, nothing would have prepared her for what she saw next; steady streams of photons flowed and arced around him, surrounding him in light, but not a usual white light that you sometimes see with pictures of angels. She couldn't find words to describe it; blue and gold sparks intermingled with the brilliance of the white, although not any old blue; it was the same cloudless-sky-blue of his eyes. Tears beaded down her face with the sheer beauty of it all. Leo stretched forward and placed a hand on her leg.

"You're beautiful," she whispered, overwhelmed and caught up in the moment.

"I see it worked."

She found it impossible to not return his disarming smile and wiped the tears from her face as she replied with a chuckle, "It was pretty awesome."

He removed his hand. "Can you remember your last dream of the boy?"

"Yes."

"How about seeing if you can return to the place you last saw him."

"Okay!" Maya shuffled to get comfortable. "Let's do this."

"That's my girl. Picture the surroundings in your mind, the greater the detail the better. Imagine you're doing a painting." His gaze caught hers. "You like art, don't you?"

"Yes, I do." Maya suddenly recalled the reflection of his face in the vase during her art lesson a couple of weeks ago. *Had he really been there?* "I'll try, but how do I get back?"

"Think of me," He gave her a cheeky grin and winked mischievously.

She blushed and quickly snapped her eyes shut. On re- opening them, she had arrived in her last dream; except, wherever this place happened to be, it was now daylight. *Funny how things always look better when there is light.* She stood in the small opening with the sparse pine trees on her left, where beams of sunlight shone between them. *Funny that! Do dreams happen in real time or is this just something to do with me?* She spotted the large tree a few metres ahead where she first saw the boy up close and waited in the hope that he might return.

169

But this was her dream, her thoughts and if she wanted to contact him, she was yet to work that one out. Squeezing her eyes shut again, she brought the image of Leo forward.

"I see it worked." She heard him telling her again as her eyes opened. "Well done. We'll try again later when you've had a rest," he continued. "As it happens, I need to speak to Gabriel." He stood with ease.

"It was amazing," Maya told him.

"That's great."

But Maya could tell his mind was elsewhere as he gazed over her and out towards the hall. *What's happened? What's so important that we've had to stop?* Leo pushed himself out of the chair and stood. Yet, Maya didn't want him to leave when they had only just begun and leapt up from the sofa. She went to protest and placed her hand on his chest, except the electrical surge she'd felt before, now raced up her arm and on towards her heart which took a perilous jump, then settled back to its natural rhythm, stopping her in her tracks.

"Maya, are you okay?"

Intense astonishment touched her pale face. "Tell me you didn't feel that."

Inclining his head, his eyes assumed a questioning look. "Feel what exactly?"

Are you serious? A fallen ringlet threw her brow in shadow and she blew at it several times.

Leo glanced down at her hand, then reached out to brush the annoying strand back behind her ear and hesitated, his fingers resting on her cheek. A clouded, puzzled look came over his face and then his hand

170

lowered, bringing Maya's gaze once again down towards his chest, her hand and the embarrassing predicament she now found herself in. *What am I doing?* Yet the way those beautiful eyes of his looked at her, the way his hand lingered on her cheek ... something was stirring inside him, she knew it was.

"I ... I'm sorry." She lowered her arm back to her side, heat rising to her face in one almighty explosion.

Okay, so that was weird. He obviously didn't feel the electricity thing because he didn't flinch an inch, yet, maybe he can sense my feelings? And if so, why doesn't he say something?

Leo wiped the hair off his forehead in a detached motion. "We'll try contacting the boy again in a little while, okay? You need a rest." He gave a single nod, spun on his heels and headed towards the hallway.

"No, Leo," she called. "I want to do it again, now, while it's still fresh in my mind."

He stopped, whirled round and grinned at her, but there was no humour in his eyes. "Are you sure?"

"Of course I'm sure, I feel great."

"Alright then." He returned and sat back in his chair. "But this time if you get the chance, talk to him, ask him where he is, tell him you want to be his friend and visit. But don't mention the book though, just in case it scares him off."

"I'll do my best." *But how am I supposed to do all this? Maybe if I try and remember what he looks like first, I might get to see him this time.*

171

"Think about the boy, Maya. Remember what he looks like."

How the hell did you know I was thinking about doing that?

Laying her head back, she flicked her pumps off and pulled her feet under her. Her fingers grasped for the edge of the armrest, except this time she didn't feel soft fabric, instead, it was damp, gritty and....

Blinking several times to clear her blurred vision, Maya stared up at the ceiling only to see grey clouds hovering above her. Springing to her feet, she spun around and realised she wasn't in the same clearing as before. She stood in a grass field surrounded by tall, prehistoric looking trees, a place she had never seen before in here dreams. Stepping forward, she felt the blades of damp grass caress between her toes. *Everything is so real. This doesn't feel like a dream. Where am I?* She circled and couldn't see any escape route between herself and the imposing mass of trees. She pinched herself and it hurt. *It shouldn't hurt when you're dreaming, should it?*

Step by tentative step, Maya headed towards the outline of trees in front of her, her breathing slowing as she began to relax. A loud crack echoed throughout the clearing bringing Maya to an abrupt halt. Holding her breath, she tilted her head to one side and heard the distant thump of feet landing on moist ground. Her breath caught in a spasm of fear. *Leo, I don't won't to be here anymore ... please get me out of here!* The pounding kept the same rhythm as it drew closer and from between the

172

trees, walked a jet-black horse. It pawed at the ground, snorted, then raised its head and whinnied, flashing sharp teeth like a lion's. The horse reared and on landing, charged.

"Don't run. Stay very, very still." A voice murmured from behind her. "If he senses your fear, he will kill you."

Maya jumped, yet she still couldn't make her body move apart from tremble as the horse bared down on her.

"Good," the voice whispered again, the same voice she had heard in her other dreams.

The horse's front hooves slammed into the earth and it slid to a halt in front of her, dirt and grass splattered against Maya's legs, mud plastered her jeans. Mist vapours blew from its nostrils as its eyes bore down upon her. A sudden gush of air blew in her face and she snapped her eyes shut, willing herself to be back with Leo. Forcing one eye open, she saw the boy from her dreams now standing between her and the horse. He reached out to the wild animal and it lowered its head in response. Maya took a step back and spotted movement in the animal's mane. She watched in horror as a small snake-like head emerged out of the coarse strands and hissed at her.

"No way!" Maya gasped. "Who, who are you?" her voice cracked.

His reply wasn't quite what she'd expected. "Jump on his back and he will bring you to me." He demanded while his hand glided down the horse's neck.

What the hell! "But you're here in front of me."

"No." He spun around to face her.

173

The horse startled, flicked its head and snorted, while the boy stepped closer to Maya.

Staring into her eyes, he continued, "I'm only here in your mind."

"Ugh," grunted Maya.

She shook her head in disbelief. *If I reach out and touch him, his body would block my hand, so how can he say that he isn't here?*

Peering back into his hazel eyes, she could tell he'd witnessed suffering that someone his age shouldn't have to deal with. It was that same look she'd seen in her uncles eyes when he returned after his third tour in Afghanistan. She lowered her gaze, afraid at what else she might see hidden in their depths.

"You need to get on his back if you want to find me," urged the boy.

Feeling pulled towards the horse by an unseen force, she shuffled towards its side and placed a shaking hand on its neck. Straight away she felt something touch the back of her hand and glared down to see the forked tongue of a snake flicking across her skin. Maya yanked her hand back and it hissed in protest, flashing its fangs at her, then it slid back into the horse's mane. *What kind of horse is this?* The whole point of her doing this was to find the boy. It wasn't meant to feel this way; oddly removed from her body and with every passing second, her mind felt like it was being taken over by someone else. Sweat beaded her brow with concentration. *I've got to stop, shout out, do something.* Her arms reached over the animal's back and she started to heave herself up. *No, I don't want to do this. Why can't I stop myself?*

"Maya. No. Stop." A voice called from out of mid-air, as a sudden breeze blew across her face.

She froze ... She'd heard those deep monotones before, if only she could remember whose voice it was.

CHAPTER THIRTEEN

Deep inside her mind, she felt the strange hold on her break. Maya glanced back at the boy and caught sight of a ball of light sparkling between the trees behind him. The light split in two; one part staying in the woods behind where it had originated and the larger sphere flickering along the trees to her right, which eventually halted once it reached the right-hand edge of the meadow. She peeked back at the boy who was glaring at her with angry eyes.

"Run to the light," the voice in her head kept repeating.

"Get on the horse," the boy urged again.

Maya took no notice of him. Her mind rattled around, desperately working out a way to escape.

"Get on the horse." His mood darkened as he demanded this time.

Hesitating, a touch of panic wavered on the edge of her voice as she replied, "I thought I ... saw something."

The boy's eyes narrowed. "Where?"

"Over there." She gestured with her chin over his shoulders and towards the trees behind him.

The boy twisted around, his back almost to her. The horse jerked its head up and stared in the same direction as its master. Her eyes widened as she watched the sphere of light fade and weave its way deeper into the thickening trees. She then squinted to look at the flickering mass of photon particles to her right.

I've got to get to that light ... Come on dammit Maya, think.

With speed unbeknown to her, Maya sprinted across the grass and towards the glittering ball. When she reached the edge of the trees, she flashed a quick glance behind her. The boy had leapt onto the horse's back. The stallion reared, its roar booming throughout the clearing. Maya ignored the pain in her feet from the pine needles forcing their way between her toes. With tears in her eyes and a burning in her chest, she ran on.

Light's safe isn't it? Light is always safe.

With every step that brought her closer, the mass sharpened, swirling and evolving into a shape. She slid to a halt, her breathing heavy as she saw a horse approach her, then stop. Taking a couple of seconds to catch her breath, Maya looked again at the boy and the stallion that were a few hundred yards from the first line of trees now. The vibrations of the great black's hooves pounding the earth, penetrated her entire body, freezing her to the core. *Now what do I do?* The white horse lowered itself, bowing down beside her.

"Okay, okay. I'll ... err."

In one mighty leap, she was upon the animals back with a fistful of its silky mane gripped between her hands. Holding on tight, the horse stood and overgrown ferns brushed against her legs as it went from a gentle trot into a swift canter. The horse dodged between the pine trees, covering the ground in a blur. Maya's legs gripped around the horse's sides; the hours learning to ride when she was younger were now paying off. She blinked several times trying to clear the moisture from her eyes and peered ahead. After a few minutes, the trees turned fuzzy and kept going in and out of focus. In the distance, spears of light shone between the thinning pines. With surprising speed, Maya and the heavenly horse exploded out from the forest and landed in a vast meadow.

A fierce breeze hit her hard in her chest making her breath catch in the back of her throat. The air swept through her hair, fanning it out to resemble flames blazing behind her. Tightening her grip, she craned her head round to see if the boy was still in pursuit.

No ... No! This can't be!

The black stallion roared and bared its teeth, which were more suited to being inside a lion's mouth than a horse's. Stretching out its neck, it went to take a chunk of flesh from the flank of the white horse, but Maya kicked her leg back, cracking her heel against the soft flesh of its muzzle, resulting in the beast jerking its head skyward. It didn't take the boy's horse long to catch up with them again and come smashing into the side of Maya's white stallion, throwing them both off balance. Maya's horse although smaller was also a lot more agile and caught its footing quickly, changing its pace into something faster than a full gallop. With a sudden jolt it turned to their right, leaving the boy's stallion skidding to a dramatic halt. Rearing, the black pivoted on its hind legs and with a mighty leap, started the chase all over again.

178

Doesn't this kid ever give up? Leaning forward, Maya shouted into the horse's ear. "Come on, come on, you can do this."

Maya's horse sped along an embankment, heading at a terrific rate towards a large hawthorn hedge. *Oh no, no, no ... not over that.* She never did get to the part about learning how to take jumps and actually stay on the horse. Yet, the horse didn't leap into the air as she had expected and instead, ploughed straight through it. Everything, including Maya, turned transparent. Staring down at the horse's shoulders, she drew in a deep breath, waiting to be torn to shreds by the thorns, but she didn't suffer one single scratch. The needle-like spines raked through her body, leaving her with the weird sensation of pins and needles. Once through the hedge, the horse slowed to a rolling canter and in the distance the spire of a church rose. Soon they were trotting up the incline of Church road and on towards The Old Rectory.

Her hands hurt as she untwined her fingers from the horse's mane and when Maya heard the stallion's hooves crunching on gravel, she knew they'd arrived. The horse came to a halt in front of the porch and waited for her to dismount. Swinging her right leg over, she winced when her feet jarred on landing. Taking no notice of her aching feet, she brushed her hand between the horse's eyes and stopped to rub his ear.

"Thanks," she said in a whisper. "Thanks for saving me."

The horse nuzzled her, then nudged her towards the porch before vanishing, leaving a wisp of mist trailing behind. Reaching for the door pull, Maya gasped when her fingers passed straight through the metal. Jumping back, she tried again, but each time she did the same thing would happen.

"What the hell!" She cried, before placing her hand over her mouth. "What's happened to me?"

Fingers stroked back her hair, soothingly. "Mum?"

"Maya ... Maya, it's me," a familiar male voice spoke.

Maya opened her eyes and saw Leo kneeling before her, concern written across his handsome face.

He tilted his head and gazed into her blood-shot eyes. "I thought we'd been too late to help."

Lifting her hand to wipe the sleep away, she cringed when she saw her dirt covered palms.

"How ... I don't ... get it?" She stuttered, and glanced at her other hand only to see the same muck covering that. Maya sniffed her palm, the scent of the horse lingered on her skin. "How can this be?" Her gaze met Leo's.

Ignoring her questions, Leo replied with one of his own. "What happened?" He leant forward, resting his arm on the sofa.

She continued to stare down at the grime under her nails in a state of shock. *It had to have been a dream, except, I didn't fall asleep beforehand. It couldn't be real, it just couldn't be.* Looking up, she saw Gabriel standing in the doorway and Sam sitting on the edge of a chair, his brow creased with worry.

Brushing the hair from her eyes, Leo repeated his question for the second time, "What happened?"

Shaking her head, Maya peered at the painting over the fireplace. The dream had been so real, the smell of the field, the pine forest and the horse were still attached to the lining of her nostrils, yet how could she still have mud and horse hair splattered all over her? Dreams didn't do that.

Leo placed his hand on top of hers, drawing her eyes back to his with his action and Maya began telling him everything, it just blurted out in rapid succession; how she'd found herself in a small clearing with monstrous trees surrounding it and after that, about the charging horse and the boy. His expression changed, growing serious.

"Do you know what happened then? I mean, the dream was real, alive." She waved her fingers in front of her face. "I don't understand?"

Leo stood and strolled over to the window, his hand stroking his chin. "This shouldn't have happened. Not like this anyway. It's most unusual."

"You're telling me," replied Maya. "It was more than a dream and it scared the hell out of me. The boy had some sort of control over me. He tried to force me to get on his horse. Why would he want to do that?"

Leo turned. "This boy is able to put thoughts into people's minds, maybe he just wanted you to go with him. I don't have all the answers."

"Well, he looked pretty angry when I broke free, when I heard someone shouting, 'run to the light.' Was that you?"

Leo shook his head. "No, sorry."

Maya pulled her legs out from under her. Her face tightened into a frown and that's when she noticed that her jeans were covered in mud and her feet were stained with blood.

Leo stared out the window, peering down the driveway. "We'll sort it, don't worry."

"Will it happen again?" Maya asked without taking her gaze off her feet.

Turning to face her, Leo replied, "I don't know. I don't understand how you managed to travel through our world."

"Whoa!" Sam blurted out and sat forward.

A look of utter shock spread across Maya's face. "I travelled through ... your ... world?" She raised her head, slowly.

Leo could only nod.

"Is this normal ... I mean, is it meant to happen?"

"It's something we hadn't anticipated." Leo looked across at Gabriel who shrugged back at him.

"Tell me what you mean, please," Maya asked.

"I can't. I have to work this out myself first and when I have the answer, I'll let you know." An expression of uncertainty crept onto his face. "I need to speak with the others. I'll ask Afriel to escort you home and I'll meet you back there, alright?"

Maya nodded and watched Leo stride towards the doorway, expecting him to turn around any minute to reassure her, except, he didn't, instead he left the room with Gabriel, leaving her with a load of unanswered questions.

"Wow, Maya, you've got some real crazy stuff going on there," Sam told her.

As if she didn't already know that.

"How'd you do that dreaming thing anyway?" he continued.

"I can't talk about it right now, Sam. I need to go and get this mud washed off me," she replied, pulling herself to her feet and heading out towards the cloak-room, across the hallway.

She stood over the sink, both hands clinging to the sides of the basin. Until now, it hadn't crossed her mind how serious or dangerous this search could be, dreams weren't meant to hurt you, they couldn't hurt you, except hers seemed determined to. Turning the tap on, she washed her hands as questions rolled around in her mind, each interrupting the other: *What did Leo mean by, 'I'd walked through his world,' and what was with the boy wanting me to get on the horse and if it wasn't Leo who sent the diamond coated horse, who was it?* She stared at her pallid reflection.

"Why me?" she whispered to herself.

After a while, she stood straight, flicked her hair over her shoulders and returned to the lounge. The reality of the past couple of weeks rushed through her mind. She couldn't do it anymore: the dreams, the attacks, the angels, she couldn't deal with it. She wasn't this strong person who could save people from an eternity of Hell. She was just a teenage girl from a small Norfolk village called Wicklesham. Tears trailed down her cheeks to drip off the end of her chin. *I'm going to fail.*

CHAPTER FOURTEEN

All night Maya tossed and turned in her sleep tormented by visions of how the boy had managed to control her, and when morning arrived, she struggled to rise. It had been too much what with the dream and trying to comprehend that she had actually entered the realm of angels and demons. Maya needed answers, needed Leo. An hour later, she peered through her bedroom window, stretched and yawned. *What the?* Afriel stood in the far corner of her garden and although he had escorted her home, she hadn't expected to see him standing on guard throughout the night. Thinking about it though, it did bring a certain amount of comfort to her, knowing that they weren't taking any chances where she was concerned. Maya glanced back at Afriel and let out another long sigh. *Right, I need to sort this out.* Closing the window, she left her room and headed downstairs.

On the kitchen table she spotted a hand written note and picked it up to read it.

Maya,

I've gone to the shop. Won't be long.

Love Mum xx

She scrunched it into a tight ball, then threw it into the recycle bin before making her way through the garden room and out of the house to face the angel.

Ignoring the fact that she was still in her pyjamas when she stopped in front of Afriel, she gulped in a large breath of air and said in a suppressed voice, "I, I need to talk to Leo."

Afriel glanced down at her and blinked, his expression giving nothing away.

"Did you hear me?" She glared up at him, rising onto her toes to match his height. "I want to see Leo, now."

"He isn't available."

"It's important." She felt a surge of irritation flow through her. "I'm staying right here until you call him."

Afriel bowed his head, a quick flash of anger crossed his face, which almost instantly vanished.

"Did you hear what I said?"

"I told you he's busy."

Maya folded her arms and raised her chin.

Without warning, Leo appeared beside her, forcing her to stumble back. Her hand flew up to her chest and rested there in an attempt to calm her frayed nerves. *This appearing out of nowhere has got to stop.*

Leo openly studied her, his face clouded with uneasiness as if he already knew why she was harassing Afriel. "It's okay. I'll deal with this."

The blonde angel snorted, shook his head and the sky boomed with a loud thunderclap as he disappeared. Maya slapped her hands over her ears.

Leo looked up into the heavens, his jaw clenching.

185

"I'm sorry about that." He lowered his head and gazed at Maya who was still grimacing from the ringing in her ears. "Afriel doesn't know how to handle confrontation yet and when he's confused, he goes off like a fire-work, as you just saw." He pulled a smile, but Maya wasn't laughing. His shoulders slumped. "What's going on?"

Maya placed her hands on the top of her head and told him, "I can't do this anymore." She pinched her bottom lip between her teeth, trying to keep a control of her emotions. "I've hardly had any sleep and I'm scared."

He raised an eyebrow.

"You said, after that last dream ... that I had walked through your world or whatever it was. What exactly did you mean?"

He spoke with a hushed tone. "I'm sorry if I scared you yesterday, it wasn't my intention, but you need to calm down."

"Calm down!" She threw her arms into the air. "You think that's going to help me?"

There was a touch of sympathy in his eyes. "Sorry."

She stared wordlessly across at him. *It's so hard to stay angry with you. It's just not fair.* "Okay. Apology accepted, I suppose."

"Good. So let me explain what I found out. You already know that demons and angels exist." He looked at her with a certain knowing concern and waited for her response.

Maya gave a nod of her head, just the one nod though.

"Most people only see this world, so I need you to

imagine if mine was within and around what you can see here, now. A world where angels and other immortals move freely amongst you. You see, Maya ... you are capable of walking in my realm, that's what you did yesterday. It wasn't a dream. There's a few humans who see us in a fleeting moment, in a blink of an eye, but most don't even believe we exist. You walked between both existences, both worlds which are also very much a part."

"Do they think you're like some kind of ghost then?"

"I suppose they could see us as such, though when people talk about ghosts, they are thinking of the dead interfering with ordinary life. The spirit world is completely different. You transcended into the same realm that we live in. Ghosts don't go there, they can't." He took a hold of Maya's other hand. "Remember how your hands and clothes were covered in dirt." He waited for her to nod and when she did, he peered up at the sky. "It's the world that you live in, except, it's different at the same time. It's a world where battles are fought, missions are carried out, brothers are lost, and it's all interlaced with this one. I know it's hard to understand."

Maya flicked her hand around in the air. "You mean that *that* wasn't a dream, not something that was made up in my mind, but ... I went into that other world? Will it happen again?"

"Probably, it happens to be a part of your gift, of who you are," answered Leo.

"My gift?"

"Yes."

"Some gift." A look of veiled amusement crossed her

face for a split second.

"In time you will learn to control it, then you can use it to help people. Think of all those souls you can save by helping us find the boy and the book."

They stood at the end of the garden in silence as fear whooshed over her. "I don't understand any of this."

"You will, I promise. Are you feeling less spooked now?"

Maya nodded, although the fear was still there.

"Good."

Leo placed his fingers under her chin which sent a ripple of warmth streaming through her chilled body. His eyes searched hers and a smile twitched at the corners of his lips. "Can you stay over mine for a few days? Sam's going to be there as well as we're all still fairly concerned about him."

"Has something happened to him then? Has the venom done something to him?"

"No ... no, nothing like that. We just thought it would be best to keep him as close as we can without him suspecting too much at the moment. And anyway, let us worry about him, Maya, you have enough to think about right now."

Yeah right, as if that's going to happen.

"So do you think you'll be able to stay?"

"Yeah, I'll try, but I'm not sure my parents will let me because they think my nightmares have returned and it's reminding them of what happened ... well you know." She shrugged.

"Yes, I do. When all this started. Well I have a

strange feeling they'll let you come." He winked and with a raised eyebrow said, "So I'll see you around lunch time."

"Oh really!" Maya answered. *How can he be so sure?*

Leo took a few steps back and with a wink, he vanished leaving behind the sound of fluttering wings.

Twenty minutes later, weighed down with three bags of groceries, Maya's mother clattered her way into the kitchen and hoisted her burden onto the table with a loud huff of exertion. Straight away Maya noticed the blank expression on her face when she turned around to look at her daughter, but what struck Maya more was the lack of any spoken words leaving her mother's mouth. *Something's not right with her. She's never been this quiet.* Delving into a bag, Maya lifted two bottles of milk out and put them straight into the fridge. She straightened and watched her mother again. *She's still acting weird. Should I ask her now or wait? What the hell! What I'm doing is way too important to wait.*

Maya took a deep breath. "Mum ..." But her mother didn't answer, didn't turn, didn't raise her head to acknowledge Maya. Instead she carried on unpacking, so Maya continued anyway with her question, "Mum, you know that new friend, Leo, from college, the one I told you about yesterday? Well he's invited me over his for a couple of days. They live at the Old Rectory down Church Road." She swallowed. "Can I go?"

Her mother turned and stared straight through her as though she were transparent.

"Of course you can, dear," she replied and gave her daughter a huge synthetic grin before returning to her unpacking as if nothing unusual had occurred.

Maya stared wordlessly at her mum's back. *This isn't right ... this isn't like her at all ... no third degree, not even a single question about it.* She bit into her thumb nail. *I don't know what I prefer; over-protective parents or parents who don't seem fazed at all. This is definitely Leo's doing and I don't know if I like it.*

A short while later, Maya strolled around the sharp left hand bend at the top of Whitehart Street, which ran alongside the Memorial Green and merged into Church Road. Since leaving hers, Maya had been wondering how she could contact the boy without the same problems occurring as they had yesterday. *What if he tried to control me again? All I want to do is get him to tell me if he knows Jack. What if my brother's still alive and we get to save him, and at last we'll be a normal family like everyone else. My dad ... would finally forgive me!* Her heart went down, it sank, almost literally at that last thought. Would her dad ever forgive her for not screaming for her parents' aid all those years ago? She could only hope.

By the time she arrived at the house and saw the front door standing open, panic crept its way back in.

Stepping into the hallway, she called out, "Hello, is anyone in here?"

She heard nothing except her own breathing, the house was silent. *Where is everyone?* Within a flash of light and a subdued thunderclap, Afriel appeared from the direction of the study, startling her.

"Um ... hi ... I was... looking... for Leo," she stuttered,

remembering her earlier outburst. *I hope he's not still angry with me. I know I would be.* Yet he smiled warmly at her.

"He's in the garden, I hope you're feeling better?" His tone was melodic and strangely soothing compared to earlier.

"I'm good, thanks," she replied. *Should I apologies?*

His golden eyes met hers. "My reaction to you earlier was inappropriate, so I apologise."

"Oh, I ... it's fine, don't worry about it. Honestly!"

"Thank you, Maya. That is most gracious of you."

And it was then that the young angel bowed before her. *Oh my goodness, weird or what!?* Afriel straightened, turned and gestured for her to follow him and once they stepped out into the back garden via the kitchen, the angel motioned with his head for her to continue down the path.

Maya found Leo sitting on a tree trunk at the far end of the garden.

"Hi," he said, his obsidian-black hair dishevelled and covering his eyes in the way she adored.

"Hi," Maya replied, dumping her overnight bag on the ground and sitting down beside him.

"Are you able to stay?"

Maya nodded. "Yeah, I am, but you already knew that, didn't you?"

Leo said nothing, except smiled at her while shoving his hand in his pocket and pulling out a chard of crystal. "This is for you."

"It's beautiful." A ripple of excitement sparked through her. No one had ever given her such a precious

191

gift before and she didn't quite know how to take it; was it a gift of fondness or to claim that she was his? And as she turned it around in her fingers to admire its rainbow of colours, a warmth resonated from its centre.

"It's from the River of Life that runs through heaven, so it will be a guide when you are lost and bring you protection when you are threatened."

"I'll treasure it," she said while clasping her fingers around the crystal and holding it close to her chest. *And there I have my answer!*

Eventually, Maya placed it into her jacket pocket and twisted around to give Leo a hug. He placed a tentative hand in the small of her back causing her heart to flutter. She didn't want to pull away and could have stayed in his arms forever except, when he had removed his hand several seconds ago, if not minutes, she was still wrapped around his neck. Maya buried her burning face against his shoulder before releasing her hold and straightening. Adjusting her jumper underneath her jacket, she began to work at a tangle in her hair. *If only I could tell what you're thinking? Whether you feel any emotions for me at all or even if you could possibly fall in love with me?*

He blinked several times as if coming out of a daze and looked away. "I think Sam was planning to cook you both something for lunch."

"Oh right, is he here now?" Maya shifted forward and lowered her gaze.

"Afriel just went to get him, so shall we head back in and see if he's arrived?"

"Yeah, why not."

Sam was already busy frying bacon, eggs, baked beans and mushrooms when they entered the kitchen. Maya dragged a stool from under the breakfast bar and sat down. She noticed Leo gazing across at her, the same way he had several times before. *What's going on with you lately, Leo? Why do you keep looking at me as if you're searching for something that you're afraid of finding? It's like you're looking at me the same way the guy in the movie does when he just realises that he's found his soul mate and wants to share the rest of his life with her.* At least that was what Maya was hoping and wishing he was seeing. A slow smile grew on Leo's face. Their eyes met and lingered there for a few seconds, until unconsciously, Maya parted her lips which made Leo look momentary confused. He turned and strolled over to the open door, rubbing the back of his neck while peering outside. Shifting on her stool, she caught Sam glaring back at her, his fingers twitching with annoyance on the cutlery in his hands. An unwelcome blush crept into her cheeks. *Oh cripes, I suppose that'll be added onto his jealousy list as well, just so he can throw it back at me some day.*

Lifting the strap of her rucksack off her shoulder to allow it to drop to the floor, Maya had at least expected to hear a muffled thud on its landing, yet, she heard nothing at all and turned her head to investigate. Leo's face was inches from hers as he bent forward with her bags straps held firmly in his grip. *How the hell is that even possible, to be on the other side of the room one second, then appear by my side within the next?*

"I'll take this to your room," he said, drawing the

rucksack to his chest and stepping away from her. "Back in a minute." And with that, he turned and practically ran from the kitchen.

Sam took one more look at Maya, shook his head and returned to his cooking. Just then, the buzz of her mobile phone became a welcome distraction. Pulling it free from her jacket pocket, her eyes widened as she read the message.

We need 2 meet. I haven't seen John and it's killing me. There's no point 2 any of this. If you don't come, then I know that life is over for me. Please meet at the lower graveyard alone at 8 2 night. I'll wait for you at the bench.

X Jess

What! What's she on about? This can't be happening! She stared at the message again.

"Do you want half of this slice of fried bread I've done? Sam interrupted.

"No. No thanks, Sam."

"Well then, your dinner is served."

Maya placed the phone face down on the worktop. *This can't be happening, not today. What did Jess mean by her life was over if I didn't meet her?*

Sam's face dropped when he saw Maya's frown. "Is everything okay?"

"Yeah, It's fine," she replied with a fake smile.

He placed the two plates down on the counter in front of Maya and sat down on the stool beside her.

"I didn't know you could cook?" Maya told him.

He scraped his dish along the wooden counter to

position it in front of him and tilted his head to one side. "Well, there's a lot you don't know about me then," he replied, with an arched eyebrow and an amused smile.

Maya picked at her food, her thoughts still troubled by Jess' message. *What am I going to do? She isn't the kind of person to come out with random threats like that, it's so not her.* Maya sliced off a piece of bacon, stabbed it with her fork and brought it to her mouth. *I can't ask Leo for help, especially after that conversation about her. What if he sent Zach to go and sort it out? That would totally be the wrong thing to do as Zach's tactics clearly haven't worked on Jess so far.*

She swallowed the piece of bacon she'd been chewing for the past minute and said to Sam, "This is great."

As Maya tried to take her mind off the text for a few seconds by loading up her fork with the next mouthful, Sam interrupted her by saying, "Thanks, I thought you'd like it." He gave her a cheeky grin while he cut into the top of his egg and they both watched its yolk spill across the slice of fried bread.

Pushing back her plate, she glanced at Sam. "Can I ask you something?"

"Yeah, sure."

"I just got a text from Jess." She picked up her phone and unlocked the screen. "She wants to meet up, reckons it's a matter of life or death."

"Right, but as we all know, she's probably blowing things totally out of proportion. You know what a drama queen Jess can be."

"She's not a drama queen, Sam." Maya narrowed her

195

eyes and pulled a face at him. "And when I saw her the other day, she looked awful. I told her to call me if she needed help and that's what she's done. I'm really worried about her, Sam."

"Okay, but Jess has always looked fine to me."

Are you blind? Haven't you seen what's been happening to her or has John effected your mind as well?

"So what's the problem then? You know Leo and the others won't let you go on your own, don't you?"

"That's just it, Jess told me I had to go alone, but I figured that she knows you, so it should be okay, right?" Maya shrugged and looked around, making sure no one was within earshot. "So will you come with me?"

Sam gulped and looked as if he was weighing up his options.

"Well?" she urged. "Please, if you're with me, then it'll be okay and I'll tell Leo what I'm doing later, I promise." She placed her hand on the top of his arm.

He peered down at her arm resting on his, then returned to look into her emerald eyes. "Yeah, like I can see that happening."

"You'll do it then." She squeezed his arm before releasing it.

He scratched the back of his head.

Moving closer, she gazed alluringly into his eyes. "Please, do this for me."

"That's unfair."

"Please ...." She fluttered her eyelashes. *I hate doing this to you, Sam, but you've got to help me.*

Sam flung his arms in the air. "Alright, alright, I'll do

it."

Maya stretched forward and gave him a quick peck on his cheek.

"When do we go?" he asked.

"She wanted to meet at eight this evening."

"Where?"

"Oh, err ... at the back of the church."

"Is she serious!?"

"Yeah, I know, weird place to arrange a meeting."

"Too right." Sam glanced over towards the door which leads on to the main hallway and the rest of the house. "How do we get away from them?"

"I haven't a clue except, I could tell them I forgot my hairbrush."

Sam raised an eyebrow.

"I know, lousy excuse, yet, at least I'll be telling them the truth and after we've picked it up from mine we can sneak across the fields that run along the back of the graveyard, nip over the wall and *hey presto*, we're there, and we can be back before they know it." She bit into her lip and twirled a strand of hair around her finger, a feeling of uncertainty creeping in.

"You've got this all worked out, haven't you," Sam said. "Except, I need you to know that I'm not happy with it."

"It'll be okay, I promise. I'll take the blame if anything goes wrong," she assured him.

Maya shot an anguished glance at the time on her phone. Another fifteen minutes and they would carry out her plan to be at the church by eight. Her stomach tightened and she felt physically sick with having to lie to Leo, although her fear for Jess was greater. Leo had appeared happy with her explanation even though he gazed into her eyes as if he saw something new and deeply serious hidden within them but he said nothing to her. Paranoia crept in as she left the study and Leo behind to find Sam. *Damn it! I wonder if he knows, but then why is he letting me go? I always hate trying to work him out.*

It took Maya and Sam thirteen minutes to walk to her house, retrieve her brush and to now be strolling along the fields that ran along the back of the houses on Church Road. Maya was pleasantly surprised with the new experience of walking through the meadows. The fading pink hue of the sunset made the view appear surreal. Trees lined the fields in the distance and untrimmed hedges separated them with the help of the odd rickety gate. A herd of Red Poll heifers lifted their heads to stare at the intruders. Maya stepped closer to Sam, who glanced at her and grinned. Lifting her gaze from the ground to glance back over her shoulder, she hadn't seen the bramble lying across the grass before it was too late and clawed her jeans, throwing her sideways into Sam's body.

Feeling his steadying arms around her, she pushed away and said, "Thanks." However, Sam drew her back towards him.

"Let me go."

"Why ... You know you like being this close to me."

She struggled against his tight embrace and eventually managed to push herself free.

"Huh, I don't believe you sometimes, Sam Brown ... you ... you!"

"Really! Has Leo expressed any feelings for you yet?" He adopted a sullen look and waited for a reply.

Maya glared at him, trying to read the expression in his eyes. *Is the venom making you act like this or is it just downright jealousy that's causing it?*

When she didn't answer, he continued anyway, "He's an angel, Maya. He doesn't have the ability to feel love like we do. When this is all over he'll go back up there." He pointed up towards the sky. "And you'll be left here alone."

Maya shook her head. "No ...."

But he was right and yet she couldn't still the anger that rose in her. *Why did you have to state the obvious, Sam?* "You're unbelievable sometimes ... argh!" She formed a fist and thrashed out to punch his arm. He jerked his body sideways at the precise moment her hand came down forcing Maya to punch out at thin air instead.

Sam raised his hands in a 'don't shoot me' pose and said, "Sorry, did I touch a nerve or something?"

"Just leave it, Sam. We're nearly there, so why don't you go ahead and find a good spot to get over the church wall and into the grave-yard," she suggested, hating herself for her outburst.

Sam shrugged, turned and wondered off with Maya watching him until he ducked down and pushed his way through a thicket of bushes.

When Maya arrived, she saw Sam leaning his butt against the ivy cleared wall to the back of the cemetery and ignored his offer of assistance, instead clambering over it herself. She headed straight towards a thick coppice of elder without waiting for Sam and ducked down.

Sam approached and fell to one knee beside her. "Where do you reckon she is?"

"She said she'd be in the lower graveyard on that bench over there." Maya pointed towards a lone wooden bench sitting in the centre of a circular patch of flowers.

Scanning the surrounding area, Maya waited, after all she owed it to Leo to be as careful as possible in the given circumstance. Three, five, and then seven minutes ticked by until she saw a slim, slouched figure stagger towards the bench.

"I think she's here." Maya told Sam and saw a slight flicker of uncertainty behind his eyes. "I ... I'll go over to her then?" A layer of sweat formed on her brow as she waited for his reply.

"Yeah, I suppose so. I'll wait back here so I can keep watch ... like ... you know?" he said with a shrug.

Maya looked at Sam and shook her head. If she was honest with herself right now, she wanted Sam by her side. Maya stood and picked her way through the undergrowth and as she approached the figure, she couldn't believe what she saw in front of her.

"Jess!" Maya gasped.

CHAPTER FIFTEEN

Maya couldn't speak as she stared down at her once blonde, immaculate and confident friend. Jess, right now, would be better suited for a horror movie and that scared the heck out of Maya. Bald patches had appeared in Jess' now short black-hair, her blue eyes were sunken and lifeless, and her cheekbones stuck out as the flesh sunk in beneath them, leaving the muscles on her face all but gone. Maya sat beside her, unable to find words for what she saw.

She gulped for air and coughed. "What's happened to you?"

Jess' head hung low as she replied, "I don't know. My doctor doesn't know either. He wants to send me to hospital, but I said, 'no way!' All I need is John."

"I'm so sorry," Maya said, in a faint tone.

"Sorry?" Jess' head lifted and her eyes met Maya's.

"Yeah ... Um ... I wish I could help."

"You do?" A flicker of life twinkled in Jess' eyes and for a brief moment her old friend had returned.

"Yes, of course I do," Maya replied, reaching forward to place her hand on Jessica's shoulder only to flinch when it came in contact with her friend's skeletal frame.

"Then there is hope for me." Jess whimpered and

rested her emaciated arms on her thighs.

Jess turned her head and smiled half-heartedly, revealing teeth that were brown and filthy from lack of care. Shivers coursed through Maya's body as she peered into Jessica's eyes again. They weren't their usual vibrant blue, instead, the black from her oversized pupils covered any former colour, which made them look like some sort of alien from a Sci-Fi movie.

It's not Jess sitting here; although it's her body, it isn't her inside – she's like ... been possessed – that's the only word for it. How did John could do this to you, Jess?

Maya stood, only to be hauled back down by Jess.

"What are you doing? Let go of me, Jess." Maya yelled. Failing to break free, she shouted out for Sam, "Sam, help me!"

Sam was already sprinting towards her.

Maya kicked out, yet Jess' grasp tightened and when she turned to look for Sam, he was suddenly surrounded by four intimidating figures. And just when Maya had thought that things couldn't get any worse, they did; two pillars of dense black fog appeared in front of her.

"Damn it, Jess ... LET. GO. OF. ME." She bent forward, trying to pry Jess' fingers off her wrist and when that also didn't work, Maya bit into her friend's hand, her nose scrunching-up at the sheer thought of what she was doing. Jess didn't flinch or cry out, instead she sat there with a wicked grin plastered across her face.

From within one of the pillars of fog, John Latruce emerged and came to stand in front of Jess.

He's not changed a bit. He's still the ugly git with the

overly skinny limbs which were too long for his body.

Beside him stood a tall, slender man, with greasy-black hair that clung to his head and framed his prominent cheekbones and the tough line of his jaw. He carried himself with an air of confidence and authority. She flashed a desperate glance at Sam and saw that the four men had overcome him, pushing her friend towards her.

"Well, well, well ... look who we have here." John smiled a self-satisfied smile.

"Go to hell!" Spat Maya.

"Already have, pretty, and looking forward to returning with you." He sneered back at her.

The stranger turned to face Sam, grabbed the boy's chin in his hand and stared into his captive's eyes. Sam's legs buckled and he crumbled to the ground, clutching his head while his body twitched and writhed in the throes of agony.

"Stop it, leave him alone," shouted Maya as she tried again to wrench her arm free.

"You humans are such fragile things, it's quite fascinating," the stranger said, with a hint of distaste in his voice.

His gaze returned to Sam and an evil grin stretched across his lips. Sam's face twisted, his screams becoming silent. "I see our hound's venom is doing its job on you, boy. The angels can't stop what will happen, and in time you will be ours, another putrid pet."

He twisted to face Maya. "Maya, my dear. It's been such a long time since I last saw you. Actually ..." He raised his head, deep in thought, resting a thin finger on his chin and tapping it. "The last time I saw you, was when I took your brother."

Maya's heart sank, the tears rising unbidden in her eyes. She stared up at the man in shock, then hatred. All the images of the past exploding before her eyes as she scanned every inch of the man in horrified recognition. *His hair's the same ... his cold lifeless eyes are the same ... the coat is the same.* Silently, she ticked each feature off a list in her mind.

Maya watched as he brought his finger to his lips and whispered, "Shh."

She shuddered. "It's you!" Her mood darkened. "Where is he? What've you done with him?" She yelled and tugged desperately to free her arm, again.

The man laughed as he watched her futile struggling. John stepped closer to Jess, grabbed her hand and ordered her to release Maya's.

As soon as she was free, Maya lashed out at the demon, but he side-stepped, causing her to fall to the ground by Sam's thrashing body. Seeing him helpless, all her anger and hatred drained from her in an instant, and her attention went to calming him.

"Sam, can you hear me? It's going to be okay!"

However, her soothing did nothing to alleviate his suffering and all of a sudden, searing heat spread across her scalp when a sizable chunk of her hair was grasped in the man's hand.

Tears formed in her eyes as she was raised to her feet by her hair. "You belong to us now and you will learn to obey."

The reek of his breath caught in Maya's nostrils, making her gag.

"I'll never obey you." She growled and kicked out at him.

"Feisty little thing, isn't she?" John sniggered, as he jigged about with excitement.

"Perhaps she needs to learn that her actions have consequences." The stranger glanced down at Jess.

Please Jess, run ... get out of here.

"May I, Fallan?" John peered down at Jess' frail figure, a look of sheer hunger glowed in his eyes. He grinned, then moistened his lips.

"You may, as she is your possession after all," agreed Fallan.

John went and sat down beside Jess, pulling her close and began to stroke her hair while whispering in her ear. "There, there, it will soon be all over, you have served your purpose well, my Jess."

A chill rushed into Maya's heart. "Get your hands off her."

He leant forward, took a deep breath and twisted Jess' head to face him. Placing his hands on her once pretty face, he positioned his mouth onto her cracked lips and gave her a kiss. Maya was forced to watch, held still by Fallan's grip.

Oh that's just sick ... Oh hell ... No!

Jessica's body shook, her skin pulled inwards and clung to her bones.

"He's killing her!" Maya screamed and glared back at the four men with Sam, who stared on eagerly.

What she saw sickened her; two of the men looked identical and had drool beading down their mouths in long strings. The third, a pig faced ugly guy, kept snorting and smacking his lips ravenously, while the fourth, towered behind them, neither moving a muscle nor looking like he was even breathing.

They're not men, which makes them in my books to be demons. Oh heck! What have I got myself in to?

"No," she cried out. "Stop it. Please ... stop it." Fresh tears streamed down her face.

John licked his lips and sighed before pushing Jess' lifeless body away. Dropping a hand by his sides, Fallan peered across at Sam.

"No, no don't! Please ... not Sam," Maya whimpered.

"Pick the boy up," ordered Fallan. "He's mine."

Sam hung between the identical demons, his body drenched in sweat and racked with pain. Fallan released Maya's hair and sauntered over to him.

He raised Sam's head and said, "This one is strong." His gaze lingered on Sam for several seconds, until he tilted Sam's head to one side revealing his neck. Fallen bent forward, his nose close to the soft flesh of Sam's jugular vein, and he took a long drawn out sniff. "The scent of the hound's venom in your veins is stronger than I first thought." He let Sam's head drop back to his chest before grabbing a handful of his hair and pulling the teenager's head back. "I bet it's causing our brothers all sorts of fun, isn't it, boy?" But Sam couldn't reply. "Oh and ... how sweet." Fallan turned to glance at Maya. "He's in love with the girl." He smiled, then returned his attention back to Sam. "We may need to keep him alive, he could be useful. However, a little draining won't hurt." He glanced at John, who stared in hungry anticipation of another feed.

Maya collapsed to the ground, every part of her screaming as she buried her face in her hands. *Why didn't I tell Leo? It's all my fault. I've killed Jess and now Sam.* A sudden sting of burning heat intensified with every second and radiated through her clothes to touch her flesh. She wrapped her fingers around the crystal and pulled it free from her pocket, remembering Leo's promise, *'It will be a guide when you are lost and bring you protection when you are threatened.'*

Fallan took a couple of abrupt steps towards her, grabbed her hair again and hoisted Maya to her feet. "What are you hiding?"

"Nothing." Maya cried, between clamped teeth.

"I am no fool, girl." He gave a bark of laughter, lacking any humour and twisted her hair, wrapping it around his fist several times.

She cried out.

No one it seemed, but Maya, noticed the figure moving towards her.

And she smiled.

Gabriel already had his arm wrapped around the pig-faced demon's neck and had hauled his bulbous figure back before the other demons were even aware.

Fallan turned, shouting, "GET HIM!"

The three demonic beasts jumped to attention, leaving Sam to slump to the ground as they leapt forward to circle

Gabriel. In the same instant, Afriel appeared beside Sam. He fell to his knees and within a flash of light and a humongous crack of thunder, they both disappeared. Strangely, Maya's ears didn't hurt at all, unlike on previous occasions, but what did capture her attention was the sound of sword's ringing out across the cemetery. She twisted as much as Fallan's hold on her would allow and saw Zach's weapon slice through the air towards John. The demon vanished before the blade fell and he re-emerged on the opposite side of the graveyard. Their fight flitting like dancers, leaving traces of white and grey mist drifting in patches between the gravestones.

Fallan's fingers clamped over Maya's trembling chin and he turned her head to face him. "Give it to me."

"You want this? Then take it," she snapped and slapped the crystal against his face.

The shard flared into a blazing light as it made contact with Fallan's skin. It burnt its way into his cheek and crackled through his jaw-bone. Fallan roared, his nails clawing at his face. Maya's stomach tightened, but she fought the nausea back.

"Where's my brother?" she demanded.

His fingers dug away at his flesh, searching for the fragment of crystal.

"Where is he?"

Fallan fell to his knees. "Haven't the cloud-hopping pansies told you?"

"Who? What?" Her voice cracked with growing rage.

"They haven't, have they? Argh ... how sweet." He smiled and licked his lips before his face contorted again.

"Your brother is the one the angels are searching for. The one they're using *you* to find."

His words sunk to the pit of her stomach. She closed her eyes. *No, he can't be!* Tears streamed down her olive cheeks. *All this time the boy in my dreams ... was Jack! Leo, why didn't you tell me?*

Fallan grabbed the front of Maya's top and pulled her closer. She looked at him in horrified silence, the anger inside returning. She heard the bones in his neck pop, reminiscent of a sizzling pig on a spit. Maya could hear the crystal eating its way down his throat, making Fallan gasp for each excruciating breath.

"Where is he, where is my brother?" She demanded.

Their eyes met and Maya watched as Fallan's turned a steely-grey in colour.

"You'll ... never ... find him." Fallan's hand rested across his chest, which expanded in short bursts.

Clenching her right hand into a fist with rising rage, she noticed how Fallan curled up in pain at the same time. Maya stood staring at his crouched figure for several seconds, trying to figure out if it was more than just coincidence that had made him stoop at the exact moment she'd closed her hand or not. Rejecting the thought, she shook her head and relaxed her fist, allowing her fingers to open and gasped. Fallan straightened, all the while gulping down air. Peering down at her outstretched palm and back at the man, Maya's eyes narrowed as she curled her fingers back into a ball. Instantly, Fallan howled, bent over and clawed at his chest.

Did I really just do that?

He coughed, choking up black liquid which dotted the ground at his feet.

But Maya didn't care. Through gritted teeth she repeated her question, "Tell me where he is."

"Or you'll what?" He gave a bark of laughter.

She smiled, digging her nails into her palm, she didn't flinch or release the pressure even though it hurt like hell. His clothes began to burn as a hole appeared in his chest, revealing his bloodied ribs. A roar burst from Fallan's mouth forcing Maya to clamp her hands over her ears, she turned her head, momentarily looking at the battle fought across the graveyard to her left.

Gabriel's sword had just ignited as it pierced through the chest of his pig-faced captive. The demon bowed backwards as white fire exploded out from its eyes, nostrils and mouth, yet it was the stench of its burning flesh that caused the acid to rise into Maya's throat. Gabriel's lip curled again in distaste. The massive angel wheeled round and glared at the others before him, his expression stern and unforgiving.

"Come on then ... boys." He mocked, a flash of humour crossing his face.

The flesh of the identical demons dripped off them to reveal their true forms.

"Is it going to be like that then?"

Maya heard Gabriel shout as she crawled a short distance from Fallan.

Gabriel's body glowed and within seconds, he stood before his enemies with his wings glistening in the moonlight. He was dressed in a white tunic, leather belt, ornately decorated with inlaid gold which hung in straps all around his waist - a good eight inches in length – white linen trousers with leather sandals covered with gold shin guards looked great on him, and a gold breastplate adorned the upper part of his masculine body.

Wow! So that's what they really look like!

Gabriel raised his sword causing its fire to intensify, the demons' confidence waned and they slowed their circling, glancing from one to the other, then back to the angel.

"Come on then. Don't keep a guy waiting." A flicker of mocking amusement showed in his expression as he gestured for them to move towards him.

Staring at each other, the demons' nodded and in a puff of smoke, vanished. Gabriel circled on the spot, waiting for them both to return, his disappointment clearly visible when nothing happened, no reappearance, no attack, nothing. His lips curled into something between a sneer and a smile.

Maya glanced back at Fallan's crouched figure, light now glistening under every inch of his skin.

He reached out a hand, gesturing to her. "I'll tell you," he said, in a gurgled whisper.

Maya crawled towards him.

Raising his head, his lips quivering, Fallan said in a barely audible voice, "Come closer."

Maya stretched forward, her face inches from his, oblivious of the danger she had put herself into. In one swift and calculated move, Fallan grabbed Maya around the throat and rolled her over onto her back. She thrashed out with her hands punching at his arms and chest to no avail. The air burst from her lungs in one large whoosh when Fallan smothered her, trapping her under the weight of his body.

Leo please ... help me.

Fallan pushed himself up into a sitting position astride her. He wiped his brow and sneered. Maya gasped in a large gulp of air and twisted her head to one side, squeezing her eyes shut as warm drops of that oil-like substance dripped from his mouth and onto her left cheek.

This is it. I'm going to die!

Without any warning, a blast of thunder ricocheted through the sky and lightning struck Fallan, the impact carrying him across the graveyard and into the surrounding undergrowth.

Shivering violently, Maya curled up tightly trying to find some warmth on the grass and gazed up into the sky. "Why ... why, Leo, why didn't you tell me?"

CHAPTER SIXTEEN

Maya felt the prickle of unease stir the small hairs at the nape of her neck while she watched the approaching figure push its way through the bushes and walk towards her. A sigh of relief escaped her as Leo crouched down to help her up and into a sitting position. He placed his hand under her chin and raised her head.

"It's over." His blue eyes scanned her face.

She glanced up, a hot tear trickled down her cheek. Her guardian angel had rescued her and at last Fallan had been destroyed. Even though she needed answers, she knew that now wasn't the time to ask them.

"It's okay, you're safe now." He wiped her tears away with his thumb.

Leo assisted Maya to her feet and as he released her hands, a shadowy figure hurled itself at his body. She heard the unmistakable sound of knuckles hitting flesh and the grunt from the impact which lifted Leo off the ground, throwing him through the air until his back hit the ancient flint wall of the church. Again, the black form struck Leo in the chest and with a *BOOM*, a chunk of the wall behind them burst into a mass of assorted fragments.

"LEO!" Maya screamed, and before she realised what she was doing, she was already running.

She clambered over broken pieces of flint and the remains of oak pews. Her foot caught the tip of a piece of wood. She fell forward, hands stretched out before her, her knees taking the full impact of her weight. Ignoring the pain, Maya squinted through the darkness, her eyes stinging from her tears, yet she still crawled closer, peering through the gaping hole in the wall, searching for Leo.

Something or someone grabbed her left ankle from behind and hauled her backwards. Maya clawed at the rubble in a desperate attempt to stop her descent, but it was useless. She was dragged down the heap, her body scraping across the debris. Movement flickered on the edge of her vision. Focusing, she saw the dark figure of Fallan standing over her.

No it can't be! Doesn't this guy ever die?

Burnt skin patterned his flesh, his jaw bone jutted out at an unusual angle, displaying bloodied and broken teeth.

"Are you looking for this?" He spluttered, holding out the crystal, and he waited for Maya's recognition, before throwing it to his left.

"NO!" Maya screeched and scrambled towards the one weapon she had.

"Oh no you don't, my little rabbit." Fallan chuckled under his breath.

His foot came to rest on the small of her back, the heaviness of it trapping her in the dirt.

Looking from side to side in a desperate search for the crystal, she prayed out loud, "Please ... please Lord, let me find it."

"What did you say?"

Grabbing a sizable chunk of her hair, he lifted his foot off her back and pulled her to her knees. "You actually thought that crystal would destroy me, didn't you?" His pale face split into an evil, lopsided grin.

Maya kept silent, yet a deep hatred burned in her stomach.

"I'm sorry, it might've worked on a demon, but it won't on an angel. Oh, and as for Leo, he's got his hands full with my brother, Nazual. I don't think he'll be able to come to your rescue this time, my poor little rabbit."

"You're no angel."

Fallan crouched down, his face inches from hers. "Oh ... but I am. Undoubtedly not one of the good ones though."

Maya shivered. Leo had told her about the fallen angels, his traitorous brothers, and now she knelt before one.

"Your brother, Jack, will be so surprised to see you. All those lost years to catch up on." Fallan yanked on Maya's hair and lifted her to her feet. "Best be on our way, wouldn't want to keep him waiting any longer than needs be. Oh, I'm sure my Master's trophy will be following you shortly because for us to capture someone like him, we have a few surprises in place. So don't worry, he will be coming back with us as well."

Come on Maya, think ... there's got to be a way out of this. Maya's eyes widened when a spark of light directly to the side of Fallan caught her gaze. Yet with one sharp jerk on her hair, the fallen angel had drawn her attention away. They say that redheads have a temper and Fallan was

215

about to meet Maya's fury full on as her anger returned. In the split second that Fallan released his hold on her; Maya leapt forward, punched him in the chest with both of her fists and yelled some indescribable word. His right foot slipped and as he reached out to pull her down with him, Maya dropped to her knees. His feet skated in a mixture of his own blood and the dirt which lay across the flints. His legs lifted from under him, his arms flew out to his side and within seconds, he landed flat on his back with a sizable piece of flint protruding through his chest. The spark of light which had caught her attention earlier did so again. Stuck between two pieces of rubble sat the crystal.

If I can reach it, then I can get out of here. I know it doesn't kill him, but it sure as hell hurts him.

Throwing herself at the crystal, Maya wrenched it free and every instinct screamed at her to run away before Fallan could get back to his feet, but she knew she couldn't outrun an angel and urged herself to stand and face her worst nightmare. However, before she could turn back to face Fallan, a hand fell on her shoulder and sharp nails dug through the fabric of her jacket, then her tops and into her flesh. The fallen angel spun her round, his breathing laboured.

"Nice try, little rabbit." He hissed.

"This is for Jack!" Maya spat and with an upward swipe of her hand, the crystal punctured his chest just above where she thought his heart should be. "May God bind you and return you to Hell."

Fallan's fingers splayed over the entry point and before he could react, light consumed him. Jumping back out of his reach, Maya watched the fallen angel rise in the air, his body twisting with agony.

"No, this can't be." He roared and glared down at Maya. "I will get you. You may have won this battle, but you won't win the next."

"Go ta hell," her voice rose to a scream and with a roar, Fallan disappeared in an explosion of light.

Standing in a daze, uncertain if he would reappear, Maya took in a deep breath and forced herself to laugh.

"I did it! I really did it!"

She cupped her hands over her mouth before turning and staggering through the hole in the wall. Sliding to a halt at the end of a row of pews, Maya squatted down and covered her ears at the sound of swords clashing throughout the building. She blinked frantically trying to clear her vision so she could see what was going on and ducked just in time when Leo came crashing backwards into the pillar to her far left. Maya cringed. The same dark angel that had punched Leo in the chest outside, did so again with such force that it knocked the air from Leo's lungs. He doubled over, clutching at his stomach. Maya heard his quick intake of breath.

"LEO!" she shouted.

The dark angel glared down at her, winked and returned to look at Leo. His enormous wings stretched wide, fanning the air.

Nazual brushed his Raven-black hair from his face. "We could finish this foolishness, Leo. Our Lord would greet you with open arms, you know this to be the truth."

Maya saw a smile tug at the corners of Leo's mouth.

What the hell? What does he mean? 'Our Lord will greet Leo with open arms?' What Lord?

White wings suddenly sliced through Leo's black T-shirt as he propelled himself towards his enemy, his fist driving into the dark angel's face. Maya heard the angel's jaw-bone crack and couldn't watch anymore. Burying her head in her hands, Maya slid to the floor and gave in to her rising panic. *I can't fight these beings, what am I thinking?* Except, while the minutes ticked by, something grew coldly determined within her. She had to help Leo. *If I distract the fallen angel at least that would be better than sitting on my arse doing nothing.* Maya forced her brain to work, gulped and peeked over the pew again.

Thick oil-like substance - the same stuff she'd seen spilling out of Fallan - now spewed out of Nazual's mouth. Gasping, he took several steps back, his hand cupping his chin as he snapped his jaw into place. Maya saw the twisted smile he gave Leo just before Nazual lunged forward. Leo blocked each blow with blinding speed and accuracy, but his enemy's attacks were relentless.

Come on Leo, come on.

Leo ducked as Nazual's blade swiped over his head, followed by the razor sharp edge of his fallen brother's left wing. Nowhere had Maya read or heard that the feathers of an angels wings were like the blades of a thousand knives which could be used like a weapon. Maya sighed in relief as Leo slid underneath Nazual and flew up behind him with his sword chomping into the dark angel's flesh. Nazual roared, wheeled round and with the remainder of his strength, threw all his rage into each returning strike, forcing Leo back until his brother's body was trapped up against a wall with his wings flattened out behind him. That is when Maya noticed for the first time the figures hovering within the shadows above Leo and Nazual.

Is this the surprises Fallan was talking about, the way they're going to capture Leo? She stared up at them and realised that they were like Nazual with their coal-black wings. *Would it really take five fallen angels to capture one pure one? They had no intention of letting him win. I can't lose him. I've got to warn him somehow.*

Maya looked up at Leo. Sweat entwined with blood beaded down his handsome face as her heart stopped its rhythmic beating. The fallen angel's hilt smashed down on Leo's sword arm, loosening his grip and Maya watched as his weapon fell towards the tiles below and disappeared. The dark angel's powerful wings lifted them both several metres above the floor, his hand closing around Leo's throat.

Maya screamed. "Leo, above you!" And pointed towards the figures floating up there in the eaves.

Nazual snapped his head around and stared straight at her, an evil smile pulling at the corners of his mouth. When he stretched out his sword, directing its tip towards Maya's chest, a breeze, where there had been none, brushed against her face, rising each strand of her hair to spread it out behind her. Standing up on her trembling feet, she sniffed the thickening air; the strong smell of death coated the lining of her throat and as she took a step back, her heart stopped beating when it didn't land back

219

on the hard tiles of the floor, in fact it didn't land on anything at all. Glancing down, Maya found herself floating above the floor.

"I could destroy her in an instant, brother."

Staring up at Nazual, Maya saw his grip tighten around Leo's throat so he couldn't reply, instead Leo's eyes met hers and she knew her fear glared back at him.

"Don't make me do this," Nazual whispered. "Join us."

Leo mumbled a few angelic words while his body began to burn brighter with each phrase he managed to mutter. Nazual's grip wavered as the impact of those words weakened him.

"Stop this, *now*, Leo. There are too many of us. You cannot take us all down like this."

Seconds later, Nazual dropped his hand from Leo's throat, his dark face set in a vicious expression as he gave his wings one massive beat to pull away from his enemy.

Leo's body burst into the familiar pillar of light that Maya remembered coming to her rescue down by the river. The iridescent beam encompassed both the angels, then broke up and shot like spear heads striking each blackened form. Maya fell to the floor and watched helplessly as they smashed through the window behind the Altar. Rainbow coloured particles cascaded down as pieces of stained glass clattered to the floor. Maya shook uncontrollably, tears stung her cheeks as she stared through the broken window and the fading light of Leo beyond.

"Leo!" She wept into her hands while a deep

220

heaviness invaded her soul.

Tonight she had lost Jess, Sam and now Leo because of her own foolishness, and all that was left were the raw sores of an aching heart.

The church remained still when Gabriel arrived and bent down beside Maya. He placed his hand under her chin, raising her head to peer into her bloodshot eyes.

"Leo?" she whispered between sobs and pointed towards the broken window.

"Shh, little one, I need to get you out of here."

He placed one arm around her back, the other under her legs and lifted her close to his chest.

"Where's Leo? Is he dea ..." Maya stuttered. "Is he dead?"

Gabriel took in a deep breath and sighed. "I don't know. I really don't know."

In a flash of light the Wicklesham church was left in darkness once again.

Moments later, in the silence, a spark of electricity danced throughout the building: repairing the broken pews, the smashed pillars, the damaged walls and lastly, like a magnet, it gathered every single fragment of stained glass, repairing it to its former glory. It was as if nothing had ever happened to the fifteenth century building.

CHAPTER SEVENTEEN

The evening passed slowly as Maya sat in disbelief. Nagging thoughts kept rolling over in her mind; was Jess' body still sitting on the bench all alone? What effects had Fallan's torture had on Sam and could angels die? She didn't want to believe Leo had, yet Nazual had warned him not to continue with whatever he was doing, knowing that it was beyond Leo's ability. What if she never saw him again, never got to tell him how she truly felt about him, what she now knew ... that she was undeniably and utterly in love with him, and that life had no meaning or purpose without Leo.

Maya's tears had all but dried as Afriel stood over her, watching her every move while Gabriel searched for any information on Leo's whereabouts. Sam, although very weak both physically and mentally, kept trying to comfort her, yet Maya couldn't look at him without breaking down, thinking she'd caused all of this, the murder of her best friend and the poisoning of her other one turning him into goodness knows what.

While huddled under a wool blanket, its warmth not giving her any comfort, Maya continued to be plagued by disturbing images of the battle between the two angels. She picked at her thoughts, desperately needing to find some little thing which might explain what had happened to Leo. She stared at the floor with a vacant look on her face, not even acknowledging the grating pain she felt every time her lids scraped across the surface of her eyes as she blinked.

"I'm worried about her, Afriel."

She heard Sam saying.

"She hasn't moved a muscle since Gabe sat her in that chair. Do you think it's shock?"

Afriel kept silent. Turned and strolled over to the fire, he stretched his hands above the flames, allowing them to lick between his fingers.

Suddenly, the blonde angel spun round to face the centre of the lounge and indicated towards the door with his head.

"Gabriel has arrived," he told them.

At that same instant, a figure appeared in the doorway. Maya lifted her gaze for a brief moment, and when she couldn't see Leo with the angel, she returned her attention back to the tiny insignificant spot on the carpet which had kept her absorbed all morning.

The broad angel stepped into the room, rubbing his hands together and glanced down at Maya. "No change, I see."

"She hasn't moved an inch," Sam replied and bent forward in his chair.

Afriel stepped over to stand beside Sam and put his hand on the boy's shoulder for reassurance. He looked across at Gabriel and asked, "Any news?"

Gabriel shook his head. "Not a thing. I've searched everywhere I know, but there's no residue, nothing. I fear the worst for him, Afriel. When I retrieved Maya from the church, I could sense that Nazual and the residue of five other traitors had also been there with him."

The young angel bowed his head and in a hushed tone, asked, "Do you think Leo has turned and now stands alongside, The Enemy?"

Gabriel shook his head. "I know you have only recently joined our group and don't know Leo as I do, but there is no way Leo would ever turn his back on Our Father, never." A hint of irritation hung on the edge of his voice.

"Forgive me, I did not mean to anger you, it is just that Leo was ... very close to Him before the fall."

"And you think that makes Leo weak enough to be turned?" A swift shadow of annoyance swept across Gabriel's face.

"No, I do not." Afriel bowed his head.

"We will never speak of this again, Afriel, is this understood?" Gabriel waited for Afriel's response before taking a couple of deep breaths and returning his attention back to Maya.

He approached and knelt on the carpet in front of her to level their eyes. "It's Gabriel, Maya," he said, while brushing her hair from her face.

"Leo?"

With a shake of his head, Gabriel tenderly touched her hand with the tips of his fingers. "We will find him. I promise you that. Others are searching and hopefully, soon, we will have some news."

Maya found her wariness lifting under the warm glow of his smile. "What happened to Jess?"

She knew Jess was dead, yet the idea that she still sat alone on that bench was unimaginable.

"I'm sorry, but that demon, John, came back for her and took her with him before we had a chance to get near her."

"What does he want with her body? Is he completely sick?" Rising anger coursed through her. "We have to kill them, Gabriel, kill them all."

Gabriel regarded Maya with the strangest, unreadable expression.

"What?" She snapped. "Isn't that what we all want?"

"Anger is good to have, but you mustn't let it consume you."

"Consume me." She sat forward, her face close to Gabriel's. "I've just watched one of my friend's die, another tortured and the person I love, go up in flames and disappear, and you tell me ... not to be angry."

"I didn't say don't be angry, I said don't let it consume you. They are two completely different things."

They stared at each other for a moment. Maya slowly sat back, knowing she couldn't and wouldn't win against his superiority.

She sighed a long slow sigh. "I met Fallan, the monster that took my brother."

Gabriel's neat brown eyebrows pulled together in a frown. "Go on."

"Why didn't Leo or any of you tell me that the boy you were after ... is actually my brother?"

"It would've been too dangerous for you."

"He's my brother, Gabriel."

"And how easily you would've followed your brother when he wanted you to jump on that black horse, then what would you have done, captured by the same demons that hold him prisoner?"

"I knew I recognised that voice." Maya gasped. "It was you!"

Gabriel nodded. "Who do you think sent Equerus, the white stallion?"

Diverting her eyes, she gazed at Sam for the first time since their return. He looked so pale and weak, yet he still had the strength to return a smile.

"I think I killed Fallan."

"We don't die, Maya. Neither angels or fallen angels, only demons the created beings of The Enemy die."

"So Leo's alive?"

Gabriel nodded. "You mentioned Leo went up in flames?"

Leo's alive! Her heart sparked into life, adrenaline coursed through her veins. "What did you just ask me?"

"You mentioned that Leo went up in flames."

"Did I?"

"Yes you did, remember?"

Maya squeezed her eyes shut, searching through the memories that had plagued her all morning, she nodded.

"What colour were those flames?" urged Gabriel.

"You know ... angelic flames." She raised her hands in a gesture.

"Maya, please, I need to know what colour they were."

"White, they were white ... okay? And the other angel's light ... was grey."

"Tell me everything that happened before that."

Maya nibbled the inside of her bottom lip, she had been trying to suppress the memories and now he wanted her to release them again. *How can he do this to me?*

"I know this is hard for you, but I really need to know all the details of the last few minutes of that fight, it's really important as it could guide me to Leo's whereabouts." He placed a warm hand on hers.

A source of energy circulated through Maya's body; a soothing energy, an energy that infused her with hope. The peace that touch gave was unexpected as she found herself drifting into a state of meditation.

"This fallen angel," she said. "Nazel."

"His name is Nazual."

"Yeah him, he had his hand around Leo's throat at the time ... they were floating in the air. It looked like the bad guy was winning when I noticed five more fallen angels arrived at that point." Her eyes lowered and a gentle smile lifted the corners of her lips as another image emerged. "Leo looked at me. He knew what he was doing."

The angel's eyes narrowed. "Go on."

"He started speaking in a weird language, the same as I hear you guys talking in sometimes. Well it weakened

Nazual and then an intense white-light appeared from out of Leo, wrapping itself around them both and piercing those other guys too." Maya sat up, her eyes wide. "BOOM," she shouted, her arms reaching upwards in an almost drunken state.

Gabriel didn't flinch a single muscle. Sam jumped further into his chair, his arms wrapping around his head and Afriel looked like he had just been slapped across his face.

Maya continued, "Within seconds, they all turned into some sort of firework display, shooting around the building until they smashed through the window." She fell silent and peered blankly at Gabriel.

"You mentioned he spoke in a different language, can you remember any words at all?"

"No, sorry."

"Will you let me take a look into your mind?"

Taking a deep breath, she steadied herself with effort.

"I promise it won't hurt."

"I suppose so," she replied, twirling a long lock of hair around her finger.

It took a few seconds of Gabriel staring unblinking at Maya before she felt a strange tingling heat inside her head and became mesmerised by the changing colours of his eyes. They went from their usual meadow green to a stunning turquoise - similar to Leo's – then to a soft purple, before returning back to their natural colour. Images formed in her mind, stopping once they reached the memories of Leo's death.

Why is it stopping here? I don't want to see this again.

However, she had no control of her thoughts as Leo looked straight at her and spoke those arcane words. She didn't have time to gaze upon him for long though, within a heartbeat, it felt as though Gabriel was delving deeper into her subconscious, erasing every single picture that had emerged and with a subdued expression on his face, the angel stood and straightened his shoulders.

Maya raised her head. "Well?"

"I believe I know where Leo is or at least where he went," Gabriel said and rubbed his chin.

"Really?" She shoved the blanket from her legs and let it drop to the carpet. "Well, tell me where then?"

"It's hard to explain. You wouldn't understand," he replied, in a vague manner. "I need to leave."

Afriel had moved to stand to one side of the doorway, his arms hanging awkwardly down by his sides.

"Stay here with them, Afriel. I've called Zach and he should be here promptly." His whole demeanour grew in severity. "Leo took Nazual to Tartarus and I'm going there to find him."

Afriel whistled softly and nodded as Gabriel disappeared.

"What's going on? What's Tartarus?" demanded Sam.

Afriel tilted his head back and sighed before focusing back on Sam. "Tartarus is where our fallen brothers are imprisoned until the day of judgement."

"Seriously!" Sam gasped.

A glazed look of sorrow began to spread over the angel's face as he continued to explain, "When an angel enters Tartarus, their life-force is drained by the lack of God's Holy Light. They are left totally powerless and hopeless. Only a few chosen, like Leo, have the right to enter and leave the prison."

"Okay, I get it. So in theory, Leo should be okay," Sam said, with a note of apprehension rippling on the edge of his voice.

Afriel's expression darkened with an unreadable emotion and he fell silent from then on.

With a long, exhausted sigh, Maya stood up. She took one final look back at the Angel before padding past them both to leave the room. At last she felt the warmth of hope that Gabriel might find Leo and headed up the grand staircase towards the family bathroom. Once there, Maya splashed water over her face, turned and glanced at her nightmarish reflection in the full length, free-standing mirror.

"Gabriel's going to find you Leo, I know he is. And even though you knew about my brother, how am I going to tell him that I'm his sister? Will he even believe me? I can't do this without you, Leo. And ..." She tilted her head from side to side. "Maya, you're talking to yourself ... you total nutter."

A black splotch in the top right-hand corner of the mirror caught her eye. Reaching up, she rubbed it with her finger and soon realised that the mark was imbedded within the glass. Lowering her gaze, Maya stared again at her reflection and without warning, she noticed the splotch move, then grow before her eyes.

"What the hell?"

It was as if she was watching the gentle brush strokes of an artist painting his masterpiece, each sweep creating life as a picture began to take form. Maya could see a person astride a magnificent black horse coming towards her along a stony road. She peered again at the rider, its dark form now smothering her own. She stepped back, then took a quick glance at the bathroom door. On seeing no one there, Maya turned back to the mirror and sucked in a large gulp of air. The boy, her brother, stared straight back at her.

She couldn't move. The horse was silent and still, unlike on their first meeting when it had charged across the meadow towards her. Tentatively, she reached towards its head to place her hand on the image, expecting to come in contact with the glass, but to her surprise her fingers touched the warm, velvety muzzle of a living animal instead. She jerked her arm back, causing the horse to snort and shake its head, and in turn waking the snakes within its mane; thirty to forty striped heads hissed and spat at her in protest, then settled down, sliding back out of sight when the horse calmed.

"That's impossible! You can't be real ... you're just an image I've conjured up in my mind."

The boy shook his head.

Her hand cupped her mouth and the words she spoke next, whistled through her fingers, "You can hear me?"

Her brother's eyes searched hers and softened. "I can."

Maya's hand dropped. She closed her mouth, opened it and then closed it again before finally speaking, "But you're in the mirror." She pointed.

"And you're standing in my path."

"That's impossible!"

Her gaze roamed across her brother's face, taking in every detail. *His nose is like mine and his eyes are the same shape as Dad's.*

"You're the girl in my dreams ... the girl who always runs away."

"Yeah ... Sorry about that."

His face lit up with a wide grin. "What's your name?"

"Maya. What's yours?"

Lowering his head, he said in a whisper, "I don't have a name."

That's awful! How could he think he doesn't have a name? She gazed again at his handsome features. *Should I tell him?* Their eyes met. *He's my brother after all and I might never get the chance again. It has to be now. I have to tell him.*

"You ... do ... have ... a name." She stuttered. "And I know it."

All the softness in his eyes disappeared. "What? How can you? No one knows my name."

"I know, because ... you're my ... you're my, brother."

"You're lying."

"No, I wouldn't do that to you. You *are* my brother and your name is, Jack."

"No ..." All colour drained from his face and his eyes searched hers. "You're lying," he said again, but he was less sure of himself this time.

"I wouldn't lie to you. It's true. You were snatched from us when you were five."

Jack leaned back and repeated his name, "Jack ... Jack," he whispered. "It sounds right for some reason, as if I've heard someone call me that before ... a very long time ago."

"Do you remember the day when that man, Fallan, took you from us?"

His eyes narrowed. "How do you know Fallan?"

"Is he like your father or something?" she enquired, desperately not wanting to say something that might damage their new relationship.

"No way! I can't stand the man."

Maya sighed and gave him a smile. "That makes two of us then." But her expression soon turned grim again. "Let me just say, that when I last met Fallan, we didn't part on the greatest of terms." There was a slight catch in her voice. "You can't tell anyone that we've spoken to each other though, or that you know me. Do you understand?"

He shook his head. "Why ... why can't I?"

"Because they'll stop us talking to each other and we need to find you."

"Find me?"

"Yeah, you know, bring you home. So do you know where you are? Where they're keeping you?"

"I don't, no." He peered at the shadowed building behind him, then back at Maya. "But I can find out."

A sudden bang on the bathroom door startled them both. Maya swirled round and saw Sam standing in the doorway, staring at the mirror. She glanced back at the image of her brother, but the horse was rearing and when it landed, Jack rode at a canter towards a house in the distance. Sam's arm brushed against hers as he came to stand beside her as he also gawked at the mirror. The image of the house grew clearer; a mansion of epic proportions stood in the background. Her heart sank as her brother disappeared.

She stared at the manor house until the image faded and twisted sideways to gape at Sam. "I've seen that house before ... on the internet."

Sam ignored her. "What the hell?" He tapped the glass. "There was someone in there. I saw a guy on a horse."

"Did you hear what I just said? I've seen that place before."

Sam's brow furrowed as he glared for a moment at Maya. "Who was that?"

She whispered at last, "It was my brother." *So that's where they've been keeping him all these years, and now we know.* Maya continued staring at their reflections staring back at them.

"That was your brother?" Sam blurted out and pointed at the glass. "That was your brother in there?" he repeated, then bent forward to inspect the mirror.

"Yes, Sam, and I need to tell Gabriel, now." Whirling on the tips of her toes, she dashed out of the bathroom, leaving Sam scratching the back of his head.

Maya ran towards the lounge, her heart pounding with excitement. She burst into the room and came to an abrupt halt. Afriel stood with his back to the fireplace, his eyes glazed a dazzling white and his body emitted the same angelic glow as Leo had done so many times before. The light around Afriel dulled within a few seconds and his eyes returned to their usual golden hue.

"What just happened to your eyes?" Maya questioned, her voice trembling a little - even when Leo had surrounded himself with the light, she had never seen his eyes turn that colour - it was beyond weird, and spooked the hell out of her.

"Gabriel has found Leo right where we thought he would be. Except, Leo did come under attack."

"So what does that mean? Is he okay?"

Afriel shook his head. "I don't know, Gabriel didn't say. He couldn't tell me."

"Who attacked him, Afriel?" Maya continued.

Afriel bowed his head without comment, his face carefully neutral.

"Afriel, who attacked him?"

He approached her, placing a hand on her shoulder. "I'm sorry, Maya. It was, The Enemy."

A sudden breeze whooshed past them both, followed by a glittering light. Afriel pushed Maya back towards the door leading out to the hall and placed himself in front of her.

Gabriel arrived with a thunderous bang supporting a wounded angel in his arms.

Is it Leo? It doesn't look like him, but it's got to be him.

She couldn't stop staring at the broken and bloodied wing which dangled over Gabriel's arm, its tip dragging along the carpet. Her sight blurred as her eyes filled. She wiped the moisture away, sniffed and tried to peer around Afriel as Gabriel lowered the angel onto a sofa and positioned its broken wing across its body. Sam stomped into the room and stared at the angel while squeezing past Maya. He plonked clumsily down on the arm of the chair opposite.

"Bloody hell! He doesn't look too good." He said with poisonous sweetness, then fell silent as Gabriel turned and glared back at him to what Maya thought was an insensitive remark.

Maya's heart slowed as her body trembled. "It's him, isn't it?"

When Gabriel stepped aside, she gaped unblinking at the wounded angel. Tears welled in her eyes, so much so that she felt them trickle down her cheeks until they hung from the tip of her chin.

"LEO!" The word exploded from her.

Throwing herself to the floor beside him, her hands hovered over the breast plate he was still wearing because she was fearful that her touch would cause him even more pain. Sobbing, she looked back at Gabriel, who reached out and stroked her hair.

"Give him time," he said.

The big angel knelt down beside her, placed his hand on Leo's forehead and whispered a few angelic words.

"He's going to be alright, isn't he?" Maya's stomach churned with unease.

Gabriel nodded.

"And now that he's back ... everything will be good ... right?" She peered down at Leo's face. "We can go and rescue my brother and the book, and finish this."

Standing again, Gabriel placed his hand on her shoulder and a soft smile appeared on his lips.

Heads turned when they heard a low groan and Maya noticed Leo's right wing twitch. His eyes snapped open and he stared straight at her, their blueness captivating Maya straight away.

He reached out and placed a hand on the side of her face. "You're safe."

"I am," replied Maya, her own hand coming to rest on his.

They ignored the strange looks from everyone else in the room, until Leo eventually sat up, stooped forward to inspect his wing and Maya noticed a look of irritation appear on his face. He glanced up at Gabriel with narrowed eyes, and then mumbled a word similar to the ones he spoke in the church. Immediately, Leo's body shimmered with a thin layer of lights. His breast plate disappeared, turning into a white cotton shirt and at the same instant, his wings also vanished. He coughed, spraying blood across the carpet and after wiping his mouth with the back of his hand, he looked up again at Maya, his face softening when he saw her stricken expression.

"I'm okay, Maya. I promise. It's just my human form that bleeds, remember?" Leo reassured her.

How can you expect me to remember that? It was like ages ago, when John had attacked us in the library. All I want to do right now is wrap my arms around you and tell you how much I love you. But Maya restrained herself from doing exactly that, fearing his response.

Sam coughed politely to gain their attention. "Maya, have you forgotten what you were so desperate to tell Gabriel about? That you know where your brother is or something like that."

"You know where he is?" urged Gabriel.

Maya nodded. "When I was in the bathroom looking in that tall mirror you've got up there, he appeared."

The big angel peered at her intently.

Straightening his shoulders, Leo asked, "Did you talk to him?"

"Yeah, but we didn't have much time. I told him that he's my brother."

"Who told you?" Leo asked.

"Fallan."

With a heavy sigh, Leo's eyes met hers. "I'm so sorry I kept it from you."

"It's okay, Leo, I'm over it." Maya bowed her head so Leo couldn't see her guilt flushed face.

He shifted uncomfortably in his chair before he said, "Did you ask about the book, whether Jack's seen it?"

Maya brushed her hair back over her shoulder and raised her head to answer, "No, I didn't ... I just about had

238

time to tell him about me when Sam came into the room." She twisted to face him and playfully stuck her tongue out.

"Sorry," Sam replied, with a light chuckle and a shrug.

Shaking her head, Maya continued, "It made Jack disappear and that's when I saw the manor he was heading to. I saw it on the internet when I was searching for the creature that attacked Sa ...." She cut herself off in midsentence suddenly remembering that Sam still had no recollection of that moment. Nibbling at the bottom of her lip, she recovered enough to continue, "Um ... attacked *me* down by the river that Friday evening."

Fumbling in his pocket, Sam brought out his mobile phone. "Here use this, I've got internet connection here."

"I don't need it, but thanks, Sam. The place is called Cripply Gorge Manor and it's on the boarders of Scotland somewhere."

"You're sure it is the same place?" Gabriel questioned with polite concern.

"Yes, I'm sure."

There was a long pause as Leo stood gazing at Gabriel and after a moment, he said, "Then that's where we need to be."

CHAPTER EIGHTEEN

Rain had been relentless since last night, the sound constantly pattering on the windows, forcing a deep depressive mood to fall on Maya and in every quiet moment, Jess' death haunted her. She strolled towards the king-size bed and sat on its edge while drying her hair with a towel. Even picking up the flattened brush reminded her of being crushed beneath the weight of Fallan. With a blank expression, Maya began the ongoing battle with her long-curls when she heard the gentle rap of knuckles on her bedroom door.

"Come in," she called and placed the brush on the bedside table.

The door opened a fraction and Leo peered around the frame before opening it wide enough to step into the room. "Sorry to bother you," he said while strolling towards her. "We need to talk. Do you mind?" He gestured with his hand to the bed.

"Uh! No ... sure." Maya shuffled up towards her pillows.

He sat down beside her, one leg bent at the knee and resting on the bed, the other swinging freely back and forth.

Twisting his head to face her, he said, "I was wondering if you could try contacting your brother again."

"What, like right now?"

Leo nodded, his hair falling forward and he immediately ran his fingers through it to push it back.

"Okay, I suppose. I'll have a go."

"Great, we need you to ask your brother if he knows where they're keeping the book. Tell him that Bazriel is the most likely one to have it. Your brother will know who he is and how dangerous he can be, but any ideas of where Bazriel keeps it would be great right now." He took in a breath and swallowed. "Zach and Afriel have managed to find the Manor and are now searching for a way in, where there is a weakness through their force-field, so we need to get ourselves ready ASAP. Once we get inside that place, everything will happen very quickly."

The fact that they've found the Manor is fantastic, but can I even contact Jack? What if he doesn't want to see me again? Then what do we do?

"Do you think you could have a go, Maya, around about ... now?" Leo asked again.

"I could try, but I don't know whether it'll work as he's the one who contacts me." Maya's gaze lingered on Leo for a few seconds before she shut her eyes.

Emptying her mind was as hard as all the previous times she had tried to do it; images of Leo, of the last battle with Fallan, of Jess and now of the fight ahead, kept intruding into her thoughts.

"Concentrate," she told herself in a hushed tone and

decided to paint Jack's image on an imaginary canvas in her mind: The oval shape of his face, the colour of his hair, a rough sketch of his lips and eyebrows, then finally his perfectly shaped hazel eyes.

"I want to see what you're seeing. I want to be where you are," she whispered.

Maya hardly felt Leo's hand tighten around hers. Her eyes shot open and the room she saw was large, but her gaze was drawn to a fire, its flames clawing into the air. Shadows scattered and bounced across the walls, touching every surface to form distorted pictures. Directly opposite the gargantuan stone fireplace sat two leather armchairs and a hexagonal, battered coffee table. She twisted and surveyed her surroundings. An impressive yet rather tatty four poster bed sat central on the opposite wall to the fire, and a large carved oak wardrobe with a matching chest-of-drawers stood to one side. There were shelves with a scattering of books clinging to the wall nearest the door which Maya crept towards. Peering at the titles along the spines, Maya was disappointed to see that there wasn't anything that caught her interest; no ordinary novels, just unusual books, boring books, books with titles she couldn't even pronounce.

This doesn't look like a teenage boy's room. Where's the sports car posters and the stacks of X-Box or Play-Station games like what's in Sam's room? Why am I here anyway when I wanted to see Jack?

Maya moved away and when she turned slightly to her left, her foot sailed through a pile of books lying on the floor. She gasped and as she stood there like a mannequin, she heard a disembodied groan coming from the direction of the chairs. Maya twirled a full circle and her feet made no sound on the wooden floorboards at all as she approached the fireplace. In the chair opposite, wrapped in a faded bedspread sound asleep, was the boy ... her brother. She watched his chest rise and fall with each breath he took.

I can't believe it! He's here, in front of me. Kneeling down, Maya spent several seconds taking in his features. *I hope he's okay? I suppose I should wake him up?*

"Jack," she whispered, without peeling her gaze from him.

He raised his arms high above his head and stretched. Maya stilled.

What if he can't see me or hear me? The last couple of times she'd tried doing this, it had felt real, she had been able to touch things, to feel the breeze brush through her hair, to smell the vegetation around her. Here everything seemed different, more transparent. She felt like a ghost. *Why is it like this?*

Pulling the blanket from his legs, he let it drop to the floor. "Skip, is that you?" he called drowsily and rubbed his forehead.

Sitting up straight, he stretched again and looked in Maya's direction. She didn't move ... she didn't breathe ... He sat staring directly at her, yet he seemed to be looking straight through her. Maya's eyes widened, her body instantly felt cold. Goose bumps appeared on her arms as she remembered how strong her brother's control had been on her the last time they met.

243

Oh my goodness, I'm putting myself in so much danger here. What if he does enter my mind again and traps me forever in this realm, in this room?

He shifted to the edge of his seat and was that close, she could feel the warmth of his breath upon her face.

If you just reach out your hand now, you would be able to touch me.

Maya remained still, too afraid to talk. She gazed into Jack's bloodshot eyes and flinched when he brought his hand up to rub the sleep from them. Then he continued to stare in her direction.

"I know you're here. Show yourself," he said, in a soft voice.

"Jack, it's me, your sister ... it's Maya."

"Come on ... I won't hurt you," he continued, but this time his voice hinted of a fake promise as she saw anger rising.

Screwing her eyes shut, Maya willed herself to become a solid form or at least to be able to be seen. On opening them again, Jack was gawking at her in horrified silence.

"It's me, Jack ..."

"Are you dead?"

"What? ... No, I'm not, why do you think that?"

"'Cause, I can see right through you."

Glancing down at her body, she gasped, and sprang backwards. "What's happened to me? Why am I like this?" A chill ran up her spine while she stared at the floor through her transparent legs. She took in a deep breath and forbade herself to tremble. Raising her head, she moved closer to Jack. "All of this isn't important right now. I don't know how long I've got, so I need you to listen. Can you do that for me?"

"Okay, but first I have some questions of my own." A puzzled look came on his face and he continued before she could decline. "The last time I saw you, you told me that you're my sister."

"Do you believe me?"

"It took a lot too, but yes I do. When you mentioned Fallan, I knew for some reason that I could trust you. Have you come to get me out of here?"

"That's our plan, but we need your help first. There's something we need which is very important," Maya told him.

"My rescue isn't important enough?"

"Of course it is. I didn't mean it like that." She wiped the sweat from her forehead with the back of her hand and rushed on. "There's a book we need, but this is no ordinary book; it's called The Book of Souls."

She noticed a sudden pained look appear on his face.

"How'd you know about that book?"

"Because my friends told me about it and we need to stop Bazriel using it."

"You know Bazriel?" he spoke through gritted teeth, struggling to keep his voice steady.

"Not personally, though I've been told that he's the one who's got the book."

"But he's only getting people to sign their names in it, your friends don't need a book like that."

"They need to get it away from here, away from Bazriel, because it's what happens to that person after they sign in it that sickens me, Jack." Maya fell silent, wondering how she should explain what she knew happened to those people without frightening or blaming him. Lifting her head, she continued, "They're imprisoning them in a place which consists of fire and torture." She didn't want to say that they were being killed off first before an eternal existence in hell, and she definitely didn't want her brother to know the full truth of the horror he was a part of.

Jack's eyes filled with tears. "They tortured them before they were made to sign in the book. I thought I was helping them, I thought they were being set free." He wiped the tears away that streaked his cheeks. "I had no choice, Bazriel made me do it."

"Jack, I know none of it was your fault. You mustn't blame yourself."

He sniffed a couple of times and swiped the back of his sleeve under his nose. "Get your friends to come here and I'll get the book. They'll never use it on anyone again."

A key rattled in his door, startling them both. Maya pushed herself into a standing position, ignoring the cramp in her legs.

Jack sprang to his feet. "Maya, you've got to get out of here. Go now."

Closing her eyes, she thought of Leo's blue eyes and a soft light brightened her face. Her vision cleared and once the spinning had stopped, the pain in her head was unbelievable. Leo sat beside her, his hand on her shoulder.

246

"Urgh, I don't feel so good." She shook her head and held a hand on her stomach.

"I think the force-field around the manor might've caused a few problems. I'm sorry, I had no idea that you would feel this bad."

Maya pushed her hair from her face. "I was transparent while I was there, like a ghost. Do you think that was down to the force-field as well?"

"Most likely. Did you ask your brother?"

"Yes, he's going to try and get the book, and wait for us back in his room."

"Great, you did great. We'd better get ready then. We'll be leaving this evening, but first, I've got something for you." He held out his hand, a smile warming his handsome face and he dropped a silver band into her palm.

"It's a ring!" Maya said with a gasp in her voice.

"It isn't just any ring, Maya. You'll be coming with us so that your brother will know we are your friends. And if you insist on doing things without our knowledge, I want to know that you have a fighting chance of survival. You do have an uncanny habit of getting yourself into trouble," he told her with a low chuckle.

"Oh!" Maya blushed and pushed her hair out of her eyes. "I suppose I do, don't I? Thanks, it's beautiful." She stared at it, rolling the band between her fingers. That's when she noticed words inscribed around its centre. "What do these words mean?"

"The inscriptions translate to ... Justice, truth and love."

"Oh!" replied Maya and pushed it on her right ring finger. It fitted perfectly. *But why a ring and what did he mean by saying, 'it isn't just a ring?'*

She glanced back at him. "I'm not trying to sound stupid or ungrateful, but how can a ring protect me?"

"It's a sword, Maya. You have to want it to existence and it will appear."

Well I didn't see that one coming. She peered down at the thin silver band again. *But how can a ring become a weapon, let alone a sword? I mean, it's impossible ... there isn't even enough silver in it to start with.* "You said, '*will* it into existence,' how do I do that?"

"Take the ring off your finger and place it in your palm," he told her.

Maya did as he instructed.

"Then tell it to appear."

She shrugged. "Do I say anything?"

Leo shook his head and replied, "That's up to you, as long as you're thinking of the sword and just the sword. It will appear."

Staring at the ring, she tried to think of the right word and in the corner of her eye she saw one of the inscribed words glitter with a blue light from around the centre of the band.

"Bah-el-tah," she commanded.

The ring sizzled in her palm and a blue light burst from out of the word, then the whole ring lit up like a firework, sparking off white and blue flames that were pleasantly warm to the touch. When the flame faded, a silver hilt had appeared in her hand. She wrapped her

248

fingers around it while watching a slender, silver blade with blue symbols along its centre, slowly materialize.

"Wow!" Maya stared at it, unable to believe what had just happened. "What does Bah-el-tah mean?" She probed, as she turned the weapon from side to side in front of her, surprised by its sheer weightlessness in her hand.

"You picked the word, Justice," he answered, while swiftly standing up and moving to one side. "The sword was designed for you. It will guide you in its use when you are threatened." Leo bent forward, took her arm with both hands and straightened it to reposition her hold. "You need only to empty your mind and you'll hear it sing to you."

"Sing to me, I don't understand."

Pulling her to her feet, his body pushed against hers and as she leaned against him, she could feel his warm breath stroking her neck when he spoke again, "Try to empty your mind the same way you do when you want to see your brother."

Maya shut her eyes, but it was impossible to concentrate ... *Oh, I wish I could be this close to you every minute of the day.* Her pulse raced, threatening to make her faint with the overwhelming sensations her body felt. Heat rose from the centre of her being warming every fibre, every muscle, and then Leo released her arm and took a step back. A cool gush of air brushed across her back, forcing a shiver. She opened her eyes, her body calming and the burning in her stomach diminishing.

"Are you still there?" Maya asked, suddenly feeling very alone.

"Yes." Leo moved back to her side. "For a minute there, I wasn't sure your concentration was fully on the sword," he said with a chuckle.

Oh crappity crap! How do you do that? Always know what I'm thinking?

"I am trying." She slipped in quickly.

This time when she closed her eyes, Maya heard a faint sound from within the very depths of her mind, the gentle buzz of harmonies and she concentrated on them.

"Good. Now let its song guide you."

She heard Leo's voice whispering in her ear.

On opening her eyes, the room shifted in and out of focus, until Maya realised that it wasn't her vision that was causing the problem, but herself that was moving. It didn't bother her though as she flitted around with athletic agility and speed she never knew existed within her. *How can this be happening?* It was like she was dancing with the sword, totally consumed by its amazing song. And then without warning, her arm thrust the swords point at a human target that had no facial features, yet blocked her again and again with ease and with a certain grace that came from centuries of combat. Maya lunged, but her target avoided her attacks by a combination of steps and a jump to the side. Each strike she made, her rival redirected her blade with ease. Her sword, although smaller and slimmer than her challenger's, struck out at him with amazing speed and accuracy. If it wasn't for the skill of her adversary, Maya knew that each of her blows could kill. She dropped the sword and heard it clatter to the floor. Her body trembled and her chest heaved. The song faded and died and her vision cleared. Standing in front of her was Leo, his sword lowering before him. Maya glanced down at the floor and saw the ring. Shaking her head, she swallowed heavily, and looked back at Leo.

"I didn't. Mean. To attack you," she said in between short gasps of air. "I didn't. Realise. It was you. It took control of me."

"Hey, it's okay." His sword vanished as he approached. "You'll get the hang of it and, you were pretty impressive you know," he said with a boyish grin.

"No, I wasn't. I could've killed you." She raised her hands and placed them on the top of her head. "I can't do this," she stated. "I'm sorry." Dropping her hands by her side, she wheeled round and dashed out of the room, sobbing.

CHAPTER NINETEEN

Maya sat alone in the lounge with her feet tucked beneath her. The sword fight with Leo earlier kept bugging her, she hadn't been able to control it, or herself. *What if it had been one of my friend's and not an angel with thousands of years' experience? I could've killed them.* Pushing her back into the cushions of the chair, she gave a deep sigh.

"That's a loud sigh from someone so young."

Twisting her body to peer around the corner of the chair, Maya saw Gabriel approach and watched as he sat on the sofa opposite.

"I couldn't help but notice you making a hasty retreat from your room earlier," he mentioned and rubbed both his hands over his knees. "Would you like to talk about anything?"

For a while she kept silent, until she summoned the composure to speak again, "Leo gave me a ring earlier, which changed into a sword, but I had no control of it, Gabriel ... none at all. The things it made me do were so dangerous. I didn't even know who I was fighting, I really wanted to hurt him."

"I think Leo's quite capable of looking after himself when it comes to a sword fight, sweetie. You mustn't worry about that."

"How did you know it was Leo?"

"He told me."

"But what if it had been someone else, like Sam?" Tears formed and welled in her eyes.

"It's important that you learn how to defend yourself against our enemies, so that you and your brother have a better chance of escaping."

"I did okay with Fallan the last time. Why don't you just give me another crystal?"

"I'm sorry, but the crystal was lost when Fallan returned to perdition with it stuck in his chest. Also he isn't the most powerful of our fallen brothers and you're likely to face something worse this next time, especially if we're going to be entering their domain." Their eyes met. "Leo and I need to know you're going to be safe." He held his hand on his chin and gave Maya a warm smile. "Your ability with the sword was quite impressive though. It was written that that weapon would be the most suited for your gifts."

"I thought my dreams were the only gift I had."

"No, there are other abilities both yourself and your brother have, and we are yet to learn about them."

"Then why wasn't I given this earlier instead of the crystal?"

"Because that wasn't the right time. Your powers are maturing faster than we had thought possible or even hoped for, and when you fought with Fallan, it had proved to us that you were now ready to receive the sword."

Scratching her head, she left her hand resting there as she continued, "Do you think I'll ever be able to control it though?"

Gabriel placed his hand on hers. "I know you will, because Leo forged that sword for you."

"He made it for me!?" Maya now felt an overwhelming sense of guilt for leaving it on the floor at Leo's feet.

"Just try it for us and don't be afraid of it. That's all we can ask of you." Gabriel stood. "I must go and gather the others and then we'll be off." He turned and left the room, leaving Maya alone with her thoughts.

She rested her head back and with a sigh she closed her eyes, focusing her mind on the joy of getting her brother back, when something landed on her arm and startled her. Snapping her eyes wide, she stared straight into the caramel gaze of Sam.

"Dammit, Sam, what are you trying to do? Scare the life out of me?"

Crouching down in front of her, he summoned a ghost of a smile. "Soz," he said and removed his hand from her arm. "They're ready to go."

Oh Sam, you look awful. Your eyes lack their usual spark. I wonder if the venom or the torture has caused it.

Straightening, Sam ambled over to stand beside Afriel in the centre of the lounge, along with Gabriel, Zach and Leo who were all in a perfect line and looking directly at Maya.

She pulled a weak smile, while peeling her tired body out of the chair. "So this is it then?"

Gabriel nodded, holding out his hand with the ring firmly gripped between his fingers. "I believe this is yours," he said, raising an eyebrow.

Blushing, Maya took it, avoiding Leo's gaze and secured it on her right finger. Stepping forward to face her, Leo's gaze lowered, his fingers touching hers, causing electricity to shoot up her arm.

You have to be feeling that to.

Leo raised his head and appraised her with more than mild interest.

There! Was that my answer in his look just then?

Gabriel gave a small cough, making them both snap their heads towards him. His expression darkened with an unreadable emotion as his gaze lingered on Leo.

He shook his head and told them, "Zach and Afriel managed to find a weakness in the Manor's force-field. Unfortunately, it's via the sewerage system running beneath the building."

There was a loud groan coming from Zach and when Maya turned to look in his direction, his face was twisted into one of disgust.

Gabriel slumped his shoulders. "What part of this plan don't you like, brother?"

"I love the plan." Zach's facial expressions stayed blank as he glanced quickly at the young blonde angel to his right. "I was just saying to Afriel, how much I am in favour of it, old boy." He slapped the shorter angel across his back, causing Afriel to fall forward, but he soon recovered his footing and returned to stand next to Sam, a look of complete surprise showing on his face.

"Humph!" Gabriel grunted and with a shrug, he resumed his conversation with Leo and Maya. "Where was I?" He rubbed his chin. "Oh yes! Once we enter, we need to re-appear in Jack's room. That's where you come in, Maya. We need you to envisage his bedroom for us, and keep that vision in your mind throughout the length of the journey or we'll end up knee high in all kinds of un-namely things." His gaze lingered on hers. "Ready?"

"No," Maya replied. "I don't think I'll ever be ready."

"You'll do just fine," Leo whispered to her and then turned to the others. "We'll see you there."

"Wait, what about Sam?" Maya interjected.

"I'm sitting this one out, Maya, because I'm still not over being zapped by that lunatic fallen angel and ...."

Maya covered her mouth as those memories resurfaced.

"No, Maya ... *bloody hell*, I don't blame you for any of this." Sam grabbed her arm and peered into her eyes. "I chose to be with you," he said. "Afriel was telling me that I'm still too weak, but I'll be here waiting for you to return with your brother. Okay?"

Everything that Sam had gone through in the past few weeks had been because of her. The pain at the jaws of the hell hounds and who knew what changes the venom was doing to him, and then Fallan. "I'm sorry I dragged you into all of this."

"Don't be, I wouldn't miss all of this for the world. I mean, how many people get to say, they have angels as friends." His smile warmed his pale face. "Go and get your brother, because I can't wait to meet him."

Leo squeezed her hand. She gave Sam a kiss on his cheek and watched him take a couple of steps back. Closing her eyes, she pictured Jack's room in her mind; the four-poster bed, the stack of books on the floor, the chair he had been sitting in when she had found him and that enormous fireplace.

Immediately light surrounded them. However this journey was longer than the others and the sudden pungent stench of excrement and high pitched squeaks from rodents distracted Maya. Her stomach churned and beads of sweat formed on her brow until she heard Leo's voice, "Maya, try and keep focused on Jack's room." She applied every ounce of concentration on her part to their mission.

When the light faded, they had all made it to her brother's bedroom intact. Maya noticed that Afriel and Zach were checking each other's clothing for any accidental faeces that might have flown up on them during their flight which made her laugh inwardly to herself, then she remembered why she was there.

Jack, Where is he?

Maya scanned the room. *Where are you?* Approaching the wardrobe, she tugged the doors wide, knowing she probably wouldn't find him in there, but how was she not to know that there wasn't a hidden passage to a secret escape in the back panel like in story The Lion the Witch and the Wardrobe that she'd loved reading when she was younger. She climbed up into it, tapped, then pushed against its back, yet nothing happened, no magic Narnia kingdom, no secret panel leading to a hidden tunnel. Stepping out, she stood back, placing her hands on her hips.

You promised to be here, Jack, waiting for me. So where the hell are you?

Gabriel crept over to the bedroom door and pressed the side of his face against it. Maya shut the wardrobe, turned and opened her mouth to say something when she felt Leo touching her arm. Glancing up at him, she watched as he placed a finger over his lips to silence her.

'But I want to know where Jack is?' She mouthed to him in silence.

He shook his head and replied in the same fashion, "Not now."

Maya gave him a sideways glare.

'What?' Leo whispered forcibly.

"Shhh!" Maya's whisper inaudibly past her finger.

Leo gave a resigned shrug and twisted his head to look at what Afriel was doing.

Maya raised her brows, taken back by Leo's very human actions before glancing over at the blonde angel herself.

What she saw was Afriel on one knee, shoving something under Jack's mattress.

"Just a portal stone," he whispered as he turned his head to notice both of them watching him. "I for one, do not wish to return via the same route as we arrived." He continued to stand, brushing the dust off his trouser leg.

Leo took a breath to speak, except he was interrupted by Gabriel who stood straight from being bent over by the door since their arrival. "It sounds quiet out there now." He gestured with his chin to Leo. "Zach, Afriel and I will head out first to make sure the way is clear and as you're the one ordered to return the book, you'll probably sense it, so I will continue with the both of you, Leo. Once we get the book and Maya's brother we'll meet back in this room. Understood?"

Leo nodded, and Maya drew in a deep breath, her heart already pumping adrenalin around her body, warming her muscles and sharpening her senses.

"Jack should be here," she told them before they left the room.

"We'll find him. Perhaps he's still hunting for the book," Leo assured her.

"Okay ... are we all ready?" Gabriel asked everyone before stepping out of the room and into the hallway.

Zach gave a menacing smirk. Afriel nodded, and although Maya thought he would be the weakest out of the three - since he appeared the most naive and innocent - she saw strength in the look he gave back to Gabriel - he was no amateur to fighting. *If anyone fits in that category, it's me.* She twisted Leo's ring around her finger; an odd sensation with each turn buzzed through her muscles. *Is that meant to happen?*

Gabriel left the room first, followed by Zach and Afriel. Leo glanced down at Maya and smiled before leading her out onto the vast landing. She trailed behind him as they headed to the oak staircase with its worn and

259

threadbare carpet. Zach continued along the landing, opening doors to abandoned rooms and peered into them, making sure they were empty. Gabriel led them down the staircase, each step creaking with their weight. Once they all reached the main hallway, the broad shouldered angel gestured with his chin for Afriel to go left, while he continued down the corridor to their right followed by Leo and Maya.

Slowing to an ambling walk, Gabriel allowed them both to catch up. "If there's a problem ahead, let me deal with it. You and Maya carry on along this hallway. Leo, are you sensing the book yet?"

"Yes."

"Let's keep going then."

Someone hollered, then Maya heard a horrifying screech coming from the direction Afriel had gone. She grasped a tighter hold of Leo's arm with both hands, pulling him closer. They quickened their pace, but that didn't help Maya to shut out the sounds of steel scraping against steel and the shrieks of agony echoing behind her. All of a sudden, Gabriel dashed on ahead, taking a sharp left at the end of the corridor.

There was a burst of light and a howl. Maya took a quick peek over her shoulder and saw Gabriel pounding down the hallway in the opposite direction to them. Suddenly her footing slipped from under her and she went tumbling down the first three steps of a flight of concrete stairs. In one swift move too fast for her eyes to focus on, Leo turned, caught her and promptly set her back on her feet. Their gaze met and Maya noticed a colour she hadn't seen in his eyes before; mauve shone within their centre.

"I can feel the book. It's close," he told her with an eager look on his face.

He towed Maya along as they entered a maze of dull, dank tunnels with crumbling paint, clinging to the walls. Hundreds of dusty cobwebs hung everywhere. Maya shivered.

Spiders ... why spiders? I hate the damn things.

Still they ran, kicking up the dust, making her sneeze with every step, until Leo stopped in front of a door.

"It's behind there," Leo told her.

Maya bent over, resting her hands on her knees and took in a deep breath punctuated with several even gasps. "Do we go in?" she said between puffs.

"Someone is in there, I can sense their presence." The tiny muscles in his jaw tightened as he swallowed heavily.

Now what? Standing straight, Maya touched the ring, making sure it was still there, ready to be used.

"Stay behind me. If I tell you to run, then please do as I ask this time and head back to your brother's room."

Her heart stopped as his fingers wrapped around the doorknob; twisting anti-clock-wise, he pushed the door open and they both entered the dark eerie space.

"So nice of you to come for a visit, brother," said a deep, rattling voice. "Will you be staying? Oh! I see you've brought the lovely Maya, how thoughtful of you."

"Leave her alone," shouted a young voice, a voice Maya knew.

"Jack," she called and stepped forward, but Leo's arm pulled her back behind him.

"I see they know each other, did you weaken, brother, and tell her the truth?" The voice rattled again.

"They've been in contact with each other the moment Fallan took the boy."

"And you know this, how?"

"You're slipping up, Bazriel."

A loud scraping noise startled Maya.

"Get on with this, old man, I haven't got all day." Leo mocked.

"Do you seriously think that I fight my own battles these days? The girl is only a small bite, but you, Leo, you're the real trophy."

Trophy! What's this Bazriel guy on about?

Coming into view were two thick-set beings. Leo pushed Maya back until they were both standing in the corridor again. He gestured in the direction they had come. "Go."

Maya sprinted along the tunnel, regret ate away at her for leaving Leo and Jack, but what else could she do. Turning a corner, she slid to a halt and watched the two men in matching tunics backing Leo down the corridor in the opposite direction to her, then Bazriel sauntered out of the room, his limp making it difficult for him to keep up with the impending battle. Maya's heart pounded, her anger rose. This was the evil that had destroyed so many lives. This was the being that tortured her brother.

My brother! I can't leave Jack in that room. I've got to go back.

Bazriel stopped. Maya froze. He turned in one swift movement and glared straight at her.

"Stay there, little one. When I've captured Leo, I'll be back for you and then we'll be one big happy family." He turned back to pursue the fight that had now erupted along another corridor.

Capture Leo? What does he want with him?

Maya peered towards the stairs and then back to the room her brother was in. *Why isn't he coming out? Please, Jack ... get out of there.* She couldn't wait any longer and dashed back to help him.

"Jack?" she shouted through the darkness.

"I'm over here," he called back. "They've tied me up."

Heading in the direction of his voice, she bumped into a table, groaned, and then followed its edge only to end up stumbling over his feet. Feeling along his knees, she found the rope and untied the knot which held him captive.

"Are you alright?" she asked.

He sat forward and rubbed his wrists. "Yeah, I take it that that Leo guy was one of your friends."

"Yeah, he is." She took a quick glance at the door, then back at Jack. "Did you find the book?"

"Bazriel keeps it locked in here, but since Fallan left, I can't find it anymore. That's how I ended up like this. I was hunting for it and he caught me." He stood and rubbed the cramp from his thighs. "I didn't say anything about you coming here, I promise."

"I know, but it's really important that we get the book. Leo said it was in here, that he could feel it."

"Wait a minute, maybe Skip can find it."

Maya could hear her brother shuffle around the room and then stop. A small clicking noise turned a lamp on which sat on top of the desk.

"Who's Skip?"

"You'll see. Skip," he called. "Skip, come here, now."

The door creaked and a little creature with large saucer-shaped eyes and big ears peered around the doorframe.

"Come here."

"Skip scared," the creature replied. "Skip can smells Holy things on her."

"Skip, you don't need to be afraid of my sister, she's okay."

The little creature entered the room, his wings tucked in by his sides. He lowered his ears and looked up at Maya.

"Sister!" he said.

"Look at me," Jack demanded and crouched down to level himself with his friend. "I need to know where Bazriel keeps the book."

Skip started to shake.

"Come on, we need to know."

"Big Masters keeps book hidden now. It's somewhere you can't go."

"But you can, right?"

His friend shook his head and trembled.

"Perhaps we can find it some other way, Jack," Maya told him. "He looks terrified."

Skip gazed at Maya, his eyes searching hers. He reached out a bony finger and touched her hand. "Skip do it for pretty sister."

"Oh, I don't think so," a voice called out to them.

Skip scrambled behind Jack's legs. Maya stared at the figure blocking the doorway. Bazriel stood with a self-satisfied grin on his face. Instinctively, Maya pulled the silver ring off her finger and held it in her fist by her side. All fear had gone, leaving only anger boiling inside her and at that very moment, she vowed that if he took another step, she was going to have him. She stepped in front of Jack, who was trying to peel his quaking friend from his body.

"Oh my dear little girl, you seriously aren't thinking of attacking me, are you?" Bazriel placed his bloated hands on his hips and laughed out loud. "Come on then, show me what my brother has taught you."

Her face reddened, blood flowed to every muscle and the song from the ring hummed in her ear.

"How about I give you an incentive? If you don't, I will capture your friends' and family and torture them in front of you before I tear them apart and feed them to my pets."

"No," screamed Maya and she lunged forward. *'Bah-el-tah,'* she commanded in her mind.

"Maya! No!" shouted Jack.

The sword was already in her hand, its song filling her thoughts, taking away all emotions. "Get the book," Maya roared.

She felt different this time, her heart beat was calm, her vision, crisp and clear, her hearing was sharp and her mind was free to see everything around her. They were no longer in the same room they had been in with Jack and Skip. She was standing on wooden floor-boards in a large, high ceilinged room. Glancing up, Maya saw five tarnished, brass chandeliers with glass globes hanging from chains and the walls were wrapped in tartan patterned wallpaper. She glared at Bazriel, whose expression suddenly turned to one of concern.

"Very impressive for a putrid human," he stated and tilted his head from one side to the other, the bones in his neck cracking with each bend. With a flick of his wrist, a black sword materialized in his hand. "You might become very useful to us in the future, especially now we have Leo."

"Go to hell," Maya screeched and took her first strike.

Bazriel moved with surprising ease for a crippled man, but this time Maya knew what was happening, this time she was in control. However, Bazriel's centuries of fighting wars made him an undefeatable opponent, and Maya knew this. Every thrust or strike she made was blocked or re-directed. To him, Maya thought, her methods of fencing were probably amateurish. The fallen angel made a cutting action towards her with the edge of his blade, she beat it back and for a split second his defence was left open for a counter attack. Making a combination of side

266

steps and thrusts to catch his thigh with the tip of her blade, she ripped through his trousers and sliced across his flesh. Then the song in her mind changed, sounding less harmonic and more minor, showing her another way to attack. Extending her sword with a strong wrist, she attempted to disarm or displace his thicker blade. Bazriel was forced back and his blade took a different line.

All of a sudden they stopped, their blades engaged, neither able to break free. He shuffled closer until their weapons pointed straight to the ceiling and their swords were the only items between them. Bazriel sneered, showing broken teeth. Maya's muscles in her arms shook with fatigue, her strength was failing and she knew her time was running out too. Seeing her weakness, Bazriel shoved Maya hard in the chest. She fell, landing flat on her back, her sword clattered across the floor. Gasping for breath, Maya rested her hand on her chest. With the sword gone, her courage also left. Bazriel approached, dragging his leg behind him. He lowered his blade and pushed the point against her throat, the sharp tip digging into her flesh, cutting into it. Maya could feel the warmth of her blood trickle down her chest and soak into her bra. All was lost, all that she had hoped to do was lost. A state of numb dread filled her.

Why didn't I listen to Leo? What was I thinking? I can't rescue Jack by myself. Please God, if I'm going to die, let it be quick.

A gust of air brushed across Maya's face. Behind Bazriel, appearing silently and with stealth, stood her brother. He stared at the back of the fallen angel's head,

267

his lips moving as if he was speaking. She gasped. Bazriel's sword arm quivered as he pulled the blade back from her throat and dropped it to the floor beside his feet. He raised his hands to the sides of his face and cried out. Maya crawled toward her own sword, picked it up and stood. She ran to Jack whose full concentration was still on the fallen angel.

What's Jack doing to him? How's he able to put fear into a being made to deliver unimaginable horror?

"Jack, let's get out of here," Maya whispered in his ear, but Jack ignored her, so Maya shouted, "Come on, we need to leave."

He twisted his head to face her and all of a sudden he grabbed his head, then cried out before collapsing onto his knees. Maya crouched down beside him and lifted his right arm over her shoulder. She heaved him up to his feet and took one last look at the beast who destroyed her family nine years ago. Blue veins bulged on the top of Bazriel's bald head and worked their way down his neck and toward his face. His arms hung lifelessly against his side, while his body rocked back and forth on the point of tipping one way or the other and Maya prayed it would be forward, so he would crash flat on his ugly face. Wrapping her arms around her brother, she closed her eyes and imagined them both back in his bedroom.

With a sigh of relief, when she opened her eyes again, they now stood beside his bed. She sat him down and plonked down next him, trying to comfort his sobs and all the time hoping and wishing that the first person to come through the door, would be Leo.

What if Leo has been captured? Surely the others would rescue him, wouldn't they?

The door flung wide with a resounding bang. Zach stormed in, covered with blood, Afriel close behind, his sword still in his hand, dripping with the same black substance which drained from Fallan's wounds.

"Gabriel, Leo?" Afriel asked, with an increasing air of urgency in his voice and slammed the door behind him. "Have you seen them?"

Maya shook her head.

Zach approached and stared down at the boy. "Your brother?"

"Yes," Maya answered, wrapping her arm around Jack's shoulders and pulling him closer to her.

"Did you get the book?" questioned Afriel as he marched to the window, his sword held down by his leg as he peered out.

"No, Jack sent Skip to get it," Maya told them.

"Skip?" Afriel asked, looking puzzled.

She shrugged. "It's his little friend."

Shaking his head, Zach grunted before moving to the door and opened it to step out onto the landing.

All of a sudden, he shouted, "Gabriel, Leo, we're all in here."

Maya's head shot up. *Did he just say Leo?* With a long exhausted sigh, she smiled when she saw Gabriel enter with Leo trailing behind. Leo's clothes and face were splattered with that same oily substance intermingled with his own blood. Gabriel marched towards her, fell to one

269

knee by her legs and retrieved the portal-stone from under the mattress.

"Did anyone get the book?" Gabriel asked as he got to his feet again.

"Nope," replied Zach. "Maya said her brother sent someone called Skip to retrieve it."

"What about Bazriel?" Gabriel continued.

The angels looked from one to the other, each shaking their heads until Gabriel glanced at Maya.

Leo stepped closer. "Maya?" He probed.

"I ... I couldn't just leave my brother in that room," Maya said.

Leo's eyes narrowed with a look of disappointment showing on his handsome face.

And without any further encouragement from anyone, a complete sentence came out in one big rush of words and in a single breath, "I'm sorry, Bazriel came back and the sword just appeared in my hand which started a fight, then Jack messed with his head and we got away."

Leo shook his head and backed off, thrusting his fingers through his thick mass of hair.

Just say it, Leo ... that you're disappointed in me, I know you want to.

Leo strolled up to them both and placed his hand on Jack's head. A steady stream of light shone out from his palm and arced over her brother. Slowly the rapid beat of Jack's heart calmed and his shoulders relaxed as the tension in his body eased.

Placing his fingers under her brother's chin, Leo raised Jack's head. "Call for your friend, Jack."

Their eyes met and Jack licked his dry lips. "Skip," he said just louder than a whisper.

"Louder," Leo told him.

"Skip," he called out.

There was a scraping of nails on brick and with a puff of soot, Skip fell from the chimney and cowered in the corner of the fireplace, hugging a large object close to his chest.

Zach sneered at the terrified creature and held out his hand to take the book from him. However, Skip turned his back on the angel so he faced the back of the hearth, flapped his wings out wide, driving soot directly into Zach's face. Leo stepped between them and placed a calming hand on his irate brother's shoulder.

"Let me handle this, bro'."

Leo crouched down and spoke in a hushed tone, "Skip, give me the book and we will spare you, I promise."

Wow! That'll put him right at ease, Leo.

Twisting his head to glance at the angels, Skip pulled his lips back into a snarl, flashing his broken teeth. "Skip gives it only to, masters."

"Grrr!" Growled Zach as he folding his arms in front of his chest.

With Maya's help, Jack hauled himself to his feet and staggered towards his friend. "It's okay, Skip, they won't harm you. Will you?" He glared back at Leo and then Zach, who threw his arms in the air and stomped off muttering to himself and brushing the soot from his clothes.

271

Skip lowered his wings and shuffled through the ash in the grate to hand the book to his young master.

"No!" A thunderous voice boomed from the doorway.

Before Gabriel could block the blade that lunged for Jack, Skip flew in its path and the sword sliced through flesh and bone. The little creature's body slumped forward, falling into Jack's arms. Bazriel pulled his weapon free, an evil grin pulling on his lips.

"Skip!" Jack screamed.

CHAPTER TWENTY

Leo leapt forward, wrapping his arms around Jack and Skip and disappeared in a flash of light. Within the split second that Bazriel couldn't see, Afriel and Zach also left, shaking the very foundations of the building.

Gabriel drew Maya close to him, his sword held ready in his hand, and when Bazriel re-opened his eyes, Gabriel shouted, "You have lost this battle, General, and if you think Leo will turn, you better think twice."

The last thing Maya saw before she was surrounded by light, was Bazriel pouncing towards them, his face twisted in rage and hatred. A venomous roar burst from his mouth, "I *will* have what my Lord wants."

The words continued to ring in her ears throughout the return journey home.

With her eyelids still squeezed tight, Maya knew they had arrived back at the Old Rectory purely from the familiar hum of voices, but when she recognised the heart-rending sobs of her brother, she snapped her eyes open, and saw Jack kneeling on the floor with Skip's body cradled in his arms. Leo peered down at him with the Book of Souls held in his hands, and as soon as Gabriel approached he handed the book over. At the same time as Leo placed his hand on Jack's shoulder, Maya darted across the room and dropped to her knees beside him. Reaching out, she tried to comfort Skip, but Jack pulled him away.

"Don't touch him," he snapped, tears rolling down his tanned face.

Maya flinched and felt a sudden sting of tears form in her eyes. "You've got to help him, please. He saved Jack's life, doesn't that mean anything?"

Just then, Sam burst into the room and stopped dead when he saw Skip. "*Bloody hell!* What's that? What's happened? Is that you're brother? Maya, are you okay?" The questions exploded from his mouth in quick succession which started a coughing fit and then led to him clutching his chest in pain.

With a sudden jerk, his body straightened and his face drained of all colour while Maya watched in horror and saw his eyes roll into the back of his head so only the whites could be seen.

Afriel shot toward Sam in a blur, his arms reaching out to grab her friend and hold him down, except, Sam's reflexes were faster; his fist made contact with Afriel's chest in one fierce punch and the angel went soaring across the room as if he weighed nothing at all. Sam with his zombie-like eyes, appeared to be staring across at Maya with saliva dripping from his mouth. He bent his knees, ready to leap towards her. Afriel appeared back by his side once again, and this time, his hands landed on her friend's shoulders.

Unblinking, Maya's gaze fixed on his. "Sam, please fight it, don't let them win."

274

"Get him out of here, Afriel," Gabriel demanded.

"We need to go, Sam," Afriel said in a calming voice.

Light lit the whole room as Afriel disappeared with Sam, leaving a shockwave which rattled the very glass in the windows and tilted every painting on the walls.

Gabriel took in a deep breath and exhaled. "You really need to talk to him about that, Leo," he said with a show of indignation.

"Is there anything else you would like to add to my growing list of concerns involving Afriel?"

"What?" Maya flung her arms in the air. "I don't believe you two! This isn't the time to be having a domestic ... what just happened to Sam?"

The two angels looked at each other for a moment, then Gabriel held the book behind his back and bowed his head.

Leo swept his hair from his brow, approached and dropped to one knee beside her. "I'm sorry, Maya." It's the venom in him, but be assured we are doing our best for Sam and will continue to do so." He lowered his head to catch Jack's gaze. "Right now we need to help Skip, okay?"

Maya nodded back at him without speaking, took a section of her hair between her fingers and started twirling it around them in silent prayer for the creature that had saved her brother's life by sacrificing his own.

"I know you have no reason to trust me, but your friend has done the most amazing thing for a demon. We've never experienced anything like it before, not from his kind. To give one's life as a sacrifice is the greatest gift any Being can do," Leo explained to Jack.

Jack hugged Skip even closer, a sudden ray of hope in his tear-reddened eyes.

"If you'll let us take Skip, we might have time to save him." A look of sadness passed over Leo's features.

Jack glanced towards Maya, raw hurt glittered in those eyes of his.

She gave the weakest of smiles and nodded. "Let him do it, Jack."

Her brother's gaze rested on Skip for a few seconds, then he lifted his friend and placed him in Leo's outstretched arms. Leo carried the wounded creature to the centre of the room and came to a halt. He stood, tilted his head back, shut his eyes and called out an angelic name.

At once, a pillar of light appeared and the being that stood before them was stunning. Maya thought she'd got use to the perfect appearance of angels, not a single disfigurement, which she'd noticed anyway, but this one was different; its gender seemed that of a well-toned man, yet he had a beautiful heart-shaped face with mauve coloured eyes and white hair, long and straight, resembling a woman. Maya was rendered speechless for the first time.

Leo approached the angel with its flowing gown and held Skip out to him. "Saphil, Skip is a very special being and deserves our care. Look into his mind and you will see the strength of his heart."

Saphil took the little demon in his arms and lowered his gaze upon the creatures limp body. He looked up at

Leo and straight away Maya knew they were communicating silently with each other, it was in their facial expressions; a little twitch here, a quick smile there which gave it away, and she hated not being able to hear what they were saying. A smile warmed Saphil's face as light surrounded both the angel and Skip before disappearing without a sound.

Returning to Jack, Leo crouched in front of him again. "We will do our best for your friend, I promise. Now we need to get you both home to your family."

"But I don't know them." Jack's body tensed, he sniffed and brushed his sleeve under his eyes, drying his face.

"You will," Maya assured him. "And you guys have so much love to catch up on." A lump formed in her throat. "Leo, what do I say to them? I mean, surely they'll ask how I found him."

"Zach is with your parents now. We have ways of sorting things out, Maya, ways that are beyond explanation, but you can be assured, that they'll be ready to greet you both back."

"What about Bazriel, won't he come for me again?" Jack asked, trying to keep his voice level.

"I'm afraid both of you haven't seen the last of Bazriel and his demons. However, I can assure you both, that we will be watching you wherever you go. And there's something else you both need to know," Leo continued.

"What?" Maya interrupted.

"If you'll let me finish, then I'll tell you." His faint smile held a touch of sadness. "That God, will call upon you both again."

"Does that mean you'll be staying?" Maya piped up, her body warming at the prospect of seeing Leo every day.

Tilting his head forward, he flashed her a comforting smile. "No, I can't. My mission here is finished."

"No!" The word blurted out before Maya realised what she was saying. *My life is over.*

A muscle popped in his jaw as his gaze drifted over her face. "I can't stay, but that doesn't mean you'll never see me again," His voice trailed off into a low sigh.

He reached out and pulled her to him, hugging her close. Maya could feel the rise and fall of his hardened chest with each breath he took and even with the gesture of him touching her hand, it drove her into a whirlwind of heated emotions, being this close to him was raising a storm inside her.

"You have amazed me through all of this, I am so, so proud of you."

What!? What did you just say? That you're proud of me! No! I can't and won't except that! At that revelation, the storm inside her quailed. *Why can't you love me, Leo, why?*

Gabriel stepped closer. "Uh hum ...." He coughed. "I'm sorry to interrupt you both, but, Leo, we really need to get the book back to Our Father."

Leo gently pushed Maya away, stretching as he stood. He reached out to assist her, but she refused and proceeded to pick herself up off the floor. When she

278

noticed his face drop into a frown of confusion, Maya diverted her gaze and instead, tried to concentrate on her brother who eagerly took Leo's hand and rose stiffly to his feet. She rubbed her thighs in an attempt to wake the aching muscles that seemed determined to stay asleep and caught a glimpse of the books cover for the first time. Maya's gaze lingered there, captured by the embossed tree swaying in a gentle breeze as if it was alive. She could tell that it had once been beautiful, a wonder to behold, something no human eye had ever observed before; one half of it was laden with healthy, green leaves with golden-orange blossoms, and the other half of the tree, Maya saw intertwined, withered branches with a scattering of decaying leaves clinging on precariously as if hanging on to the very brink of life itself.

"What will happen to all the people who signed their names in that book?" She made a slight gesture with her hand towards it, her eyes unable to break free.

Gabriel lifted the book to take a look. "Those that are still alive, which I doubt are just a few, if any at all ... will be given a choice to make, and that choice will determine whether their souls remain in this book and the property of The Enemy's, or whether their name will reappear in The Book of Life."

"A choice?" Jack stepped in.

"They will be told the truth which is written for all to see in the Gospels, the truth that the Son of God died for their sins, if only they are willing to believe. 'Whosoever will; let him take the water of life freely.' It is up to man to choose the path they wish to follow," Gabriel continued.

"And the ones that don't want to believe, surely their names will still be in that book, so if it's in heaven with God, won't that make them safe too?" Maya interjected.

Leo shook his head. "No, Maya, those that were killed will stay The Enemy's captors, at least up until the day of judgement, when man and angel, fallen or otherwise will stand before God. As for the book and its existence in heaven with God, the answer to that question is also no. It will be taken somewhere far away from The Almighty, and placed under lock and key until that day when everyone will answer for the path they have walked and the deeds they have done."

Maya watched as Gabriel tucked the book under his arm.

"What about my part in it?" Jack's whisper hardly rose above a rasp. "What about what Bazriel made me do? I forced some of those people to sign in it." He was crying suddenly; soundless, exhausted weeping. "I didn't want to do it ... but the pain in my head ... when Bazriel touched me ... he promised he would let them go home afterwards. I didn't know...." He croaked between sobs.

Tears found their way down Maya's cheeks, she stepped towards him, wanting to console him, love him. With a gentle grip on her arm, Leo drew her back, and instead approached her broken brother. He placed both his hands on either side of Jack's face, their eyes meeting.

"I'm so sorry," Jack continued.

"I know, and so does God, because he can see into your heart, Jack. He forgives you."

Leo lowered his head, his forehead touching the top of her brother's and Leo began whispering words Maya couldn't quite hear, but she knew whatever he was saying were words of comfort from the expression of relief and joy appearing on her Jack's face. She wiped her tears away.

I'll never forgive you, Bazriel, for what you've done to Jack and my family. I will somehow see you suffer for this. Then she remembered the threat Bazriel had shouted at Gabriel as they fled, she could hear it ringing now in her ears as if she were back at the manor; 'I will have what my Lord wants.' *What did he mean by that? Did it involve Leo, like the trophy thing? Gabriel had said that Leo wouldn't turn? I'm so confused!* She bit into her bottom lip. *Should I say anything or just keep quiet? Yet I might never get the chance to ask them about it again.*

"Is there something else bothering you, Maya?" Leo asked while helping Jack into the sofa and then spinning to face her.

Dammit, I should've known?

Nodding, she cleared the tickle in the back of her throat and asked, "Why does Bazriel want to capture you?"

Gabriel raised his eyebrows and gave a little whistle.

Leo gave nothing away, his expression didn't change although his eyes dulled a fraction.

Maya continued, "When I fought Fallan and you were fighting in the church, he mentioned that Nazual and a few others were set to capture their Lord's trophy, then when we were confronted by Bazriel and his men, he ordered his men to capture you, his Lord's trophy." Maya looked

281

from one angel to the other but had no response from either. "I also heard Gabriel telling Bazriel that you wouldn't turn, Leo, and Bazriel replied, 'he would have what his Lord wanted.'"

There was a moment's astonished silence before Gabriel coughed several times and answered, "I need to watch what I say when you're around, sweetie."

Leo gave her a lingering look. "That's another story, Maya. Maybe someday I'll tell you."

"I don't think that's fair, after all I've done for you."

Leo's eyes narrowed and Maya became more and more agitated by his lack of empathy, that's when suddenly, words blurted out as her emotions took control. "I need you to stay here with me, because I can't live without you." A muscle in her neck tensed, she lowered her gaze as a hot tear trickled down her cheek.

"Gabriel, why don't you go ahead and take the book back." Leo told him, without taking his eyes from Maya's. "I need to talk to, Maya."

"Leo?" Gabriel approached and placed a hand on Leo's shoulder. "A word, please?"

Leo nodded, giving Maya's arm a gentle squeeze before retreating to the far side of the room.

Oh my goodness, what have I just done?

She felt something brush against her elbow and twisted her head to take a quick peek only to find Jack standing behind her with his hand open. She gave him a weak smile, wrapped her fingers around his and in an instant, Maya felt the weirdest of sensations tingling throughout her head.

282

"I've been wondering how to say what I have observed."

Maya heard Gabriel telling Leo in a low whisper. She stared in shock at Jack, who placed a finger on her lips to silence her.

"It's okay. I think somehow when we joined hands, my gift was strengthened so now you can hear my thoughts and also what they are saying."

Maya glanced back at Jack who seemed completely unfazed at what was happening. He shrugged and turned to watch the angels.

"Observed?" questioned Leo.

Maya snapped her head around, concentrating once again on their conversation.

"Please, don't be vexed with me when I tell you this."

"Come on, Gabriel, it isn't like you to mince your words, spit it out, old boy."

"Maya has feelings for you."

Leo's expression was one of confusion. He combed his hand through his hair.

"She has fallen in love with you," continued Gabriel.

Maya gasped. *Did he really just say that? Gabriel's known all along!*

She squeezed Jack's hand. Her brother bit down on his lip.

"In love?" Spluttered Leo.

"In the way a man and woman fall in love."

The muscles in Leo's jaw tightened.

"My brother, when you look the way you do, in your human form, it's fairly understandable why the female

283

species fall in love or lust over you."

No ... no, I love him. Leo, I love you.

"This form was not of my making."

"I know and if you'd had your way, you would've come here looking like a middle-aged bore." Gabriel's shoulders bounced with silent laughter.

"What, like you, you mean."

Gabriel's mouth slammed shut, his eyes widened as he glared straight at his brother. Seconds later, he placed a hand on Leo's shoulder and with a smile nodded. "You're getting better at humour, I'm proud."

Oh for goodness sake!! Don't change the subject now.

"But back to Maya. I've noticed the way you have been looking at her lately." Gabriel's eyes searched Leo's. "Lust is a dangerous temptation, brother, be careful."

Leo glanced back at Maya. "Go, Gabriel. I'll see them both home."

Swallowing heavily, a blush rose to Maya's face, she released Jack's hand. *How can this be happening, how can it end like this ... my feelings for Leo are genuine.*

Jack stepped toward the sofa, shaking the life back into his fingers as he went. With a shrug, Gabriel shook his head and vanished as Jack fell back onto the sofa, his attention diverted to the painting above the fireplace. Biting down on her thumbnail, Maya wondered whether Leo would ever want to see her again knowing her true feelings for him.

How could Gabriel do this to me? And what if Sam's right about angels ... that they can't or they are forbidden to fall in love?'

Leo approached and gazed into Maya's eyes.

"I'm sorry," Maya said, in a voice breaking with emotion.

"Sorry for what?"

Maya bowed her head. "For you having to find out from Gabriel how I feel about you."

Cupping her chin, Leo searched her upturned face. "Please, don't be. I'm the one who should be apologising because I don't understand the feelings you have for me. Although, I have sensed how your body reacts when I'm close. Is this what you call love?"

Oh hell, how do I answer that? 'No it's not, Leo, that's pure and outright lust.' She skipped the blushing part and went onto the full-scale burnt look.

Clearing her throat, she answered, "It's a part of it ... I suppose. I could help you. I could show you what love is." *What am I saying? I don't even know what it is myself.* She cringed.

He lowered his hand and tilted his head, the colour of his eyes lightened several shades, making Maya's breath quicken and before she could react in any way, he seized her hands, enfolding them in his own, holding them tenderly pressed against his chest. Electricity sparkled through his fingers and into hers, this time though she didn't jump or flinch, instead Maya leaned into him, into the tingling sensation that surged through her body. Their heartbeats joined in rhythm for a tantalising few seconds, until he broke the connection by lowering her arms.

Shaking his head, he recovered with effort. "It is forbidden." A look of regret flashed across his face. "I

285

can't."

"But you feel something, right?" She pleaded, tears already in her eyes. "These last few days, I've noticed you looking at me in a different way. And every time you touch me ... it's like these electric shocks go right through my body ... you must feel them too?"

At that precise moment, when their eyes met, she saw an inner battle – a battle far greater than any he had ever fought before, a battle against everything he believed in.

He nodded, and that one single gesture made her heart leap, then settle to its original beat, giving her hope.

"I must get you both home." He turned his face away from hers. "Jack, are you ready to meet your parents?"

You can't just leave it there. I can't lose you now. "Leo?"

Leo turned and for the first time she sensed his vulnerability. Jack stood, strolled over to her and he pushed his hand into hers.

"It'll be okay, sis'," he whispered and a smile warmed his face. "You'll see."

Preview

The Book of Souls

Truth

2

Prologue

As the first call of dawn echoed across the land, the eerie, damp gloom of night was replaced by the soft glow of day. The angelic being sat on the ridge of a mountain overlooking the vast valley below. He squeezed his eyes shut to listen to the sorrowful songs of humanity ringing in his ears. For centuries the songs had been the same, but in the past few years the pitch had changed, tearing at his very core.

Never before had he left the Court of His Father. There again, never before had his feet stood on the cool, moist earth, but this *one* particular song continued to eat away at him. Why did it affect him so? The others in the Holy Court seemed to block their cries, their voices continuously singing praises out across the heavens. Why did it only hurt him? Or that is what it seemed.

He watched the sun rise, felt the warmth of its rays touch his skin for the first time, then rose to his feet and gazed into the seamless, summer sky. Power coursed through his body like the wind from a tornado, whipping around him, raising him into the air to ride the thermals. Hovering above a narrow coastal path, he came to a wooden fence where the land suddenly plunged into the sea. He dove, faster than lightening, then straightened out, kicking up the waves on either side of him as he skimmed across its surface.

The heavenly being laughed, flying for endless miles before the earth rose again, taking him across land, fens, rivers and cultivated fields; the song growing stronger, the soul drawing him closer.

Structures tall and short, made of brick, wood and concrete lined the sky-line. He soared over the striped huts of a street market which filled the air with an exciting mix of smells and busy buzz of mortal conversations. Peering down at the humans, he heard each of their soul's singing a different tune, each song personal, but none of them, the one he had left the comfort of his home for. Following along a cobbled street lined with Victorian terraces, beamed cottages and shops, he flew towards an ancient building with its carved structures and statues. Up he soared to the west end entrance and glided down land on top of one of its parapets and waited.

Day 2: He had watched humankind's comings and goings with intrigue throughout yesterday. Drops of moisture **like fine specks of dust** fell from the heavens, refreshing him. He tilted his head back, following the course of the stars and counting them within a single blink. Then there it was, the mortal he'd been waiting for. Leaning over the parapet, he peered down at the one with the heartfelt song of regret, of desire, of a love which was out of reach. That lone mortal was why he was here. He had to inform the human of the truth, the truth to the Being who held the key of survival to all mankind.

Chapter One

Rain spat sporadically over Maya. Her bare feet froze to the cobbled courtyard as she stood in her soaked pyjamas. *Where the hell am I?* She blinked several times before wiping her eyes and peering up at the building standing in front of her. Maya stared up at the Cathedral but where and which one she couldn't tell at this close proximity and in the gloom of such a lousy morning.

Something moved, catching her attention, way up in the shadows on the left hand parapet. Maya squinted, her eyes adjusting as she focused on the movement above. It wasn't tiny like a bird, but the size of a man or maybe even bigger than that and it shimmered with a faint light that emitted from its own body. Stopping dead, it seemed to lean forward and peer down at her. *Who the hell's up there this early in the morning? And how did they get up there in the first place?*

An odd sensation coursed through Maya's muscles; a tingling, warming buzz which wasn't unpleasant. Then a song saturated her whole being, a song that seemed to stem from her very soul. Harmonies from the ring that Leo had made for her when they'd rescued her brother from a fallen angel named, Bazriel, a couple of months ago, along with a book called 'The Book of Souls' which had been stolen from the courts of heaven, soon joined in. The ring looked like a simple plain silver band except for

1

the three angelic words engraved around it. The first word she'd learned 'Bah-el-tah,' during the rescue, had turned the ring into a slender, silver blade with blue symbols sparking along its centre. Leo told Maya that Bah-el-tah in his tongue, translated to mean Justice in the English language and he also mentioned that the ring contained other secrets which were yet to be revealed to Maya. When she lowered her head, looking down at the band on her right ring finger, she noticed the middle word glowing brightly from the engravings, but before she could read it, her vision blurred making her whole hand distorted.

"NO!" she called out. "Not now. I need to know what it says."

"Maya ... Maya?" A familiar voice called from amongst the shadows.

Maya's eyes snapped wide to see Jack, her younger brother standing over her, his hands resting on her shoulders. Peering up, she noticed the expression of concern on his face.

"You shouted out in your sleep again and I ... I couldn't find you this time. I couldn't see where you'd gone. I tried."

No wonder he's looking the way he is! She turned around to find herself standing in the middle of her bedroom, her hair and clothes dripping wet.

"Are you okay?" Jack asked.

Blinking, Maya gazed into his hazel eyes. Ever since her brother's return, they'd been inseparable and her ability to manipulate her dreams or as the angels had informed her, *'the capability to walk within the realm of the angels and demons,'* made no difference, until now. *He's always tracked me down, so what's stopped him this time?* She knew the angels kept watch over them both while Leo and Gabriel returned to do heavens business as they called it, except, when Maya dreamt, both herself and her brother were undetectable from the angels and demons unless they wanted to be found. Maya often wondered whether it was the subconscious part of her brain which blocked their whereabouts, or Jack, with his mind controlling ability. Her money would be on her brother. Searching his face, Maya's mind raced over unanswered questions she might one day have to ask. *Do you possess that kind of power, Jack? Gabriel told me that we both have other abilities which would surface in time, so is this one of yours? Yet, that was no human that'd found me at that Cathedral, and for it to stop your interference, it must've been a lot more powerful than even the angels. Damn it, Leo. I need to see you, now.*

She blew out her cheeks and closed her eyes, hardly daring to believe what she'd just experienced. With the back of her hand, she swiped her bedraggled red-locks from her brow and swallowed heavily.

Peering down at the ring again, Maya wondered why it had responded to the Being's song and even joined in. *What does it mean? The song ... the word ... what's it all about?* Twisting the band around her chilled finger, Maya noticed that the word which had shone so brightly earlier, had returned to its dull state along with the others. She took a step back and lowered herself to the edge of her bed. Jack came and sat beside her.

"Why couldn't I find you, Maya?" Jack asked again.

"I don't know. I didn't even know where I was, except that it was raining," she replied, giving him a weak smile. "All I could hear was some weird song buzzing in my ears."

He turned to look at his sister and shrugged. "But I couldn't get anywhere near you. Whatever it was, it had a lot more power than anything I've ever felt before. Even the angels."

"Don't scare me, Jack."

"I'm sorry, but it wasn't me it wanted."

A shadow of alarm touched her face, she knew not to question how her brother acquired this information as it probably had something to do with his gift.

"Do you really think it was after me then?"

He shrugged again and stayed silent which only confirmed her worst fears; whatever or whoever was peering down at her from on top of that Cathedral, wanted her and wanted her alone.

A gentle knock on Maya's door made them both jump. They watched the latch rise with intent and then with a creak it opened to reveal a rather sleepy, balding head with his sleep incrusted eyes peering at them from around the door.

"You two okay?" Maya's dad, croaked.

"Yeah, sure," Maya replied in a hushed voice. "I was talking in my sleep again, you know, that same old rubbish I keep doing lately."

"Oh right ..." Her dad yawned, his hand polishing the

4

top of his head as he continued, "Well, don't be ..." he sighed loudly. "Don't be long before you both get back to bed. I know it's the start of your summer hols, but I've still got work in the morning and it's ...."

"Two Thirty, Dad," Jack piped up.

"What your brother just said, Maya," he finished in mid-flow of another yawn, then disappeared closing the door behind him.

"You'd better get back to your room, little bro. I'll be okay."

"You sure? I could stay and kip on the floor if you'd like."

"You don't have to do that. I'm sure I can cope, and anyway, you're only next door if I need you."

"Okay, but you know I'm not goin' to be able to shut my eyes now, don't you?"

Maya shook her head as she watched him leave her room.

"I really need to speak to you Leo, so please be at the Old Rectory tomorrow," she mumbled to herself while peeling her legs out of her soggy pyjamas and replacing them with a fresh pair of bottoms and a vest top. Finally, Maya slumped backwards on her bed, wrapped her duvet around her chilled body.

Is it worth me coming up with an excuse this time? I know Dad would've said something to Mum by the morning and she'd want to know the details about the dream, but I wonder if I can tell them the same thing over and over because they never seem that bothered with the explanation I give them. She knew the angels had something to do with it as they had with many aspects of her life since their arrival but was it right for her to do this, lying to them was hard enough.

She called out to her guardian angel again. "Leo, I'm coming round yours in the morning, so you'd better be there. I've had enough ... you've been away a lot longer than a couple of days, more like two weeks, and I don't care if you come up with some excuse like ... angels don't live their lives around a twenty-four hour clock, well I do .... Oh this is stupid. Good night, and if you're listening at all, you need to get your butt down here because something unnerving has just happened to me and I'm scared."

Every still moment she managed to make in her mind throughout the night was filled by the continued humming from the ring and when morning arrived, Maya gave up on any further attempts of getting to sleep. She stretched, yawned and sat up, before silently cursing when her fingers snagged amongst a few knots in her hair.

"Oh joyous holiday!" She groaned and got up.

On entered the kitchen, Maya's dad stood up from his chair, scraping it across the kitchen tiles in the process.

"You're up early, dear."

"Yeah, I couldn't sleep." She glanced at the clock above the table. *Six! It's way too early to be up on the first day of the hols.*

Maya watched her father place his mug in the sink, pick up his briefcase and then their eyes met. "So what've you and your brother got planned today?"

"Don't know yet. Might take him down to the river with Sam, he said he's got some fishing rods, so I thought it might be fun," she replied, and flipped the switch on the kettle.

"That sounds a good idea. Anyway, I've got to go." He approached Maya, leaned forward and gave her a peak on her forehead, his neatly trimmed beard scratching her skin. "See you later, sweetie," he said with a chuckle.

She had seen such a huge change in her father since Jack's return, before, he couldn't wait to get out of the house to get to work as the managing director of Lotus and two months ago, when she arrived home with Jack in-tow, Maya had never seen her dad break down like he did then; Zach one of the angels, had to help him back to his feet. Her dad was no small weed, his six-foot, seven-inch frame always reminded her of an international rugby player, and there he was on his knees weeping. She saw a side of him she never thought existed. There was guilt in those tears as well as pain and forgiveness. He had wrapped his arms around her first and held on tightly, never wanting to let go. In that embrace the guilt she had carried around with her for nine years - concerning her brother's disappearance - evaporated. It was as though the chains that had weighed her down all those years just fell to the ground, freeing her at last.

"I'm so sorry ...." He kept repeating until Maya forgave him.

He clasped her head in his hands, their eyes meeting for what seemed like the first time since her brother was taken from them. "I will never leave you again."

7

Tears welled in Maya's eyes. "I know." She nodded. "Jack's home now, so we can all be a family again, can't we?"

Her dad glanced up at her brother who was held in his mother's embrace. "Yes, we can. I love you so much, Maya, and I know I haven't said that enough to you."

He kissed her forehead and stepped over to his son. Leo inched towards Maya and drew her close to him. In all the nine years they'd lived without her brother, Maya had never heard her father say those three simple words, I ... love ... you. A lump formed at the back of her throat, tears welled in her eyes and a sudden giddiness made her collapse into Leo's strong arms. Her dad loved her and had always loved her.

Pouring the boiled water into her mug, Maya stared hypnotically at the tiles behind the kettle while stirring her tea. It felt oddly safe and comforting having Jack back and even though the angels had prepared her parents for his return, Maya still knew she had a certain responsibility in keeping him out of trouble, which wasn't easy with his mind controlling gift. She'd spent hours explaining to him the correct way to behave amongst their own kind, humans that is. *I suppose being brought up by fallen angels doesn't help, but what's it going to be like after the hols when he starts school?*

Maya dreaded that thought, spending many an hour stressing over it, knowing that she couldn't just go and ask her parents for advice like every other teenager could. She wished Leo hadn't made her promise not to mention anything about her involvement with the angels or the recovery of The Book yet, she understood why and would never intentionally put her parents in danger.

Anyway, they wouldn't believe that both Jack and I help angels to fight off fallen angels and that we have powers that humans shouldn't possess. But I wish I could talk to them all the same. After all, the book's safely hidden away for all eternity, Jack's home and there hasn't been any sightings of Bazriel and the fallen ones or their pet demons since. So what's the harm? Yet somehow, my life continues to get more complicated by the minute.

Maya shook her head and threw the teaspoon into the sink before making her way into the lounge to sit down. Curling herself into the sofa with her legs tucked beneath her, she started reminiscing again. Nine years she'd had to come to terms with the belief that her brother was dead, all those years of feeling the pain of loss whenever she peered into his bedroom at night, hoping he would be there, and that it was all somehow a bad dream. How quickly that time had been forgotten by her parents as they settled into a normal family life, yet, deep down, she knew they would never really be that kind of a family. One day, her and Jack would be called upon to help against Bazriel and stand side-by-side with Leo and his brothers. *How had Leo put it? That my family's bloodline is the same as the chosen family of Jesus, we are God's chosen ... the ones that he decided would help him do all those miracles ... I think? I still don't quite get it. Too much to learn in such a short time, will blow anyone's sanity away.*

Glancing up at the clock above the mantelpiece, beside the last photo they'd taken of Jack before his kidnapping, she sighed, *as soon as Jack wakes, we're going to find Leo.* She took a long sip of tea, savouring its flavour and waited for her brother to come downstairs.

Three hours later, Maya, followed by Jack, marched along the drive towards the Old Rectory. She climbed the three steps up towards the door first and noticed that it felt different from two weeks before and couldn't understand why. Placing her hand, palm flat on the smooth oak, she felt its warmth and knew that the unnerving sensation originated from the door itself.

Narrowing her eyes, Maya wrapped her fingers around the metal door-pull to her left and said a little prayer ... 'Please let them be in.'

She had never been one for praying before Jack's return or even before Leo arrived, but since discovering that her life was intermingled with the everlasting battle between heaven and hell, good and evil, Maya found herself doing it more and more often these days. Pulling sharply down on the oval rod, she heard the bell resonate throughout the house and turned to gaze at Jack who stayed statue like on the drive, staring right pass her and on toward the entrance with his eyes wide.

"Do you see that?" he asked and pointed at the door.

"See what?"

"There's a pattern appearing on the door, right now, while I'm watching it."

Maya stepped back to take a better look. He was right. An ornate labyrinth pattern which never seemed to begin or end, became visible. Her eyes widened. *That's so weird. Does this mean Leo and the other angels are inside or not?* She grabbed the bell pull again, gently yanking down on it this time, then ran down the steps to stand beside her brother. When she heard the thud of footsteps getting louder as they approached from within the house, Maya took a deep breath, steadying herself with effort. *What's up with me? I don't usually feel like this when I call on Leo!*

The tarnished brass doorknob twisted as Maya and her brother watched on. It creaked open and her jade-spoked eyes widened in astonishment, her heart missing a beat. Standing before her wasn't Leo or Gabriel as she'd hoped, or even anyone she recognized. It was a complete stranger. *Have I done the right thing in coming here? What if he's one of the fallen and Leo's been captured by Bazriel. Oh cripes! That never even crossed my mind.*

Lightning Source UK Ltd.
Milton Keynes UK
UKOW02f1903120317
296467UK00003B/40/P